Smoke Follows Beauty

by Brian Ames

In these stories Brian Ames has given us an unusual, sharp and priceless look at the multiple levels of human experience. His characters weep, laugh and dance, but most of all, they make the effort. As a reader, I am surprised and illuminated.

> - Alex Kuo, author of *Lipstick and Other Stories*

Brian Ames delivers his characters brilliantly and gently to the page; they've clearly got him in their grasp, and he has them in his. Gorgeous!

> -Susan Burmeister-Brown,
> editor, *Glimmer Train Stories*

Smoke Follows Beauty Defined

Campfire smoke – lifted on an unsettled wind – blows into the eyes of those gathered about the circle of dancing flames. One no sooner moves than it changes direction and starts blowing at him again. "Smoke follows beauty," he coughs, as he lifts his chair and moves again. "Yeah, and Beauty was a Horse!" On can always rely on campmates for that quick quip.

Smoke Follows Beauty are 22 tales meant for telling around the campfire. But, the name means so much more than that corny camp joke. In a closed system, one cannot finish any real physical process with as much useful energy as one had to start with. Some is always wasted. A perpetual motion machine is impossible.

In the title story, there is the pristine Cascades wilderness rendered gray and devastated by Mt. St. Helens; against this backdrop the beauty of youthful innocence on the brink of chaos in the life of the young protagonist. In other stories, a rifle muzzle cracks, smoke rises from the barrel, and where once stood a beautiful bull elk – living and breathing and gorgeous – there is now only slain game to be gutted and packed out. The fact is, smoke follows beauty is a poetic rendering of the second law of thermodynamics – everything runs down. Entropy happens. The tendency of creation to decay is natural and acceptable. That's the way it was set up. Get on with it.

Smoke Follows Beauty

Brian Ames

Pocol Press
Clifton, Virginia

POCOL PRESS

Published in the United States of America
By Pocol Press
6023 Pocol Drive
Clifton VA 20124

Publisher's Cataloguing-in-Publication

Ames, Brian, 1963-
    Smoke follows beauty / Brian Ames. -- 1st ed.
    p.cm.
    ISBN 13: 978-1-929763-10-8
    ISBN 10: 1-929763-10-7

    1. Hunting--Fiction. 2.Outdoor life--Fiction.
    3. Saint Helens, Mount (Wash.)--Fiction.   I. Title

PS3601.M446S66 2002   813'.6
                                 QBI01-701243

Cover art copyright 2001 by Todd Mueller.

Epigraph © 1994 by Roderick Romero. Published by Windswept Pacific Entertainment dba Full Keel Music Co. (ASCAP)/Hoodooh Chile Music.

Acknowledgments

The author wishes to acknowledge gratefully the editors of the following publications in which some of the stories in this work appeared: "The Bones of Elk," in *Weber Studies*; "Waterlogged" as "The Body," in *Dan River Anthology*; "Killing Lucky" in *Literally Horses*; "Memory of Hard Rain," in *Glimmer Train Stories*; "A Known Turn in a Road" as "The Impostor," in *South Dakota Review*; and "The Elk that Walked Through Camp" and "Hunt at the End of the World" in *Cenotaph*.

One hundred thousand special thanks to Alex Kuo, Mike Wiegand, Rick Johnson, Yvonne Leach, Wayne Ude and Marion Blue, who encouraged me. And to Natalie Ames, my friend and spouse, one million.

My hunting partners are Kent Brown, Curt Butherus and Art Butherus. A big round of applause to them, please.

Contents

"Old stories at the end of the road
new skin stretched across these old bones. "
- Sky Cries Mary, 1994

For my grandfather, Art Butherus

Listen

Listen.

In a light eastern Cascade foothills snowfall, if you wait long enough, you can hear it. The language of trees, utterances of fir and maple, the soft hum and sigh and clearing of the pine's throat. An opinion offered from cedars.

Fallen needles and decomposing leaves are the adjectives and past participles that have been edited from the conversations of trees. What remain - nouns of heartwood and verbs of sap - reach into the mist and tell a story, if you wait long enough, patiently enough, to hear it.

Sit here on these bones of a tree. This fir trunk was thrown down in an autumn windstorm roaring down out of Clover Springs - see how its limbs splay, like fingers and toes, at the sky? See the root ball at the base, still clutching twelve cubic yards of earth? When it hit the ground, there was a loud sound in the forest, even though there was no one around to hear it. But sit quietly, and you may be the first.

The fallen trunk rests here against a tall red cedar. Here, in the relief of its bark face, is a series of ever-changing glyphs. One time you look at it and see the shape of a brown bear's head. Look again: it's changed into a leaping salmon. Again: a thunderbird.

Gather your thoughts here next to this grove of aspen. They will speak to you of the cycles of deer and elk, for they know the touch of elk's teeth and have felt the rubbing of felt from deer antlers.

Examine the last unfallen leaf from this tangle of vine maple. Note its symmetry, and sense the last gasp of its chlorophyll engines, a pang of deciduous regret that joyous gossip will die down for winter.

Over here is a strong western hemlock, pointing at the sky. At night, it tracks the movement of stars, the zodiac. When wind comes up, it sends messages to Polaris.

Here is a gray snag with a hawk's nest. Put your ear up to the bare wood for seven days, and the faint meter of the forest's history will tap out a rhythm in your temples.

Junipers and hickory on the south of a ravine will tell you rumors of the ocean. They've heard fabulous and wonderful things from the creek at the ravine's base, which heard them from a stream, which heard them from a river - the stories changing at each fork, becoming more fantastic or more tragic at each bend.

The same plants to the north of the ravine know nothing of the outside world. This is the result of coriolis, the same principle that makes

9

you walk lost, in circles. You will need to listen to the moss on the north side of a dogwood's trunk to regain your way, to receive summation, repatriation from the consequences of your choices.

A yellow tamarack pine will tell you a legend if you let it. A Douglas fir will help you find water if you're thirsty.

You just have to listen long enough.

The rustle of wind migrates across a mountain hillside. The resulting babble you hear in the needles and leaves and moving branches is not the words I'm telling you about. They are deeper in the wood than that.

Listen.

The Bones of Elk

Early, pre-dawn. Wilhelm has just climbed, muscles still stiff from yesterday's exertions, out of the passenger side of his uncle's mud-spattered Jeep. The two have agreed Wilhelm will hunt down the ravine here. His uncle, Ivan, will drive up the road a mile or so and hunt the opposite ridge. They will meet back here at 10:30 to break for lunch back at camp.

Ivan pulls away, his big tires crunching in the mud and gravel of 1600 Road. The crunching goes on and on then fades to an occasional *pop* as he rounds a corner. The Jeep's one working taillight slips from view. Wilhelm stands there for a minute, looking around in the dark, blowing steam, looking up at stars. It's cold, about 22 degrees.

Still standing by the side of the logging road, Wilhelm removes his wool gloves and stuffs them in one of the oversized pockets of his red hunting coat. He takes out a box of shells and, balancing his gun on his forearm and in the crook of his elbow, opens the bolt and feeds them into the magazine. One, two, three, four. Sliding the bolt forward a bit to avoid engaging the fourth shell, Wilhelm places a fifth shell - a 7-mm bullet his father reloaded almost 30 years ago - in the chamber. He pushes the bolt forward to fully engage the shell, snaps the bolt down with the thumb and forefinger of his right hand, and in the same fluid motion, clicks on the safety with his right middle finger.

Sliding his left arm through the sling, Wilhelm hoists the rifle onto his back. He digs into another pocket for a can of snuff. Packing a substantial bolus of tobacco between his lower lip and gum, he slips his gloves back on and works the snuff around in his mouth with saliva. He looks around again in the dark, taking in the shadows, the stars, the absolute lack of further sound. Wilhelm's eyes grow accustomed to subtle diversity in the play of starlight over different surfaces, different albedos. Starlight reflects from a fallen, bleached limb and the pre-dawn retina records this. Starlight reflects from a stump covered with moss, the distinction between the two clearer as moments pass.

Above him, to the north, the road-bank rises sharply twelve feet and flattens out in a thirty-acre clearcut. Below, south, the forest drops away at a hundred feet every seventy yards or so for three quarters of a mile, until the grade terminates in a ridge above a clearcut where his father shot a spike a few years back. He'll hike down to that ridge over the next hour and a half, pausing every two-hundred steps for fifteen to twenty minutes, so game will know to be on the move. Then he will wait at the ridge, looking down on the clearcut and back up into the woods, for an hour and a half, then hunt up as he returns to this spot. It's a good strategy and it could work.

The first step into the woods is always a struggle of decision.

Here, on this logging road, Wilhelm knows where he is. He knows that in four and a half hours Ivan will return. The two will go back to camp and start a campfire, have lunch, and debate where the best hunting will be in the afternoon. He knows that if he follows this road, 1600, back down out of the hills about twenty miles he'll be at the Nile River Road, and if he takes a left at that intersection and follows the Nile River Road two miles he'll come to the intersection at State Highway 410. He can take another left there, drive a little less than a hundred miles, cross the Cascades at Chinook Pass, and pass through Enumclaw to arrive safely at home.

If Wilhelm steps into the woods, he steps into uncertainty.

He could walk in and get turned around and wander in this immense wilderness until his ghost took up residence with the ghosts of other hunters who have made the same mistake. He could shoot an elk in the absolute bottom of one of these ravines, but shoot it badly, and track it for miles. He might lose his way so comprehensively that no compass could ever guide him out. He could stumble on a fallen limb. His hand could tangle with the safety and click it off. In tumbling, fighting for balance, Wilhelm's own rifle could betray him - one shot to the head. His eyes would be wide and dismayed.

Resolved, Wilhelm takes one measured, quiet step off the road onto forest duff. And another. Down, ten, twenty, thirty yards in the dark soundlessly. Frozen patches of snow are here and there; these he avoids. At about step number seventy-five, he misses seeing the faint white of a fallen section of limb - even though the earth has spun and light is rising a bit. A *crack* fills the woods as his boot snaps the stick and he stops instantly, listening for indication that he may have spooked game. There is no further sound but his own heartbeat in his temples.

Wilhelm realizes he is standing near where two seasons ago Ivan found the carcass of a five-point bull. Shot but not tracked, it had been abandoned bleeding to death to fight off coyotes in the night with its last breath. The wild dogs had eviscerated the bull; by the time Ivan brought Wilhelm to see the abomination, torn hide stretched across the bones of elk, and odor, were all that remained.

He sits down on a nearby stump and waits for more light. Up through the limbs of pines and Douglas fir, aspens, maples, he discerns the rising of morning. Like watching the hour hand of a clock, if he watches with focus and intensity, over time, he may detect the evolution of dawn.

Animals around him are waking up and moving. Squirrels and small birds start to pip, infrequently at first. The spans between their sounds grow briefer, and light sloughs darkness away from east to west. As Wilhelm waits on the stump, morning blooms in full on the eastern slopes of the Cascades. A chipmunk scrambles up a fallen Douglas fir trunk, spies him, and begins to scold Wilhelm for his intrusion. Wilhelm scopes him with the rifle but the chipmunk continues in its ill-informed arrogance. *There'd be nothing left of you, kleiner Bruder*, Wilhelm thinks. He gets up and moves on to let it know everything's all right, to quiet it. This, after all, is the chipmunk's home. Wilhelm is just passing through.

Wilhelm switches shoulders with the rifle and hikes slowly down a little further into a small clearing. As he emerges from shadow, it is clear elk were bedded down here under the trees near the edge. The mountain grass is pressed flat against the frozen ground. Their sign is everywhere, tracks and droppings, fur and odor. He closes his eyes and imagines them, making soft sounds as they sleep in the moonlight. The fog of their breath rises toward Sirius.

Only moments ago, they may have risen and moved off through the clearing into the opposite woods. Did they hear the careless snap of his twig an hour ago and wake with a start? Or were they dreaming wapiti dreams, waking leisurely in the cold, and move off to graze for moss and aspen bark?

Crossing the clearing, Wilhelm enters the forest again. He hikes another twenty minutes and comes to the final ridge. It plunges three-hundred feet to the clearcut below, impassable without intense physical exertion. Road 1608 is a half a mile across the clearcut, and one night Wilhelm, his father and Ivan dragged his father's year-old spike elk out of there, full, in the dark. The thrill of that night rushes back to him, the three of them pulling and grunting with ropes, breaking their lantern so they had to finish in the dark. They pulled the elk's six-hundred-pound chassis a mile and a half uphill to the trucks. Somewhere about halfway up the road Wilhelm put his back to the spike. Even dead, one of its antlers gored his left calf, clean through his jeans and thermal underwear and into the muscle. Later, back at camp, they strung it up by the hind legs high between two trees and cut off its head with a chain saw. "That'll fix ya," Wilhelm said, lifting the head by the prongs and

13

speaking into its beautiful face. His calf throbbed. The elk's eyes stared back without acknowledgment, having faded to dull black.

Selecting a wide stump to wait and watch, Wilhelm slides his rifle off his shoulder. He removes his gloves again, unzips his coat, slips in another wad of tobacco. From the stump, he surveys the area, down into the clearcut, up and around into surrounding woods. Before long, the cold creeps up from the stump into his buttocks, numbing them. It spreads into his guts and torso and out through his capped head. His feet and hands get cold, too, as heat is exchanged for frost. He's longing for the moment the sun rounds a stand of trees curving out to the left and falls full on him.

Viewed from across the valley that spreads below, over the fold of another ridge that reaches its bottom at Nile Creek, he'd appear a red dot in the greens, whites and golds of the autumn ridge. He's seen other hunters from these distances. It reminds him that the land is immense.

He sits and quietly waits for the ungulate sounds of approaching elk. His mind wanders across variegated, unrelated topics.

Wilhelm thinks for a moment about tonight's campfire. They will sit around listening to Hank Williams, eat like kings, tell jokes and laugh, spit tobacco in the fire. His campmates will drink bourbon and beer. He'll drink diet cola. They'll watch the characteristics and maturation of fire in the pit, pondering its properties in poignant silence. As the fire consumes fuel, they'll wander off at times and look at stars. Wilhelm will chart the constellations again for his father, show him the nebula in Orion's sword through field glasses.

Thoughts come to him, unbidden, about the exigencies of the real world at home.

In his career, has he sold out hawking his company's products, telling half-truths and obfuscating reality while becoming more and more ensnared in the web of interoffice politics? He thinks of people there with power over him and evaluates where the boundary is between hard work and sycophantia. And comes up with no answer at all.

He's traveled throughout the world in his work. His favorite place is this stump, right here, right now.

There's a woman he runs across from time to time, an acquaintance, prettier than his wife. This other woman has sent certain signals that she is available and amoral. Wilhelm wonders whether he should fuck her, once, twice, and pretend that he hasn't when he comes home. The thoughts make him hard for a while, sitting on the stump with images of this woman, nude, moving like a cat in and out of his brainstem.

He looks down at his rifle. It's a Winchester 7-mm Remington Magnum with WesternField optics, the gun handmade in New Haven, Connecticut. He bought this gun from his father, and in it he imagines he can feel his father's strength, his discernment, his authority. The grain of its stock is beautiful, even with a few scratches. Its barrel and muzzle mean business. It smells of gun-oil, a good odor.

To look at the rifle is to view an underestimated object, Wilhelm thinks. Three and a half feet long, it can fire a projectile the size of a small rock at two thousand feet per second into a paper target and make a precise hole three-eighths of an inch in diameter. Or it can fire a bullet into the body of a thousand-pound Roosevelt bull elk, pierce the hide, glance off a chip of bone and ricochet around inside the animal at incredible velocities. The pressure of its flight liquefies flesh and organs into jelly.

Thinking in clichés for a moment, Wilhelm considers the process of taking his own life with the rifle. Clicking the safety off, inverting the gun, putting the muzzle into his mouth and reaching down. Remembering to push, not pull, the trigger. Lots of people have done it. Thinking about the mechanics, the methodology of it, seems otherworldly. Five seconds from now he could be gone. It's seductive, disturbing, preposterous.

Training the crosshairs of his scope on a jetliner passing overhead, Wilhelm thinks of the possibilities.

He hears the *thwap thwap thwap* of a raven's wings generating lift before he sees it. Then it's there, floating, then straining against light mountain currents as it surveys its kingdom for prey. Jet black, the bird reminds Wilhelm of the helicopters of Armageddon, which brings to mind God, or the ferocious articulation of the vengeful and righteous God of Wilhelm's youth, who still is there in his head. It means that he is still a sinner, and always will struggle with the stark fence between right and wrong, always will wrestle with faith.

He hopes a bull elk will rush out of the forest and present its chest, fifteen feet away, like happened last season. Wilhelm was sitting on a rock outcrop below 1706 Road about two miles from here and heard crashing in the woods above and behind him, from the west. The bull had been jumped by other hunters. It emerged from the trees, drawing up short and staring at him full on. Wilhelm was unprepared, facing the opposite direction, sitting with his legs crossed under him, rifle across his lap. They both were absolutely still. If Wilhelm moved, the bull would

15

bolt. So they waited for what seemed like moments but was probably only a few seconds.

Slowly with one hand Wilhelm clicked the safety off. In one fluid motion he turned to his side and brought the rifle up and around in a great arc. The bull turned to flee. Wilhelm fired. Then, carelessly, he fired two more rounds at it, but the bull was gone. Wilhelm leapt off the rock and sprinted through the forest after it. But by the time he had run twenty yards the bull was two ridges over. Wilhelm looked around for signs he'd wounded it and through the hammering of adrenaline, heard himself say *shit* and *fuck* over and over again. There were no signs of blood anywhere, and he knew he'd missed anyway, and he knew it was a once-in-a-lifetime opportunity blown.

Wilhelm hears a rodent up in a tree a few feet away gnawing on the sweet flesh where a pinecone attaches to a branch. His gaze follows the trunk up and sees it, and the cone separates and is falling, falling, falling, then hits the ground with a small *pop* and rolls downhill for four or five seconds and comes to rest. Wilhelm is reminded of the end of all things.

Glancing at his watch he sees that it's 9:25. He's supposed to meet Ivan back at 1600 Road in one hour and five minutes. So he gathers his rifle, hoists it onto his shoulder, refreshes the chew in his mouth, and begins the climb out. As many times as he has done this, he never recalls that one of the laws of the hike out is that since you've been there before and you're not really quietly hunting and surveilling, it takes about one-third as much time as the hike in. So at 9:45, he's bridging the rise directly below 1600 Road. At 9:46 he's standing there on the gravel again.

Wilhelm has almost three-quarters of an hour on his hands, so he decides to climb the rockpile next to where 1600 switches back on its final approach to Little Bald Mountain. The rockpile comprises loose chunks of shale, feldspar and granite, with alpine vegetation struggling here and there. In summertime, it would be full of rattlesnakes. But in late autumn, risk is in the shifting of a loose stone under boot. So his ascent is careful. Each step is a process of selection for foundation and evaluation for stability.

Ten minutes to the top, at 5,465 feet above sea level, on the eastern slopes of the Cascade Mountain Range in Washington state, part of the Ring of Fire seismology network that surrounds the entire Pacific Ocean, on a planet called Earth third from a yellow star in an arm of a galaxy that forms a molecule in the universe, which may be one of a zillion universes, all of which may be neurons firing in the mind of the Most

16

High.   One is prone to hyperbola, hove to on a large boulder at the summit. Gazing out for miles and miles and miles. Breathing clean air.

From here, the land stretches out, where God could sleep. His holy green comforter unfolds in ridges and canyons of blanket, stopping where the golden sheets - bare, rolling hills flowing off the east slopes - begin. If God reclined here on the Seventh Day, his head dreamed nodding on the future site of Union Gap, his toes in Commencement Bay. His left arm lay out with his hand on Spirit Lake, right arm running up Umtanum Ridge across where Ellensburg is, into the North Cascades. If he came back here to sleep, His Tahoma belly would rumble as villagers below shook in fear.

Wilhelm knows that God is watching him here, now, and is around him and above, below, to all points of the compass. At every degree of every axis he looks and sees God the Father, God the Son and God the Holy Spirit. This morning is an oracle of the omnipresence of the God Who Provides, Redeems, Judges, Reconciles and Spins The Cosmos.

He hears noise below, the opening of a door. It's Ivan, arrived at the Jeep, which is hidden around the bend just barely out of sight from where Wilhelm is now. Again, shouldering his rifle, he rises from the boulder and heads down the rockpile, back into his own small life.

Waterlogged

We were Boy Scouts, Jackie, Rusty, Mark and I, and some others, around twelve years old. This was old enough to know about a few things, but young enough to not really comprehend that life can be complicated. Things were simple for us. We came from the 1970s suburbs. Our parents were old enough to have missed being called up for Vietnam, and square enough to have missed out on dope and protesting. We were good kids, Boy Scouts.

We paddled with vigor, canoeing Oregon's Willamette River between Eugene and Champoeg State Park, near Oregon City. We were unaware of the odor of our pre-teen sweat. Our objective was the 50-miler patch, a larger-than-average badge given for troops that traversed fifty or more miles on land, or the same distance by canoe. Scouts wore them centered on their red flannel camp coats, just below the Order of the Arrow circle, if they joined that advanced outdoorsman's group. Wearing the 50-miler patch was a big deal.

We were actually going much further than fifty miles - almost a hundred and fifty I think, in ten days - and we all felt cheated when it was made clear we were going to be doing all this paddling and camping for only one patch.

Our scoutmasters, Misters Selfe and Taylor, were with us. So our ignorant spirits couldn't get into too much trouble. Sure, a couple of us tipped a canoe over in a stretch of rapids and all our stuff, even that wrapped in visquene, got wet and we had to hang it out all that night and it was still damp the next day. And there were too many paddle fights to count, where we'd smack each other with glee, paddles glancing off the river with tepid spray and thwapping into big orange life jackets we hated wearing in the heat. We fought mosquitoes and sprayed all kinds of bug-off on our bare arms and legs. We got enough sunburn to call down the risk of fierce melanoma.

Sometimes it rained too, and that was pretty miserable because rain on the river in the Pacific Northwest, even in summer, is colder than crap. Everything gets soaked and your hands get clammy and prunelike, numb, until you whack them by accident on the side of the aluminum canoe - then you can really feel the bastards.

On hot days, we played tadpole baseball. Here's how it works:

You find a sort of calm spot, some estuary on the inside curve of a large bend in the river, where the water is shallow and brackish, usually surrounded by cattails and Queen Anne's lace. Down in the water it's warm in these spots, and river frogs have laid their eggs in the spring. By the time we come through unable to quell our spasms of energy, it's August and hot, and the still water is even warmer here. The eggs have hatched into good-sized tadpoles - black and slimy and shiny, with two little pre-legs poking out of their fat torsos and translucent tails where their hind legs should be.

You look down in the water from the stern end of your canoe and there are so many of them it looks like a squadron of bombers. The water is filled with them and you think, shit, if they were people it would be this huge crowd like down at the Fourth of July at Fort Vancouver. They mill all about each other and slip in and out of and around each other until you can't really tell where the one you were just looking at went. They have big honking eyes the same color as their skin. Their eyes bulge and they look stupid. When you touch one it feels like your dick when it's soft, only slippery.

So you reach in and scoop out a handful - you can't grab them because they just squirt right out of your grip. So you have to make a cup with your hands to get ten or a dozen. Then you shout *Ready?* to your mate at the fore end of the canoe, and he says *Yeah!*, and you toss them at him, only not right at him but off to his side a little like you're aiming for the strike zone.

And he swings that paddle, blade turned so it pushes air, and finds the sweet spot and that's all she wrote for most of a handful of tadpoles. Sure, a few he misses and they plop into the water behind him and swim off to become frogs or heron food or eat each other or something. But depending on how bunched-up-together you pitched them, he's going to connect solid with more than a few, and what you got then is a flying wall of tadpole guts. Tadpole baseball. You both had to dive in and let the river wash the innards off your skin though, because if you didn't you'd have blow-flies divert from every big turd or dead fish in the area and head straight for you.

That's about as sophisticated and complicated as things got on a canoe trip. Sunburns, mosquitoes, tadpole baseball, setting up camp and making fires so we could have hobo dinners, shit like that. We didn't know nothing and we were a couple of years yet from discovering girls and cars and cigarettes - although once in a while we rolled up rope in tubes of grocery bag paper, touched the end to the fire, and puffed away on those when the scoutmasters were off doing whatever scoutmasters do when they're not around bothering us. I still remember the taste of that burning rope and paper. The memory is a pleasant one, invoking campfires, experiments with cussing, whittling, half-cooked carrots and potatoes in the hobo dinners. And earning that cool 50-miler patch.

We'd get up in the morning and throw on the same smelly clothes. We'd spray more bug-off on, run our filthy hands through our greasy hair, break camp, and stuff all the stuff in the canoes. Then we'd throw a bucket of water on the fire pit. If the scoutmasters were down by the canoes, a couple of us might pee in the pit and try to avoid the cloud of smelly urine steam that exploded from the cinders. Then we'd throw some more water on it and make one of the younger tenderfoots put his hand in there and swish it around in the black ashes, with the water and piss, to make sure it was cold or at least not hot to the touch. That way we'd make sure our troop wasn't responsible for any wildfires getting out of hand.

Most days each had their own one memorable feature. For instance, I think it was Independence where we pulled ashore of an evening and weren't really out in the wild country, strictly speaking. Instead, we were kind of at a city park and there was a coed softball league playing on diamonds at one end. So instead of pitching our dining flies and tents right away, and getting a fire going, we headed off for the diamonds to watch the games.

This one sort-of fat chick was batting and she hit the ball pretty good, only the shortstop snagged it after one hop, firing the ball to the first baseman. She came barreling down the first base line like a bat out of hell. The first bagger was this little kid, but sure enough, he caught the ball square on just about the time she flattened him. She was big, but in knocking him to hell, she must have tripped on him or the bag or something, because she went down too. We waited for the earthquake to hit.

So the first-base ump called her out and she got up covered with grass stains and first-base diamond dirt and started limping back to her side of the field, and left us with the memorable feature of the day: On the way over, covered with dirt, this pudgy girl was rubbing with both hands up and down all along her front, all over her boobs and crotch - I guess probably sore or trying to rub off the dirt or something - calling over to somebody, "Mona... Mona..."

Well, we just about puked from laughing so hard. All the way back to the camp we were choking and squealing "Mona... Mona..." rubbing our dicks and pretending to knead our breasts. All through dinner, "Mona... Mona..." All damn night, "Mona..." That night we'd just get

settled down and someone would moan in their sleeping bag, "Mona...
Mona..."

"Shut yer face and quick playing with yerself," we'd all shout, and
dissolve into helpless giggling, calling out again, crooning for Mona
under tent flies in the Oregon summer night. Years later, any one of us
would just call out the name of Mona, our fat goddess of laughter, and
start cracking up, even kids who hadn't even been there and had no idea
what the big deal was, laughing like idiots.

One morning we got up and performed the same routine, getting into
our stinking clothes, breaking camp and so forth, and setting out on the
river just above Albany. None of us knew what the day's memorable
feature would be, nor were we really even aware that each day had a
memorable feature. That just automatically happened.

It was a sunny day and we paddled out around 9 a.m. a couple of
miles upstream of the town. As we entered town and drifted through, we
passed under a large bridge span for Highway 20, which connects Bend
inland and Newport on the Oregon Coast. The river was deeper here so
not very swift, and we were bored and, canoe by canoe, slowly faded over
toward the east bank of the river, where at least the shore might prove
more interesting.

Rounding a bend, Jackie saw something bobbing up and down in the
water; he later said he thought it was a muskrat. He and his canoe mate,
who happened to be Mr. Selfe, paddled over near where he saw it, but
couldn't see anything anymore so they started to head back over to the
rest of the canoes, who had pretty much ignored the two of them and still
drifted lazily down with what little current there was.

Jackie told the story of his discovery that night and I'm not sure how
much of it was true, or how much he made up, but either way it's pretty
cool.

As he and Mr. Selfe head back over to the group from where they'd
spied the muskrat, Jackie dips his paddle in the water, feels the tug of
some slight resistance, and lifts this rotting guy's head out of the water a
little by his chin and neck. It's not very deep and the body's just below
the surface, so it bobs a little, bounces on the bottom, and more fully
resurfaces. He's bloated like crazy, and blue, with the lips and eyelids
eaten off by fish. The only thing that's not blue is this guy's teeth and the
gasping hole that used to be his mouth. It looks like he's biting at the air
or Jackie's paddle, and the mouth looks like it's as big as his whole head
used to me, but his whole head is bloated up so big he's almost like a
cartoon balloon dude.

21

For having just found a gross bloated floating blue dead guy, Jackie and Mr. Selfe were pretty calm. In fact, they called a couple of us over - telling us to keep a little distance, Mr. Selfe, I'm sure, thinking about how many future nightmares he could avoid for a troopful of impressionable puppies like us.

"Toss us your rope," Mr. Selfe called out. "Then head up the bank over there and find someone to call the police. There's a man drowned over here."

So I tossed him our rope, and me and Rusty paddled like hell over to the bank, pulled the canoe up on the shore, and headed up a trail that climbs a bluff to a row of houses overlooking the riverbend, with the bridge in the distance.

We looked all over the place for a person to tell and finally, we found an old gentleman tying up bean vines in a side-yard garden.

"Sir," we said, and he looked up, squinting in the sun with a farmer's tan, white hair, and sweat on his brow and cheeks. He looked like he'd been struggling with the beans all summer, our interruption his first break. "Sir, we are looking for someone who can call the police for us."

He acted like he didn't understand, and I was wondering if he looked like an Oregonian but maybe was really an old person from another country and didn't speak English. "Sir, we need to call the police because we've found a body down in the river, sir."

He comprehended now, but still answered slowly, through a veil of caution. Nowadays, he would have been suspicious. Back then, in the mid-1970s, he could still trust Boy Scouts, but a body, now that was a disclosure to be acknowledged with great care and due process.

"Couldn't be," he said. "I was just down there yesterday..."

"Sir, it's true, there is," one of us replied. "We've just found him. Will you please call the police for us?"

He shunted off into the house and didn't come back. It was getting hot, and me and Rusty were looking at each other wondering whether he went in and called, or whether he went in and keeled over from all the excitement - and now we had two bodies on our hands or what.

Rusty and I exchanged one more glance that said what the hell, of course he called the police. Besides, we couldn't stand the thought of what we were missing down at the water.

We both shrugged at the same time and bolted for the trail down the bluff, cresting the rise at the bank and glancing up at the canoes gathered to one side of the guy as we struggled for footing on the dirt and sand all the way down.

22

Mr. Selfe and Mr. Taylor were on the bank with the rope pulling the corpse out of the water, and it was snagging and, I suppose, little pieces of the more rotten matter were dropping off into the water. The guy still had some of his clothes on and he was wrapped in chains, so the chains were catching on driftwood and rocks and stuff. Finally, he came free and then they had him winched onto the bank just as it became clear the old bean gentleman on top of the bluff had come through: two Albany black and white cruisers arrived. Four cops popped out and took over.

The scoutmasters spent quite a while with the cops talking about the discovery, and what this whole mess of Boy Scouts was doing in the area, and how long this fellow's been in the water - a couple weeks', the cops guessed - and why he was wrapped in chains. Suicide, the cops supposed, one pointing his thumb back over his shoulder at the Highway 20 bridge.

The cops took our scoutmasters' statements and got their addresses and phone numbers, thanked them for helping out.

"You want your rope back," one of them asked Mr. Taylor.

"Er... no, I don't think so," he said. It's time for us to go or we'll never make camp, never keep on pace.

Tucked away in our sleeping bags that night, with a silver moon filtering through camp and peaking in under the sleeping flies, we told ghost stories with new burgeoning comprehension. In them, the ghost of Mr. Blue Bloated Chains came clanking right through camp, grabbed the weakest, youngest tenderfeet, and feasted on their brains by sucking the matter right through their eye-sockets, which he had ripped out. The younger kids were practically shitting themselves with fear while us older kids snickered bravely to hide our confusion.

We boys were very brave and very mature during this scary day - that's what the scoutmasters would report to our mothers and fathers when we returned three or four days hence.

Still, as camp quieted that night and the silver rays of the moon changed position, the last Mona moaned, the last ghost story just an echoing whisper, we older boys pulled our sleeping bags clear up over our heads too.

And never slept a moment since.

Properties of Knives

Paul sees knives everywhere. A blade in the orange sliver of moon hanging over a summer twilit horizon. In icicles hanging from the soffits during silverthaw. In the sharp challenge to the sky above alpine cirques. In his reflection, in the corner of his eye: in his peripheral vision, briefly, as he turns.

He will ask a friend of his, whom he has always known simply as Hat, to make a knife for him.

Right now, Hat says, he carves ornate handles from hardwood or deer antlers. Sometimes he imbeds the handles with narwhal or walrus ivory and won't disclose his source, happier to perform scrimshaw in private on the prohibited bits.

Paul asks his friend how much one of these knives costs, getting right to the point.

"I only do the handles," Hat explains, ignoring Paul's question. "I can buy ten or a dozen good blades from a wholesaler, then carve my own. Sell them at community fairs, over at Leavenworth next month maybe."

Paul knows his friend has been hard up, looking for income for a while. So hoping to be helpful, he suggests taking out an advertisement in the back of magazines like *Blade* and *Blacksmith*. Hat nods, yeah, and explains that he's seen a lot of knife periodicals, but the really good knifemakers hammer their blades themselves - come up with a blade design of their own - then sell them for hundreds of dollars to collectors.

Still trying, impatient with his friend's excuses, Paul offers an opinion, not well-formed: Hat should set up a forge and get going on it. Commence this knife-making business.

This leads to a discussion about the so-called lost art of Damascus Steel, executed by forge-welding many layers into a billet, folding and re-folding the mass to double the strata and re-welding by forge and hammer. As an art form, the cipher was lost to Europeans for centuries. Discoverers had only found fragments of instruction for the two-thousand-year-old process. Even so, blades hammered into five-hundred layers of the material are remarkably stronger than others, and pleasing to the eye.

They briefly consider the favorable aspects of titanium blades as well. Hat promises that setting up a forge for himself is "somewhere down the road." His friend honors Paul by divulging a secret: he yearns to make a living making knives.

Paul's own interest is to acquire one of these knives, Hat's blade or not. His friend goes on, recalling an old master knifemaker he met at one county fair or another. An enormous Belgian or Luxembourgian named Willem, so zealous was this artisan that his face was permanently blasted red from constant proximity to the brilliant coals of the forge. The man's eyebrows, lashes and hair had melted away. His ears were festooned with metal rings and clasps, individual teeth filed to vladic points. The teeth of Nosferatu.

"Bet flossing's easy for him," Paul quips, just to say something.

"No man, he cleans his teeth with a file," Hat says, agreeing to the humor for a moment. They laugh together.

Their conversation returns to the properties of metal, of which Paul knows nothing. Hat wants to make knives; Paul has half a mind to start collecting knives. It should be a simple thing. Paul is running out of things to say.

"What you want to do," he starts out again, "is get your forge set up and start making blades, then start figuring out how you can make them with magical properties."

Hat doesn't know what to say in response, so he just looks back at Paul for a second like Paul's got a head full of traffic, like he just stepped out of a UFO.

"You know, like Tolkien's knives that used to glow when orcs were around," Paul says.

"Yeah, well, Jesus Christ, I just want to make some knives," Hat finally says.

Paul tells his friend about a thought he had one time that he couldn't escape from for an entire evening, to take this old rusty machete he inherited from his step-dad's tool shed during a big pre-garage-sale clean-out. All night he lay in bed thinking about how he'd remove the handle and grind and polish the blade, then make a new handle. Carve it out of a block of old wood or something, and put some varnish on it. How locating it in his garage, picking it up and looking it over the next day, he couldn't figure out how the hell he'd do all that, and tossed it back into a pile of garden implements.

Hat's ride suddenly shows up and they say so long for the night. Because there is this oddity: Hat possesses no driver's license.

On another occasion, Paul gives Hat a ride home.

"I want to show you my shop," Hat says as they enter his driveway. Loose gravel pops under the car's tires. They turn past a mobile home. Paul stops the car in front of a shack where Hat has directed. Hat works the padlock on a plywood door hanging skewed on rusty hinges. Their protest as he opens the shop is the only sound, save the click of a bare bulb as Hat tugs its string.

Hat's shop is a dog's breakfast. There are hand-tools and other implements of purpose unknown to Paul lying everywhere. Bits of wood and antler are strewn across a desktop. A couple of grinding wheels stand inert. The floor is dirt. Hat points to an empty, dark corner.

"That's where the forge will go," he promises.

"When you get around to it," Paul adds, and Hat nods and studies the spot. There is a brief interval with nothing but their breathing, wisps of exhalation rising from their open mouths. Then Hat springs into action, eager to share the process of blade sharpening.

He extracts a new blade from a felt slip-cover. Holds it in the bulblight for Paul to see. Light explodes off the steel like a small nova.

"It's beautiful," Paul stammers. He is fascinated by knives and, as indicated earlier, may start collecting them. He has a few: a commemorative of the two-hundredth anniversary of George Washington's inauguration with his silhouette and signature etched in the blade; a red Swiss Army knife lousy with marginal utility (blades, drivers, awls and dozens of other gewgaws); a couple of old crappy pocketknives; and a Genuine Buck Knife made in the USA he received, to his delight, one Christmas.

The Genuine Buck Knife is for elk hunting. Paul is supposed to level the crosshairs of his optics about mid-shoulder on a bull elk, fire a 30-06 bullet through his rifle, approach cautiously after it drops in case the elk kicks out in pre-death panic, then slice the stomach open with the Genuine Buck Knife and hew its guts out - a carnal editor in a Cascades clearcut. Then he has to haul the heavy bastard out and string it up and pull its hide off in strips. So they can stick it in the freezer and barbecue hamburger and smoke jerky at their leisure.

As Hat snaps on a toggle that starts a grinding wheel spinning, Paul is reflecting that *Australopithecine* didn't have it so easy. Four feet tall, he had to hunt prehistoric bison and cats with big teeth in teams armed with dull spears and clumsy blades while his woman gathered Pleistocene tubers in the Great Rift Valley. Half the damned time he didn't come back.

The brilliant friction of metal and grinding stone startles him back to Hat's shack. His friend presses the blade into the spinning stone and sparks arc through the filmy air and descend to dirt. Paul's eyes are as wide as pies. Hat sharpens the fresh blade and shouts over the din that the next steps will be to seat the blade's tang in a handle of Brazilian cherrywood he fashioned earlier in the day, then fine-hone the blade with a whetstone. There's just that much left to do. Hat shuts down the grinder. The sudden absence of sound is a cavern. Hat holds the blade up in the light.

"What do you think of that?" Hat asks.

"Stunning," Paul says.

"Go right through you."

Paul is remembering Hat's words as he takes his own Genuine Buck Knife from the top drawer of his bureau. He loves to hold it, to feel the weight of it in his right hand, to heft it, to find its fulcrum and take pleasure in sensing its balance. To admire the curve of its blade, the blunt shine of its hilt, to kiss it with spit and a whetstone. The handle is black. The blade is a clear mirror. He can look in it and fool himself that he can see all that is pending. The Genuine Buck Knife possesses all the properties he wanted his machete to have, the mysteries he wants Hat's forge, hammer and carving to fashion.

Paul wants a Promethean knife that will steal fire.

Paul is an aircraft engine mechanic. This he knows: A modern commercial jet-aircraft engine is a construct mostly of hundreds of whirling blades. Giant turbofan blades at the intake pull air into the engine. A series of progressively smaller blades, rotating and counter-rotating at startling speed on hubs around the motor core, compress the ingested air until it is hypercharged with oxygen and superheated by the pressure. The action of the blades on in-rushing air is akin to the pressure of a knife on skin at the instant a cut actually happens and the surface spreads. Titanium is selected for the blades because of its robust properties at high temperature - 3,000 degrees Fahrenheit at the core - and the metal's ability to handle intense stress. Factory metallurgists make the smaller blades by hand.

Once the screaming vapor is being delivered through the machine, pumps spray fuel through a burner into the stream, and the controlled explosion is vectored out the back of the engine as thrust. This, along with compressed bypass air, in turn moves the airplane forward, and upward as its wings generate lift. A summary of the process is *suck, squeeze, bang, blow.*

If one of the engine blades develops a mind of its own, goes rogue, departs its spinning hub, this can, and infrequently does, produce a phenomenon called *uncontained engine failure*. Everyone involved has a very bad day.

"Blade of dishonored/samurai has clear knowledge/how to restore it."

Hat explains he has been executing haiku about his blades, thinking this shit up as he hammers out billets. The forge is in. It throws impossible heat from the corner of the shop. Paul feels that he is wrapped in hot wool, that the breaths he takes are weighty. The odor of heat and molten steel is all about them.

"I wonder whether/knives, or their blades, are sentient./Yes, it must be so."

Paul doesn't get, at first, that Hat has fashioned another haiku just as he fashions the blade on the anvil before him. Paul's look is all question.

"Think about it," Hat says. "The sentience of knives. The Inuit's ulu understands how to sustain life, sloughing blubber from the chassis of the kill. The stab of Brutus carries on today between colleagues in the pursuit of business. Skywalker's blade of energy perceives the Force, knowing right from wrong."

"The scalpel of hope removed a lump from my mother's breast," Paul agrees. Hat nods and his hammer clanks. He sets the implement down and plunges the proto-blade into a bucket of water. Steam explodes. Hat indicates the tattoo on his forearm, a dagger through a heart.

"The tattoo needle, a form of knife that impregnates the skin with color," he says, "communicates forever, sending a signal that must be carried, good or bad, neutral. It forms a semaphore of skin."

"What the fuck are you talking about?" Paul asks.

"What are *we* talking about, my friend? It's *we* who are talking."

He winks as he says that last, and Paul perceives something in him that has fractured and fallen through itself. He wonders, and not for the first time, but for the first time *seriously*, whether it's such a great idea to hang out with Hat. They are as far apart as stars.

Hat has convinced Paul to help him out at his knife-vending booth at the summer's street fair. In the middle of all that heat rising off asphalt, people strolling past, elephant ears and dripping corn-on-a-stick, Hat's hawking home-hammered knives. A man comes up wearing a black T-shirt that reads "POWWOW NATION - Confederated Tribes." As he admires Hat's handiwork, Paul is surprised to hear how his friend engages the Indian.

"You know what Indians and knives have in common, don't you?" Hat asks the man.

The Indian looks at the woman with him. Perhaps he believes he is about to hear a joke. Politely he sets the blade, whose reflection he has just examined his own face in, down on the flannel counter. He and the woman begin to move off.

"No, really," Hat insists. "I'm not kidding."

The pair pauses.

"It's like this," Hat says. He lifts the knife the Indian man was holding and hefts it in his left palm so that the blade rests in the meat of his hand. "It starts with Moses," Hat says. "You know Moses?"

The Indian nods.

"Moses used the knife of Jehovah's mercy and power to part the Red Sea, you remember the story." Hat grasps the knife handle with his right hand. "Indigenous people on the move," he continues, "crossed the Bering Isthmus from Asia to North America, never believing the blade of continental tectonics would gut them, carving, as into a ham, a body of impassable water." He pauses and eyes his prospective customer levelly. "This is the Bering Strait," he adds. "I have heard that some suggest the two events - Moses and the Bering migration - are connected through some occulted apocrypha." Hat slides the blade through his palm. "American Indians are the Lost Tribe of Israel."

The Indian and his woman each take two steps back. They cannot take their eyes from Hat's bleeding palm. Paul, too, is mesmerized. Blood fills the cup of Hat's hand and spills. There are street sounds and the distant delighted screams of children on the carnival rides. No one else has noticed Hat's act but this universe of four.

"Sharp!" Hat says, wraps his new wound in clean, white cloth. "None sharper."

The Indian man looks as if he doesn't doubt it.

After the two prospects have left - without buying a knife - Paul remains silent. No passersby indicate anything more than a fleeting interest in the array of Hat's blades. There is a gulf of silence between them, Hat unwrapping and rewrapping the stained cloth around his palm and Paul searching for words. Finally, he finds them.

"Maybe this knife business isn't the thing for you, Hat."

"How's that?" Hat asks.

It was difficult enough for Paul to express that first thought. He had made no preparation in the eventuality he might have to follow it up.

"That cut thing," he stammers. "It was... violent."

Hat's laugh fills the booth. "The censor knows he is a dagger that cleaves creativity from the heart of the artist, and discovery from the eyes, ears, touch of the beholder," he giggles. The binding falls from his wound as he points at Paul with the forefinger of his unwrapped hand. "Careful you don't become the censor." And Paul sees that there is no wound, that Hat's palm is clean and unified and whole.

Back at Hat's place. It's early evening; Paul and Hat have brought in all the cases from Paul's car. Everything Hat was selling at the street fair remains in those cases, with the exception of one kinzahl - like the knife used in the attempt on Rasputin - Hat sold to a flat-topped, peg-headed man with a USMC-*Semper Fi* tattoo.

"Not much of a living made today," Hat observes.

"No," Paul says. He has been rendered pretty much monosyllabic since Hat revealed his wound-less palm. There isn't much to say, there never has been. Paul believes that these are the last moments he will spend in Hat's presence. This knife making has altered the man who was once his friend, made him something freakish, a grotesque, a sleight-of-hand performer.

"Let's take a look at what we have left," Hat says. Paul can't believe his ears. Everything's left, everything except the kinzahl! Nevertheless he nods, yes, let's have a look. Hat hauls one of the cases from the rug to the dining room table and pops the hasps. He coos at them, his darlings, as he unwraps then configures the blades across the table. He pauses, steps to the window, and draws his front curtains.

An equation occurs to Paul: a drawn curtain neatly halves the elemental matter of light with the same measure of thought given by a tableknife through a pat of butter. And so they are in halflight.

"Be honest with me," Hat says, returning to the collection. "Which is your favorite?" No longer even capable of uttering a single syllable, Paul simply points. He has selected one that resembles, very much, his own Genuine Buck Knife. "Mine too," Hat agrees, and selects it. "Do you want to know how I did it? The palm trick, at the booth?"

Paul remains silent. He is wondering whether it's possible for something to go terribly wrong in the making of knives, so that the blade becomes simple and knows only savant rage, the cast mercury of Manson. The cry of the Stones' Midnight Rambler: "I'll stick my knife right down your throat, baby, yeah, and it hurts..." What was in the mind of the pocketknife, shaping the bow of a toy sailboat, which slipped during summer camp and sliced his left-hand middle finger to the bone? He ran crying to the first-aid cabin, blood draining in red rivulets down his arm - then later won the sailboat race. Is the scar he carries today the price of that small victory?

"I'll show you," Hat promises. He again slices his own palm, the same one, or appears to. He holds the blade up dripping. "Give me your hand," he commands, and Paul obeys immediately.

The cut is stunning, as cold as icebergs calving. Paul's blood wells in a new, perfect furrow. "O god of razors!" he thinks. Voltage springs up his arm and collides with the ancient, reptilian part of his brainstem. Hat clasps Paul's palm in his own, so that their blood commingles.

"Brothers," Hat says. They are joined forever and ever.

"Lovers," Paul, managing two syllables, counters.

And as their blood joins and merges like a confluence of tributaries, Paul prays that his knife knows to stay sober and clean, to do no harm, to clean up its own damned messes. To remain loyal and never twist a quarter turn in his lover's guts, their guts, together.

He wonders this as their palms remain fast: Will his knife know that it is the knife of eternal separation, held aloft by an angel to enforce exile from Eden? Or will it know, like the blade slung from Orion's Belt, that through it, by way of another galaxy in another time, lies Heaven, lies reconciliation?

Killing Lucky

Corey has a friend who is a horseshoer, a farrier, and this man drives a broken-up pickup the color of sweet corn. Harlan is his given name, and he makes his living driving from farm to farm in southeast King County, in the state of Washington. He'll be lifting the fetlock of a three-year-old appaloosa mare in a barn in Cumberland, his pager will go off, and he'll be off to Selleck, or Black Diamond, to hammer shoes onto another horse in pasture sunlight.

Harlan's leisure pastime is training and showing a one-year-old gelding, a paint, in arenas around western and central Washington, maybe driving down to Oregon or up to British Columbia once a year for a show of which he is particularly fond.

He's proud of his horse, and shows Corey snapshots one night as the group fellowships outside Black Diamond Presbyterian Church. In one photo he is roping a calf. In another he's standing, with chaps and a cowboy hat, outside his own barn. And there's the shot of a mutual acquaintance of theirs, mounted on the gelding, smiling shyly at the camera, not quite comfortable in her saddle.

Corey knows next to nothing about horsemanship, even though in Boy Scouts he earned the horsemanship merit badge at summer camp one year and, for a time, owned a horse of his own. But he never took to it, and today prefers to admire horses - their shape and power and compulsion - from any distance behind a fence.

By way of explaining his own philosophy one time, Harlan, who moved to the Pacific Northwest from Mississippi by way of Texas and Louisiana, once gave Corey a good piece of advice: Do what's right in front of you; do the next indicated thing, and you'll be fine. Corey, at any moment, can hear Harlan drawling it. Solid. Sensible. Corey practices, but never quite gets it right. He suspects his friend doesn't either, all the time.

Standing here on the back porch of the church smoking cigarettes, Harlan engages Corey in whimsy: he sees the Maker of All Things in horses, in their strong chests, in the splash of earthen colors, in manes and tails and erect ears, in the cycling of their strides at gallop. In the soft light of early morning drizzle, he sees the same deity in the calm raising and lowering of a quarter horse's head as it forages and consumes pasture grass.

Harlan notes that on Palm Sunday, Our Lord road into Jerusalem on the foal of a donkey, a form of horse from his perspective. And at the end of time, four horses will thunder into chaos bearing apocalyptic warriors.

It's obvious to Corey that this southern man, migrated north with the gentleman still in his blood, derives great satisfaction from his proximity to horses. Equestrian activity brings meaning to his life, a smile to his chapped lips, a bounce to his two-legged gait. It fills spots that used to be empty, and Corey wonders what he will choose, himself, or stumble across, that can fill the same holes in him.

"You oughta think about gettin' you a horse," Harlan says. "Do you some good."

"No." Corey drags off his cigarette. "No, a horse wouldn't be right for me at all, Harlan. Not at all."

When Corey was ten years old his Boy Scout troop went for a week to Camp Cooper, across the Columbia River at The Dalles and down into Oregon, to earn the horsemanship merit badge. He still has the badge today on his olive sash, with twenty-five or so other badges, a little embroidered circle an inch and a half in diameter, with a saddle on a red background and a light green border.

Camp Cooper specialized in horses, kind of a dude ranch for little kids, and they would camp in cabins with their fellow patrol members and sing Kumbaya around campfires at night. During the day, they would sign up over the week for a curriculum to earn three or four merit badges - could be first aid, woodworking, forestry, any of the outdoors arts. But, all other badges aside, everyone at Camp Cooper went expressly to get the horsemanship badge, the course of study and application culminating in an overnighter, with horses, out in the wild hills above camp.

During the week leading up to the overnighter, the boys received instruction from rough men who seemed old to them then, but may really just have mostly been in their twenties and thirties. They taught with an affected impatience that led the boys to want to please them, to want to cinch the saddle on just right, to memorize flawlessly the parts of the horse and the names for their meters of movement - walk, trot, canter, gallop. They wanted the boys to know the reason the height of a horse is measured in hands rather than inches, and why the height of a horse terminates at the withers, and what it means when a horse lays its ears forward, down.

The boys strove, as little men, to bask in the glory of an affirming comment from the big men: to brush the horse correctly, to properly apply a hoof pick, to avoid folds or wrinkles in the saddle blanket.

They learned quickly and forever to mount the horse only from its left side.

Near week's-end, each scout was assigned a horse for the overnighter. Corey's was a roan gelding named Buck with a white blaze on its muzzle. He rode Buck up into the hills on hot trails, in single file with the other boys and the instructors, walking some, trotting, and breaking into a gallop at intervals, ducking low-hanging limbs as the shout moved backward in the column: "Tree!"

That evening each of the boys was assigned various tasks, the most fundamental being to prepare the horses for the night: removing and hanging their bridles, tying them to a suitable tree with a halter, removing saddles and blankets and the proper storing thereof, feeding the horses, and thanking them with comb, brush, hoof pick and soft words of gratitude.

They lay down in sleeping rolls outside under cover of stars and a half moon. They told scary stories to each other. The soft snorts and whispers of horses lulled them to sleep.

The boys woke early in the morning in pre-dawn rain, their sleeping rolls soaking, and cold, even for summer. The instructors ran around half dressed, pushing the boys to tie their rolls quickly, wipe the cobwebs from their minds, and saddle the horses.

By the time Corey rolled his blankets and tied them, and wandered over to where Buck was tied to the tree, light was coming up. In it he could see steam rising from Buck's back. Approaching him from the front, Corey patted and hugged Buck's muzzle, the horse's smell deep and fascinating. Lifting the bridle off a broken limb from the tree, he struggled to untangle it, to make sense of the rawhide strips and rings, clasps, the bit. After a moment of fumbling, Corey held up a configuration that seemed to be correct, at eye level for him and the horse, and attempted to place the top of the bridle over its ears. Buck's head rose suddenly, and he let out a snort, backing Corey off.

Corey tried again, and a third time, with Buck protesting more with each attempt. So he set the bridle down at the base of the tree and reached into the saddlebag for a plastic sack of oats. These Corey offered to Buck, and stroked his muzzle, sighing sweet persuasion into his ears. Trying again, Buck acquiesced, and the bridle slipped over him in perfect fit. Now, though, the gelding wouldn't open his mouth far enough for

Corey to slip the bit between his teeth. For ten minutes Corey tried to pry Buck's lips open, conscious always of the latent potential for a bitten finger. The horse's mouth remained closed.

Other boys were saddling up, nearly ready to move out. Conspicuous, Corey stood there coaxing Buck, growing impatient, trying again. One of the instructors came over.

"What's wrong?" He made no pretense of his annoyance that Corey was holding up the ride back to camp, to shelter.

"He won't eat his bit," Corey shivered in the cold rain, motioning to Buck's mouth.

The instructor poked his face close to Corey's. "Horses don't *eat* bits," he spat. Scorn and longsuffering in his tone pegged him as a martyr, and he was letting Corey know it: *Of all the stinky pre-teen kids over all the years who have come to Camp Cooper, here is the dumbest, most incapable tenderfoot and I gotta deal with it. Look at me hangin' on a cross.*

The instructor's four words having their intended effect, Corey stepped back while the instructor slipped the bit between Buck's teeth and lips without effort.

"Saddle this horse up, boy, so we can get goin'."

The day Corey met his two future step-sisters they were riding bareback through hay in the acreage of his future step-dad's pastures. They saw Corey, his sister and his mom pull up in a 1969 Buick Skylark, and galloped competently over, pulling up on their reins as Corey, thirteen years old, got out. His future step-dad stepped off the back porch and came over to the group, assuming the task of introductions.

The older girl, eleven, sat on a mid-sized black gelding and the younger one, eight, rode a Shetland pony of varied coloring, a female. They dismounted; Corey shook their hands. Both of them were pretty, the older girl strikingly so. Feeling awkward and inadequate, ugly, Corey asked about her horse.

"He's Lucky," she said, the gelding's name, confidently. "That's Cindy," she added, pointing at the pony. She offered to let Corey ride her horse.

Lacking, but wanting to demonstrate confidence, he agreed. Next came the trick of mounting a horse without stirrups and a saddle horn for leverage. Corey made several awkward attempts while the girls, including his own real flesh-and-blood sister, giggled into their hands.

"Here," the older future step-sister offered, bending and clasping her hands in a make-shift stirrup. "I'll boost you up."

Miserable, Corey stuck his left sneaker on her cupped hands, grabbed Lucky's mane with his left hand, and propelled himself off the ground with his right leg onto its broad, black back. In doing so, overzealously, he nearly threw himself over the horse. But clutching at the coarse hairs of its mane with both fists - nearly pulling some strands away - he finally found balance and righted himself. So far, so good.

Corey clicked in his mouth and squeezed his legs together a little, snapping the reins lightly, and Lucky walked forward. Gathering faith, Corey snapped the reins a little harder, laid them on the left side of his neck, and the gelding turned right and began to trot. With no saddle, this took some getting used to, but soon Corey had nearly completed a full circle. He approached the three girls, his mom and future step-dad waving. He waved back, slapped Lucky's neck with the reins, clicked again, and kicked the horse's stomach with his heels.

Lucky took off like a rocket sled, throwing Corey backward on its rump. Corey stayed on for a few moments only by coincidence, clutching the reins and bouncing left and right, the backbone hurting his butt. Then the horse turned left too quickly. That day, Corey understood the concept of inertia, flung headfirst over his right withers and piling into the hay on his left shoulder.

Humiliated, he ate barbecued ribs on the deck of the farmhouse that night in silence, while the three future sisters laughed and made friends.

Later, after his mom and step-dad were married, his real sister got a Shetland pony named Frosty one Christmas. Not wanting Corey to feel left out, his step-dad made him a gift of his half-Arabian, half-Quarter Horse mare, Molly.

Now all four of the kids had horses, and they enrolled in 4H the following spring to learn how to show and care for them.

The Clark County Fair ran the first two weeks of August. It was a calliope of rides, freak carnies, game booths, food booths and commercial and livestock exhibits. Like every fair in the United States. And like every fourteen-year-old boy, Corey wanted to spend his time at the fair riding rides, running around with a troupe of other gibbons his age in shorts and tank tops, playing games, trying to peak down girls' shirts, eating scones and corndogs, and watching the big Clydesdales crap.

Instead, enrolled in 4H, he had to join his sisters in hot jeans and goofy western square-dance shirts, and cowboy hats, and ridiculous nametags, with their four horses, for exhibition riding. The judges would sit around drinking lemonade under an awning, and give the kids marks for executing proper turns, running their horses through their gaits, the tidiness of their horse-care, and so forth.

Came Corey's and Molly's turn to ride, and she hadn't traversed twelve yards around the outdoor arena when his hat blew off into the dirt, an automatic deduction of one point. Three kids got a blue, red and white ribbon, respectively, and the rest of them got these lame orange ribbons that said PARTICIPANT with the 4H clover above and CLARK COUNTY FAIR below.

The next summer Corey was fifteen years old and more concerned with earning spending money than showing Molly. He picked strawberries and baled hay, scraped weathered paint off of eaves to prepare them for painting, mucked stables, picked tansy, those sorts of farm-maintenance chores.

Tansy ragwort. *Senecio jacobaea*, a native plant of Europe also known as Stinking Willie. It's a noxious weed that can grow between one foot and six feet high, with dark green leaves and a yellow, thirteen-petaled bloom. The entire plant contains concentrations of poisonous alkaloids and livestock that partake thereof, over time, develop irreversible liver damage. Cumulative consumption can kill the largest animals.

One of Corey's tasks was to spend an afternoon a week pushing a wheelbarrow around the pasture, pulling tansy out by the roots, and burning it. It was a difficult chore to keep up with, because each plant can produce 150,000 seeds that remain viable for fifteen years. So it's always going to be around, and it's always going to be a farm chore and on hot summer afternoons when he'd bend to pull the three-hundredth tansy ragwort plant out of the earth, he believed that he'd always be doing it, forever.

That summer his mom and step-dad flew off to Hawaii for a delayed honeymoon. Ten days, fifteen years old, Corey had the run of the farm to himself.

The first day after they'd departed Portland International Airport for Honolulu, Corey went out by himself to muck the stables, brush and feed the horses. Lucky stamped in his stall. He gnawed on the wooden half-walls of the stable and as the posts that provided structural support for the barn. He was sweating when Corey groomed him out, froth building up in the teeth of the comb. Corey brought some water in, and some fresh hay. Lucky ignored it.

The next day the horse was absent, and Corey noticed the indicator light on the switchbox for the electric fence was off. He saddled Molly and road the perimeter of the pasture. Near a back corner, he found where Lucky had burst through the fence and clambered off through a thicket. Lucky had broken through vine maple limbs and torn the ground up completely as he exited the pasture. Corey had no idea where to begin looking for him.

The boy called his step-dad's father, who calmed him down a bit and called *The Reflector*, Battleground's weekly newspaper, to place an ad for a lost horse. Calling his son and new daughter-in-law in Hawaii, Corey's step-grandfather assured them everything that could be done was, in fact, right now being done, so they should stay there and enjoy their holiday.

On the morning *The Reflector* came out, the phone rang at the farm. The caller believed they had found the lost horse, and asked Corey to come over to verify Lucky's identity. The horse wasn't in very good shape, the caller added, gave directions, and hung up before Corey could press for details.

Lucky lay gasping in a foreign pasture, a crust of dried froth around his mouth, his breath heaving. The farmer who took Corey down to the horse said that he had been standing that morning, had fallen a couple of times and raised himself up again, but hadn't risen for a couple of hours.

He'd been waiting for *The Reflector* to show up at his mailbox, knowing he'd find an ad, and had already called a veterinarian.

"This horse has been into tansy," he stated, neutrally, a fact. "He isn't going to live much longer, son."

Corey watched Lucky's labored breathing, and the horse's whole body shuddered. His eyes rolled back into his head, showing only the whites as he coughed and sprayed mucus out his nostrils over the hay stubble.

Corey turned to the farmer and asked him whether he had a rifle. The farmer nodded and turned to walk for his house. Corey sat down on the ground next to Lucky and spoke softly to him, solaced the animal, tried to anaesthetize his pain and confusion with sighed banalities.

"You'll be all right soon, Lucky," Corey whispered, wondering in his mind whether he had the courage of murder for mercy. Distracted from the horse for a moment, Corey indulged selfish fear and black fascination, brooding on what it would look like and sound like to fire a round into this horse's head, the hole appearing, blood flowing out, and his body shaking and then still. *Could I do this thing, make this right?*

The farmer came out of his house with a .22 caliber rifle at the same time the vet pulled up. They met in his driveway, and Corey saw the farmer motion out into the pasture and the two set off toward the boy and the horse. Corey's attention snapped back to Lucky, now observing him, intently, out of his left eye. *Does he see me?* Corey wondered.

Corey cradled Lucky's dark head in his hands, lifting it to get his arms underneath.

The weight of it pulled Corey back down on all fours, right down there where he could sense the sour smell of Lucky's fear, the musk of his pain. Then Corey saw Lucky's eye focus sharply. Fierce black, it started, contracted, then began to wane and lose its center. Light flew from it in a galloping jet across a prairie. Wind blew through his mane across a landscape of release.

Corey marveled at this and hoped the farmer would hurry with the rifle. Yet the boy trembled still with indecision, and hoped that the farmer would never come. Then Lucky died in Corey's arms.

His death rattle sounded.

Listen to What the Crow Says

I am waiting. Cold bites into my flesh, through multiple layers of wool and nylon. The hard surface of the redwood stump I chose an hour and a half ago as a seat, compliant with the fatty tissue of buttocks at first, has become a numbing fakir's cot. I feel like I'm frozen in place, that if I move, I'll crack. My breath, in steam, flows out and floats away.

Equipped with rifle, field glasses, compass, buck knife, wool coat and cowboy hat, I'd hiked in for thirty minutes from a logging road. I moved slowly, in the foggy dark, pausing to listen every few steps for the crack of limbs, the signature of startled game. I resented the fog. Deep and smoky, it would make discernment difficult, masking gender and making yearlings and cows indistinguishable from mature bulls. It would steal the precious seconds one has to verify that an animal can be taken. To fire a well-placed kill shot. Even so, weather changes frequently here at five-thousand feet, and I'm optimistic: the worst day hunting is better than the best day doing... well... just about anything else.

Sitting here, I've thought of everything, some things a number of times, turning matters over and over between my ears - a dangerous place to linger. It's rough, because as I wait for game outside, I'm inside my head. And that's a strange neighborhood. Even for five minutes, let alone ninety.

Dawn has happened around me, so now shapes that seemed only questions have taken on definition. The odd mists have evaporated in snatches of sunlight, and the fog seems to have broken for a while. Dark places I earlier wouldn't look at now teem with squirrels and small, flitting birds, and are filled, overflowing with color. The knot of these woods, irresolvable in the darkness of pre-dawn, began to clarify with the rising of light. Now, in full morning, it looks simple. The progression of dawn in the forest is like the rite of a small boy who finally learns to tie his shoes: mystery, complexity made routine. A knot comprehended and solved.

Elk-hunting comprises long stretches - hours at a time - of attempting to sit motionless, silent, on a stump or log providing a secreted, but systemic, view of a ravine or hillside one believes the animals will graze in. Hunters look for fresh sign - moist scat and hoof prints with motes of dry earth in them - that will indicate the recent presence of animals. Then they survey the area for a reasonably comfortable spot to wait, one where two or three hours can be passed before time and failing anticipation overwhelm them and they must move on. This is happening to me now, but I will myself to tarry. How many times have I risen from one of these long sits to have the forest exploded around me with fleeing elk? How many times were they about to wander into my field of vision, into range of my ordnance, but startled by my gathering and movement, leapt off to another ravine? A rule for the long-term investor: wait five more minutes.

So I do, and the time stretches out and I stare at the second hand on my watch and count its long sweep. It seems an eternity, and I glance up *knowing* an elk is about to wander into the clear. But five minutes pass, forever, and I rise with the creaking and stretching of tendons and bones and believe it's true - I am about to crack, to shatter like a frozen mirror. I take an aching, noisy step and, still, there is silence in the woods around me, disproving the rule this time.

I take some steps into the ravine I've been surveying for ninety-five minutes. Fog is gathering again, deeper than before. Soon I'm on a game trail, its cut clear on the forest floor, dividing salal and other undergrowth with a ribbon of pine needles, spotted with deer and elk tracks, droppings. There are so many trails, they lay like a matrix over the forest - to follow one would be impossible. I wonder, in the presence of such an extensive network of trails, why game isn't spotted constantly, why deer and elk don't criss-cross in front of me every ten seconds. But I also know that even a small number of animals are capable of making them, so the number of trails and the proliferation of their web is a false indicator of population.

Moving slowly across the ravine on this trail, I cross over some limbs and around a stand of mountain juniper, pick up another trail, and begin to climb out of the canyon. The fog is yet fog denser here, and enveloping. The woods around me gather and close. The trail moves into the trees: so do I. Dry lower limbs scrape across my coat and face, some crack as I press through a tight spot, and the trail continues. And as the route winds past a fallen hemlock, blown down in a windstorm, I spot a black object ahead of me, directly in the center of the trail.

A crow, dead, lying on its side with wings stowed and feet tucked in. It is clearly not a raven, the Passeriform most common to these woods. Its size - about ten inches from beak to tail feather - confirms this. A raven is larger, sometimes more than two feet long.

I pause for a moment and wonder that its body lies here - any animal's corpse in the forest is almost instantly consumed by other animals, either in an act of depredation by a pack of coyotes, or carried off by a wildcat. And then it occurs to me that this crow must have just

41

died, maybe only moments ago, falling from one of the branches above me. I look up and examine the overstory, as if the answer waits there. But silence, and no revelation, rewards my query.

Looking back down at the bird, I prod it with my boot. It is pliant, lending more credence to my theory that this crow has recently expired. I stoop toward it, note that its eye has gone milky but the sheen of its feather oils, even in the fog, remains. Its beak is slightly open and I can see the tongue inside. On my haunches now, my body starts to protest this position, so I drop to my knees and examine, more closely, the bird. Even in death, it is pretty, but not as majestic as I would expect a raven, lying in state, to be. For a moment, I wish I had come upon the resting place of a raven rather than a common crow.

As I look at its body, impressions formed from my own culturalization dart in my imagination:

Crow is the yard bird - he is the black cawing, cloying grouper at school recess. Crow is inelegant. He shouts at his children, demanding compliance through intimidation and psychological manipulation, a form of witchcraft. He casts his spell by shrieking at his little crowlets, and they grow up and pass this curse on to their children and thus crow is the father and mother of a black cycle over and over and over again. Crow's biting *caw* pokes like an unexpected needle. He is the target of bad boys with BB guns, on power lines. Crow eats the entrails of road kill, sets back on the asphalt, hitches his suspenders, flutters out of the way as an automobile thunders by: he hopes for another mishap. Crow cannot properly articulate his feelings, but settles into fury and takes his toys away after disagreement. Crow is not discreet and blabs indiscriminately to friends, who soon become enemies: Do not tell him your secrets! Ubiquitous crow is no gentleman but, rather, a philandering rook. Crow is flatulence. Spring-Heeled Jack was a crow, and remains a crow to this day. Crow is the Rodney Dangerfield of all birds, the jackass of jackdaws.

Raven, on the other hand, is the velvet beauty. She is the ebony messenger across the divides and folds and heritage of our mountainous world. She is courtly, a sophisticant without effort. She raises her children gracefully, and they pass this on to generations of ravens. Poe quoted her respectfully as she is the queen of all black birds, as well as jays, choughs, magpies and nutcrackers. Raven's seductive *honk*, silky, is a warm invitation to communion and intimate relations. She sounds like a warm, wet tongued reed. She is the arbitrator, the mediator, the agency of good offices. The bringer of good news. Through her clemency, reconciliation is sought, achieved and treasured. Your secrets are safe with her! Rarer than the crow, she is comely, a good witch.

Sloughing this hyperbolic train of thought, I pick him up, forsaking a cleanly upbringing that suggested found animals might be disease-ridden. What affliction could linger here, bacterially, in these unblemished woods? I'm shocked to find he weighs almost nothing, less than a small sack of sawdust, I would guess, then realize that I have never in my life held something as simple and plentiful as a bird. He fits well in my gloves, and his body still is soft. I remove one glove, wanting to feel and smooth its feathers, experience tactile - if unilateral - intimacy. His surface is cold. I lift him closer to my face, run my index finger across his beak, pinch it closed between my thumb and forefinger. Stare at his cloudy eyes.

Even though it's not a raven, an idea evolves that I might take him with me, out of the forest, home, to stuff and place on my mantel. I have a budding interest in taxidermy, and he would make an interesting conversation piece. I'd keep him cold in one of the ice-chests back at camp until we break, take him home and put him in the freezer. Keep him on ice until I've read up on taxidermy and can execute a first experiment. It's reasonable, compelling. I decide to do it.

I stand with the crow, turn and start to hike back up the hill, in the direction where I know the road lies, where the truck waits for my return. It will take me probably forty-five minutes to hike out of this steep system, depending on how thick the woods are above me. As I take steps on the climb out, I have to pause every fifteen yards or so to catch my breath. And during one of these pauses, which are usually void of intelligence but useful only for dumb, mute physical recovery, I again engage in whimsy on the subject of crows versus ravens:

As the crow flies -

This expression is used to define the shortest distance between two points. People will ask how far is it to Point B, from here, Point A. Other people, who have the answer, will say, oh, it's nine miles as the crow flies. They're not talking about getting there by road, which may be twelve or nineteen or a hundred and twenty miles. They're talking about overland, a straight line, a geodesic - or more precisely, an arc of a great circle of large distance, perhaps across oceans.

As the raven flies -

This could be a deeper, more profound mystery. It could change our sense of direction and migration forever. The shortest distance between two points is a straight line unless you move the two points together. Try

43

it with a sheet of notebook paper: mark two points, then fold the paper so the points come together, make contact. Point A becomes unified with Point B. That's the way a raven flies.

I consider this algorithm, pleased with myself in the way that people are when they believe they have stumbled across some profundity with the sharpness of their intellect or the labor of their hard work. They don't pause to think of how many times before, in all of human history, some ancestor thought the very same thought until soon the wisdom of "discovery" became folklore, or something much worse. Columbus on the shores:
I seem to have discovered a new world. Natives scratching their heads, on the mantel of North America for thousands of years: *Who's this goofball?*

Still, this is *my* thought, right now, and it proves I can come up with something inventive once in a while. Somewhere in it may lie the answer to the problem, then, of time travel, and I postulate that Einstein had the soul of a raven - an insoluble mathematical proof, to be sure. I am no physicist; I'm sure I'm confusing elements of the General Theory of Relativity - in which objects accelerating with respect to one another explain apparent conflicts with relativity and gravity, and gravity is held to be analogous to acceleration, and there is the fourth dimension of time and it can be made to slow and bend around massive objects, and reverse itself. The thought is delicious.

Sir Isaac Newton, who believed that every object attracts every other object in direct proportion to its mass, was thus proved misguided by Wild-Haired Albert at his Princeton blackboard, pumping out chalk hieroglyphics. Newton, beaned by the apple, must have had a simpler soul, the soul of a crow - yet I am drawn powerfully to this crow in my hands: I am five hundred times more massive, yet pulled inexorably to his field.

This is hard thinking, a knot only solvable by the fingers and mind of God, and I lose the train in a wreckage of synapses as my body and lungs and heartbeat recover from the last spurt of climbing. And the crow - whom I shall name Sir Isaac of the Fireplace Mantel - is still here in my grip.

Shaking my head from the mental labor, clearing my ears with a snort, I weigh anchor again and climb. Twelve more steps and I break out of the tight woods into a moderate clearing, and the way plateaus for fifty yards or so before the final climb to the road. The fog is still thick, and it muffles the routine sounds of the forest morning, sounds usually bright and pointed, of small animals going about their business.

I stride across the clearing at nearly a fast pace and hold the crow's corpse to my chest with my right hand, stabilizing the rifle with my left thumb hooked in the sling.

And sense a change in the clearing that grows and gains focus as rustling in my right palm, between the light curl of my fingers.

Release me.

I stop for a moment, and stare at the bird.

Release me.

I examine his wings, his tail, the gloss of his feathers, his unclouded sentient eyes, his moving beak, and he speaks, commands, pleads: "Release me."

The crow's wings flap and the surprise shocks me, and I lose my grip and the crow slips from my grasp, but I grope quickly and snare a wing and hold on. And the crow struggles, then settles, then fights again and I look into his magnificent, intelligent black eyes. And let go.

He gathers - an eminence - then flies away through the clearing, disappearing into fog through pine branches at the perimeter.

Flight Into Terrain

The sky is gray, threatening rain again as Kevin and his brother, Tim, jump out of the 4Runner at the end of a spur off 254 Road. This is the most ambitious point of all elk-hunting in the northeast corner of the Nile game management unit, a quarter-mile hook of road that jumps off a steep climb through thick woods and settles out into open air - the transition from western to eastern Washington state perceived in the declination of coniferous trees. This line runs ridge for ridge behind them, and every year they come here, once, to sit and wait for elk to pass through.

The mud road has ruts that have filled with melt from the season's first snows. It terminates in a wilderness cul-de-sac at the bow of a steep ridge. Over the edge, at the bottom half a mile away, the north fork of Nile Creek rushes down to join the Naches River. From this spine, across the valley to the west, lies thick forest and elevation. Turning to the east, the face of the opposing ridge, bare grass and sagebrush, rising and folding to lower hills and valleys. Bethel Ridge, sprouting antenna and fire-observation structures, is barely discernible miles distant in the falling light.

A quiet, inconsequential rainfall starts. Kevin and Tim load their rifles and separate. Tim will walk back up 254 Road on the ridge and double over on the bare hill to the east. Kevin will remain in this area, near the 4Runner.

Two seasons ago, they hunted this same system one afternoon and arrived to find perhaps an acre of the area, just as the hill falls away from the cul-de-sac, scorched from fire. Remnants of orange plastic emergency tape still fluttered from charred trees and bushes. Halfway from the center of the burned circle, toward the west, a crater of bare earth, hardpanned, the soil's elements and composition morphed by heat and impact. A small airplane crashed here. Tim had retrieved two feet of the tape, wrapped and knotted it around his cowboy hat, and wore it like a ribbon for several subsequent days.

Each of the following seasons morbid curiosity has drawn them to this spot. As in past years, there is no fresh elk sign here - spoor is at least two months old, and the only hoofprints are baked into the ground like fossils. Yet they must return, Kevin supposes, to ponder the enormity of impact, of the release of energy, of last confused moments, of loneliness.

Kevin wanders about for a while in his boots, wool trousers, hunter-orange coat, scanning the ground for fresh sign. Pees on a rock, exposed. Selects a boulder to sit on and pass the time, ears on the alert. Alive.

He sits, then closes his eyes and sees, on a similar hillside ten-thousand miles from this spot, a duty-free cart smashed from cube to pyramid. Intact bottles of Courvoisier, their labels scorched and turned up at the edges. Full cartons of Marlboro cigarettes, compressed at one end, their plastic wrapping partially melted. A torn fragment of fiberglass. A little orange flag flapping on a wire stick. A woman's shoe.

The scene of disaster.

Korean Air Lines Flight 801, a Boeing 747 carrying 231 passengers and 23 crew members, descended perfectly through gusty rainfall from two-thousand feet early in the morning on August 6, 1997, on approach to Guam's Won Pat International Airport.

Passengers, most of them tourists from Seoul flying to Guam for a week of sun and respite from business concerns, were belted in their seats - as were flight attendants - for a routine landing. In the cockpit, the pilot and first officer checklisted Guam landing procedures in Korean, ticking through the process. Gear down. Flaps at thirty degrees. Throttles back.

On Nimitz Ridge, a poacher searches for small deer after midnight. Rain and light wind have hampered the night's illegal activity. He's tired but still hopeful.

The poacher hears the approach of a large airplane without alarm. He's hunted here many times, directly in the flight path, and notes nothing strange about the constant sound of the jet's engines.

Suddenly he hears an enormous crunch, then a universe-filling boom accompanied by brilliant orange light, and the compression wave knocks him to the ground and he's uttering, confused, in Chamorra, *God is Great, Hail Mary Mother of God.*

The co-pilot of a Ryan International 727 hauling freight into Guam leans over to peer through breaks in clouds at the approach to Won Pat. Occasional lightning pulses inside the towers of cumulonimbus and he reviews, with his pilot, the descent track and glideslope for landing.

The co-pilot turns to his partner. A red flash registers in the sweep of his peripheral vision. Quickly, he turns back to the flash. It firms up as a glow from beneath clouds at the center of the island, throbbing. They contact Agana tower.

The Korean jet has just passed through seven hundred feet at 140 knots when a dense, profound two-pointed thud shudders through the entire airframe: Manifestation of the port outboard engine clipping trees and dirt, then separating from the wing pylon. The anomaly transfers through the structure of the airplane in shock and sound waves, reaching the cockpit a second before a hillside looms, fills the windows.

The pilot jams the throttles forward. The jumbo jet's nose rises a little. But the seamount of Guam has risen from the Pacific Ocean and grabbed this airliner - perhaps offended that aeronautics is practical science - out of the sky.

Four-hundred tons of aluminum, titanium, fiberglass and human souls pile into the ridge in flaming pursuit. In an eternity of three seconds, the fuselage severs at the juncture of foil and skin and again just in front of the empennage. Exploding fuel flies everywhere. The forward third of the fuselage ejects the cockpit, then twists in the hillside's refusal back on the rest of the craft. The empennage careens forward into the middle section like the stowing of a telescope. The starboard wing, still generating lift, jumps up, up, up and around in a wide arc. It drops two engines and slams atop the left-hand wing.

The air is hot, thick, tropic. Sawgrass and other vegetation grow abundantly in this part of the world. After passing a controlled-ingress station staffed by soldiers with
M-16s, a Guam police truck carries the team down a red-clay road. It winds along a ridge on Nimitz Hill next to an oil pipeline that moves fuel from processing plants at the south of the island to Anderson Air Force Base, at Guam's north end.

The team jumps out of the pickup's bed as it rolls to a stop. They walk past refrigerated morgue tents with American Red Cross signs on them, then down a steep thoroughfare bulldozed through thick plants and carpeted with loose gravel. They round a corner. A grim vista cuts through the humid air. It hits Kevin like a fist of ice.

The burned remnants of Korean Air Flight 801 lie in front of them, impossibly.

The area is teeming with Red Cross volunteers, Army and Navy personnel, National Transportation Safety Board people, surveying and salvage contractors, local law enforcement, representatives of Korean Air and the airplane's manufacturer. A Red Cross volunteer, a kid, maybe a teenager, walks up with a handful of towels and a grocery bag of bottled water. "You'll want these," he says.

The air is oppressive with the stench of death. The team has arrived thirty-eight hours after the accident and all retrievable human remains have been collected. Yet there remain more than a hundred corpses still crushed beneath the sections of fuselage too heavy to move without cranes.

The airplane is a tableau of disintegration. How could anyone have survived this, as did a handful? Working in airplane factories for twelve years, it's easy for Kevin to swallow the illusion that the beefy structure of a modern jetliner is inviolate. He ponders that every step of the manufacturing process is meticulous, more so than in any other industry save, perhaps, the assembly of space vehicles or submarines. It's troubling, unnerving to ponder how the careful integration, on a clean factory floor, of stout intercostals and stringers, thick airplane skins, huge titanium structural members, powerful fasteners, could terminate in this chaos. Simple clay should yield to the authority of such a perfectly engineered machine. It seems oddly counterintuitive that it doesn't.

How could this have happened? The orange black-boxes, the cockpit voice and flight data recorders, already have been quickly retrieved from their hiding place above what remained of the aft galley and shipped to Washington, D.C., via Honolulu for readout. Perhaps they will provide clues.

The immediate area resembles a city dump: pieces of wreckage, clothing and shoes, luggage, paperbacks, seats, stuffed toys, panels, a landing gear strut, loose paper, blowing litter all cross the gouged earth where the airliner dug in and slid to an abrupt stop. Orange flags mark the resting places of passengers or crew thrown clear during impact. Analysts trying to understand the dynamics of the crash will chart these locations to shed new light on survivability factors.

Kevin and the rest of the team walk around, slipping on the hills of mud, cutting their hands while grasping sawgrass to get their balance.

Stepping around wreckage, the team is directed to the flight deck, a hundred yards from the rest of the airplane. It had been flung from the rest of the fuselage, tumbling end for end, coming to rest upside down near the bottom of a ravine. The bodies of the pilot and co-pilot, completely broken, have been removed. Now inspectors are taking readings from the analog components in the flight deck to determine whether they indicated altitude and airspeed properly up to the instant of impact. An open, stained Jeppesen Manual flutters in a slight gust, lying next to torn electrical wiring yanked out by the inertial force of the flight deck's break-up.

Kevin makes an electronic impression of the readouts with a digital camera: airspeed is 140; altitude 0656. One man is removing some of the digital components, which will have to be hooked up to power back at the Air Force Base and read out through a computer. He hands Kevin a plastic sack enveloping the ground-proximity warning computer and asks him to take it back to the Red Cross tent. Kevin performs this service for the investigation, pleased with his contribution. Up to this point he has felt vestigial - a non-engineer encountering a compelling engineering challenge.

Rain starts to fall lightly through the heat. Kevin slips back up the hill, fighting again for balance. Cresting the bluff, the wreckage lies again before him as he sweats. Volunteers have located another piece of matter, placing the tissue carefully inside an olive-green body bag, nesting it respectfully on a stretcher and then - four of them for remains that may weigh all of two pounds - carry what may be the last earthly evidence of an anonymous life across detritus, up the hill, and into the morgue tent.

A chorus of wailing fills the quiet of the hillside. Every worker looks up and snaps attention to a group of mourners who have been brought to an overlook some two-hundred yards away and slightly above the wreckage. The governor of Guam has arranged tours to the site for family members flown to the venue by Korean Air. As they grieve and throw flower petals, some faint and the sound fades, and the hair on the back of Kevin's neck settles. One woman has lost twelve family members - she is utterly alone now and will show up on CNN hollow-eyed, barely believing.

The workers return to the enormity of the task at hand, clinicians. B must follow A and precede C in order for them to carry out their work here, in order to contribute to the prevention of another air disaster. They are professionals and must distance themselves from emotions that will overwhelm them when they finally slip, exhausted and dehydrated, between hotel sheets tonight thousands of miles and time zones from those whom they love.

This Kevin knows: To fly on a modern commercial jetliner is to enjoy the safest method of passage in humankind's history. The data cannot be disputed. It is far more dangerous to climb behind the wheel of an automobile every morning and commute. Flying is safer than riding a horse, safer than bathing.

But that's a numbers game, he realizes, and the demise of an airliner and the lives of many - if not all - the individuals on board touches a chord deep in humankind's nature. The instantaneous and constant feed from the news media abets all of this: If it bleeds it leads.

Nervous flyers, uncomfortable with the notion that someone else has assumed control, number among themselves a minority group that believes the absurd: to mutter this incantation *This airplane will not crash This airplane will not crash* guarantees the fulfillment of that declaration.

Sit next to one sometime.

You'll sense his faith through his fear, and see his head snap up, looking abruptly around whenever the airframe bounces unexpectedly on turbulence.

Experts in airframe structures burrow in under the giant wings of the 747 to verify the jackscrew settings on the flaps indicate they were set at 30 degrees, appropriate for routine landing. Powerplant engineers find all four engines had ingested dirt and debris, blades bent out and back, with no signs of fire. This means they were operating properly.

The tenor of the investigation, wide open at first, begins to focus on the interaction between the crew and the landing environment, guiding mechanisms, tower communication and weather. A study of Doppler radar charts reveals enhanced reflectivity in the area at the time of the crash. Cells of rain, some heavy, may have contributed to poor visibility. Investigators wonder whether the pilot and co-pilot might have been confused by "black holes" - areas without visual reference on the ground - streetlights, headlights from moving vehicles, that sort of thing. Some wonder if the flight crew believed that the VOR - the outward vectoring

51

beacon to the runway, three miles distant from the airport - was the footing of the landing strip itself. Why did the officers on the flight deck believe everything was O.K. at 656 feet of altitude when they should have been at 1440 feet at this point? The cockpit voice recorder and the flight data recorder reveal only that this flight was routine in every aspect, except for a premature, but fully controlled and intentional descent.

The hoard of journalists dwindles as the story becomes banal. There is a brief report from Texas that an eleven-year-old girl flown to one of the leading burn units in the world has succumbed there. Now the number of survivors stands at twenty-eight.

A week after the crash, the United States government has turned over the wreckage to Korean Air. The portions of the investigation interested in the structural sequence of events and airplane performance have concluded. The airline contracts with a salvage company to take possession of the wreckage as Typhoon Winnie gathers to the east and heads for Guam, Saipan and Rota.

The outer arms of Winnie slap at Guam for two days, gusting winds and rain at fifty to sixty miles per hour. Kevin has received clearance to leave the on-site investigation and return to Seattle. He makes arrangements to fly to Honolulu on a Continental Micronesia 747, then to change airplanes and fly back to Sea-Tac.

But the typhoon has wrought havoc on airline schedules, limiting their ability to move equipment and passengers around the South Pacific. Unthinking, he checks out of his hotel room, refuels his rental car, and arrives at Won Pat airport a couple hours before the scheduled departure of his flight.

Queuing with hundreds of other hopeful passengers at the Continental desk, Kevin hears that flights have been canceled. Most airplanes can't get it or are stuck at other airports, so there are fewer options to fly out. Continental staff accommodates each of those waiting, in turn, with suggestions about other airlines and routes. Kevin winds up at the Delta ticket counter and lucks out with a DC-10 flight to Narita, then Honolulu, then Seattle - eighteen and half hours in coach class and layovers. He'll take it.

Banking over the Puget Sound area on a summer evening, the beauty of Kevin's country leaps up at him. Crystal off water, ebbing pink-white from Rainier and Baker, green, and then the city and lights rising and rising towards him. Turning over Elliott Bay, the airplane begins its approach to Sea-Tac International Airport. Kevin looks out the window at the wing and hears the hum of actuators as the flaps are engaged and articulated, and senses the retardation of the craft's airspeed. Motors turn and the gear lowers. The airplane drops further toward the ground.

Three miles from the runway, just after crossing Interstate 5 and Boeing Field, Kevin thinks, *this is where, this close, they were right here,* and then they are landing and he is home.

The smell stays with Kevin, even now. On a hillside in eastern Washington, a hemisphere away from Nimitz Hill, Kevin can smell it. He wonders whether the ghosts of the occupants of the light airplane that crashed here will be cold in the coming winter, now only a month off. Or are they looking down from heaven, pulling for us to release our obsession with mortality? Or is there an abrupt explosion, then nothing?

Tim's familiar voice calls from the 4Runner, disturbing this inky, pointless line of questioning.

Kevin rises, shakes it off like his night terrors, shoulders his rifle, and heads in.

A Quilt of Polaroids

It was nine seasons of elk hunting the Nile game management unit before the crippled man with the cowboy hat at Eagle Rock said anything more to me than good morning or good afternoon.

Cresting Chinook Pass from western Washington on Highway 410, we would drive our rigs down out of the high mountain country around Rainier. We'd pass over the American River several times on bridges as it tumbled down from the Cascades. A wall of forest on both sides of the straight highway, we'd pass through Cliffdell, running past Whistlin' Jack's at 70 miles per hour no matter how icy the road. Ten minutes later, we would pull into the lot at the Woodshed, Eagle Rock's restaurant, tavern and grocery. Light corn snow falling.

Here we would throw out some money for overpriced, last-minute provisions before heading across the Naches River and up into the hills fifteen miles on roads used for logging during summer. Periodically during the course of the twelve-day hunt, we'd come back down to Eagle Rock and wait in line for the single coin-operated phone with other hunters in fluorescent hats, coats, and days-old stubble, all calling their wives or sweethearts and telling their little sons about all the game they were seeing. We'd stock up on more cases of beer, and some supplementary lantern mantels, maybe refill a five-gallon container with unleaded gas.

The crippled man with the cowboy hat always smiled and tipped his hat, but limited his speech to good morning and good afternoon. He'd come out of a trailer at the north side of the grocery half of the Woodshed, behind the dumpsters, in his hat and Levi's, and a button-down logger's shirt, and say good morning as he limped past you. Or he'd be in the bar in the restaurant half of the Woodshed, or behind the counter in the grocery, and say good afternoon.

We never came out of the high country for an interim shopping trip without consolidating our water back at camp and bringing the empty cans back to the Woodshed to refill. Always have a full supply of water at camp is the rule - you never know what the weather's going to do during elk-hunting season. More than one hunt has been snowed in for a few days beyond what was anticipated.

The evening the crippled man with the cowboy hat said something more to me than good morning or good afternoon, we'd come out, my uncle and I in his red Jeep, to refuel and fill up with water. It was evening, after the second hunt of the day. We drove the fifteen miles of logging roads in the dark, the Jeep's running lights cutting into the night, tires and shocks and chassis shaking on the washboard road surface. Rodents darted across the road, and sometimes deer leapt out to run in front of the Jeep, startling us, then disappeared back into the woods just as we were about to overtake them.

The temperature had fallen from a clear high of 40 degrees, dropping quickly through the 30s and 20s in the half hour since the sun had disappeared behind the mountains. It now flirted with 15. The heavens were exploding with inescapable perfect starlight and the Milky Way spanned north to south like a banner. Watching long enough on nights like this, we'd see shooting stars, satellites. Pulling into the gravel parking lot, we recalled one rare time from a previous hunting season where we stood in front of the Woodshed gasping in awe at aurora borealis, which pulsed like a veil of crystal lava above the Wenas and Manastash Creek areas to the north.

It was so cold that moisture froze in our noses, even inside the Jeep. A blizzard of condensation blew from my mouth ever time I exhaled, gray ice collecting in my mustache and beard. Even so, the hunters were lined up for the phone. Our headlights swept them as they stamped their feet, impatient with the fellow on the phone in the booth.

We'd each called home the night before, so the line wasn't our concern. Pulling up to the pumps, we climbed out, bones and muscles sore from the day's exertions in the hills. My uncle started to refuel the Jeep while I grabbed the two water containers and walked over to the corner of the grocery. A steel pipe rose from the asphalt there. A spigot on top was connected to a four-foot length of green garden hose. Bending over, I slid the first water container over and reached with my other hand to collect the end of the hose, rubber stiff in the cold, and shoved the tip down through the container's orifice. Then I reached over to turn the spigot. Nothing.

The crippled man with the cowboy hat had noticed us from his station behind the counter inside. He limped out to me.

"Good afternoon," he said, smiling. "Pipe's frozen."

"Yeah." I smiled, too. But then I added - feeling foolish that he'd found it necessary to come out in the freezing air and interpret the malfunction for me, like I was some city boy - "I just figured that out."

He didn't mean anything by it, though, and either overlooked or didn't catch my slight sarcasm. Soon we were talking about the hunt, and how it was stacking up against previous years' hunts, and sharing our opinions of how the state department of fish and wildlife was being run.

"Game management," he said. "Now there's something you don't have to know nothing about to get a good-payin' job, and once in a while get to ride around out in the woods in a nice rig."

"Yeah," I said - knowing nothing about requirements for jobs with Fish & Wildlife and assuming that as public servants for the State of Washington, they were probably just trying to do what was best - but wanting to be affable. "Get a degree in biology in the classroom, and suddenly we're all hunting spikes. There's more and more restrictions every year."

We both nodded. He knew what we were talking about. I just strung words together. I really needed to get him to refocus on the problem of the frozen pipe, on the issue of refilling water containers.

My uncle finished fueling the Jeep and drove over to the side of the grocery, where I wouldn't have to carry the heavy containers, full, so far. Climbing out, he saw that I hadn't yet filled them. He guessed right the reason.

"Listen," he said, "I got something that'll take care of that."

He walked around to the back of his Jeep and opened the tailgate. He wrested a propane torch from clamps on his rollbar and hefted it in his big ungloved hand as he returned.

I was freezing, the cold creeping right down into my marrow, even with layers of thermal underwear, a T-shirt, a Seahawks sweatshirt and my red wool coat. "That'll crack the pipe, won't it?" I asked.

The crippled man with the cowboy hat shook his head.

"You just do it real slow like," my uncle said. "Apply the flame with care. Don't touch the pipe with it. Run it along so the tip of the flame is just shy of the metal."

He dropped to his knees and twisted the release knob on the torch half a turn, then lit it with a pop from the crippled man with the cowboy hat's cigarette lighter. An eager jet of energy thrust out of the end of the blow torch, blue hot at the core and trailing to gold and orange. He fiddled with the knob a little, fine-tuning the torch until it burned exactly to specifications known only to him. "Watch," he said. Then he began to run the flame up and down the pipe, near the metal but not touching it, the acute light shining as points on the dark irises of his eyes.

The crippled man with the cowboy hat knelt down next to him on one knee, watching in silence. There was no room for me to kneel down and watch closer, so I stood there looking down again at the operation. A couple of other hunters began to take interest in my uncle's industry and walked over. Before long, a small group had formed. My uncle didn't notice any of them. He just continued thawing the pipe.

After twenty minutes, he turned off the torch. The jet seemed to suck itself back into the torch and flicker there for a few seconds as candleflame. Then it disappeared with a tiny pop.

"Try it now," he said.

He and the crippled man with the cowboy hat stood and stepped back. I turned the handle and heard the rush of flow up from below. In stops and starts at first, then steady, water raced out the end of the hose. I thrust it quickly into the container's hole, and the gathering of hunters applauded my uncle. I heard one of them say, "Fuckin' A," and offer to buy my uncle a beer in the Woodshed.

The group went inside the tavern. The crippled man with the cowboy hat separated from them at the grocery door and went in. I filled the first container, transferring the hose to the second in a rapid motion, trying to minimize the water spilled on the asphalt. No sense in adding to the ice there. After the second container was full, I shut off the spigot and screwed the caps back onto both containers. Then I hefted them one at a time into the Jeep.

I turned and walked to the grocery door, pulled it open. A little heralding bell jangled on the doorknob, and I stepped onto the hardwood floor into heat for the first time that day.

The grocery half of the Woodshed at Eagle Rock came from the same mold as so many rural stores. Scrubbed plank floors resonated with the sound of your boots, and two aisles had the basics of food, first aid, toiletries, candy bars, supplies. Newsracks contained the last copies of Yakima's daily newspaper. At the counter you could buy a dozen different kinds of pepperoni sticks and jerky, or maps of the logging roads for miles around. You could buy a sweatshirt that read *Eagle Rock University* for $25. A stand-up cooler branded with PEPSI running up the side glowed in one corner next to a door to another room. A piece of paper tacked on the door read *Showers $5.*

The walls had all the usual stuff. Painted canvas signs from beer distributors hung for the latest Bud Lite sale. Neon signs advertising other brands of beer hummed in the windows, and there were four or five mounted heads - an elk, a couple of deer, a mountain goat. At Eagle Rock though, management - the crippled man with the cowboy hat, I presumed - had mounted Polaroid photos of hunters and their kills across the store, each picture like a block of a quilt. Dating back to the early 1970s, Polaroid snapshots covered every portion of the walls not

57

otherwise occupied, chronologically, until the present day. Hundreds of grinning hunters and hundreds of dead elk, deer, goats, bear - even some pheasants, grouse and chukars here and there. On the larger border at the base of each snapshot was written the date and hunter's name.

The older photos were grainy and faded. As the years wound on and I crossed the store, the clarity of the pictures improved with the pace of Polaroid technology, I suppose, until there were seventeen clear photographs of last year's hunt, and a snapshot or two of remarkable clarity from this year's, snapped in the past few days.

Lost, wrapped in the quilt of Polaroids while my uncle drank in the bar, dreaming of my Polaroid joining the hundreds on the walls, I didn't notice at first that the crippled man with the cowboy hat had come up to stand beside me.

"Pretty cool," he said.

"Yeah." I didn't look at him. I kept looking at picture after picture.

"You'll get one tomorrow," he said. "Bring it by, and we'll have your picture made too."

"That'd be great." I was already skinning a one-year-old spike in my mind. "In fact, if I had my way, there'd be no room up here for any other pictures over the next few years."

He chuckled laughed and nodded. "That'd be somethin', now, wouldn't it?"

"Sure would."

He was quiet for a moment before speaking again.

"You know, there's more pictures than this." He seemed to evaluate me. "Some very interesting stuff."

I looked at his face, and in it he was holding cards, eyes dancing a merry polka.

"You wanna see one of them?"

"Sure," I said.

He motioned with his hand for me to follow, and shuffling away with his limp, the crippled man with the cowboy hat led me through the $5 shower door and into a little-used back room of the Woodshed. There were old liquor boxes, and milk crates filled with manila file folders discolored with age and water-damage. There were some knick-knacks and books on shelves, and an old gray metal desk.

I was anticipating that he'd pull out a snapshot or two of animals with strange antlers, like the bull my step-dad saw in the woods a few years ago. This animal had one normal antler, but the other was twisted out and down, the end spread flat like a spatula. It reminded my step-dad of a caribou's rack, and not knowing whether he could shoot it or not, he allowed the elk to lumber back into the gloom. We joked about the poor animal that night around the campfire, how it was a mutant from the atomic age, migrating cross-country from the Hanford Nuclear Reservation. How difficult it must have been for the sorry bastard during the rut, ugly, unable to attract a cow to copulate.

"Cost you five dollars to see," the crippled man with the cowboy hat said. He turned and I noticed he had a big jar, the kind filled with those nasty pickled eggs you see in some taverns. It was filled halfway with five-dollar bills and a few one-dollar notes, and a couple of slips of paper that may have been IOUs.

"Okay," I said, my curiosity getting the best of me, thinking he supplements a pretty small income with this. Wanting to contribute, I handed over a fiver to him.

He reached down and opened the desk's top drawer, retrieved a single Polaroid, and handed it to me.

It was him in the photo, and something else, a being, a spaceman. The being was entirely whitish-gray, and the head was proportionally too big for the slim torso, and the eyes, which were not shut, were almond-shaped and dull black. He was holding the being by its neck with one hand, and had his rifle in the other hand, and the crippled man with the cowboy hat was staring at the camera unsmiling, not like the hunters in the other Polaroids, who were beaming. The being had a single, dark hole in its chest, where the bullet had pierced him.

I turned the photo over in my hand, evaluating, I suppose, whether it was genuine.

"It's real," he said.

I wasn't sure what to think, how to respond. Had this guy just duped me for five bucks? Anything's possible with photography these days, I thought. But he seemed sincere. If he was shining me on, he was doing so in perfect earnestness, and with total credibility.

"How ... what is it?" I asked.

"You tell me." He took the photo back and replaced it in the drawer. He indicated, by motioning back toward the door, that our time here was through, and that not much further would be coming by way of explanation. So we went out together, and I went next door to the bar to retrieve my uncle.

On the road back to camp, I was silent and thinking hard. Not even the jarring of the ruts and folds in the road surface could pull me out of it. My uncle, talkative from the alcohol, jabbered on about God knows what.

I interrupted him in mid-sentence:

"Hank, have you ever been in the woods, sitting on a stump, and you just get this creepy feeling like something's coming up behind you, and you want to look but you don't want to at the same time. Maybe the squirrels and birds have stopped making sounds for a minute and you're sure something's there, and finally you turn slowly around and there's nothing?"

"Sure," Hank said. "All the time ... why?"

"Oh, I just wondered." I lapsed again into silence.

Next morning in the pre-dawn darkness, Hank's Jeep faded from view up the logging road. I stepped into the woods with my rifle and a tumor of doubt in the back of my throat.

Memory of Hard Rain

A Noahic rain is falling, and I have nearly an acre of sodden leaves to rake, a task procrastinated for weeks as broad-leaf maples, oaks, hoary birch and aspens have shed and shed and shed. In some places, the leaves are a foot and a half deep, and saturated, ten times their dry weight. My rake will be useless; I need a bulldozer. As I look around the yard, the rain splatters on my neck, cold, and drips down the sides of the bill of my ball-cap, running down my temples to linger in my beard. I should be in rain gear, but the work will be hard. The gear wouldn't breathe, and I'd be lathered in sweat in no time. Standing in the downpour just thirty seconds, I'm soaked to the skin on the shoulders and arms, and God turns up the volume, and I hear the velocity and pointed beat of raindrop on leaf quicken in a rush that moves, in waves with the wind, from every corner of my property. And blows more leaves into the disorder.

Last spring and all through the summer I would tilt my head back and admire the trees. Full green in canopy, tall, strong, each leaf a vital component of the high season's health and hope. As fall cycled and leaves changed from green to yellow and red, chlorophyll ebbing, a kernel of distrust intruded on the pleasant act of surveying what was mine. As they began to fall, one by one, I'd spend a Saturday morning raking them into neat piles, transporting them to the curb in a refuse bin for the county to take away. This labor was manageable until the first autumn rainstorm, when they fell in vortices too large and numerous to track. Then the leaves became things to be despised, each one an object of rising dislike. Morning after the first storm came, and I stepped onto my back porch and gazed in a stupor at what had used to be a carpet of green lawn. The fury of the preceding night had covered the grass with corruption.

I apply the rake to a tangle of dead leaves, and pull. They clump and roll, water squirts out, and I look up at the gutters of the house and they're overflowing, torrents washing in waterfall across my view of the eaves and soffits. Leaves in the gutters, plugging the downspout holes, and the weight in them worries me: they might separate from the house. I know the pipe under our driveway in the drainage ditch that runs across the front property line, parallel to the road, is plugged, and water has ponded, sought alternate routes. I'll have to address that issue today as well, before I have an erosion problem that undermines the asphalt.

Prying neighbors walk by on the street, cloaking their nosiness behind simulated geniality: *Looks like you're having fun there*, they say, two of them in matching L.L. Bean raingear. They execute fashionable exercise; I bust my ass and strain my back, puffing away on a pack and half a day. They all own leaf-blowers or hire landscapers to cart their yard waste away. Another pair passes. They refrain from comment, but have a look on their faces as if I am hiding something crazy, perhaps building an ark in the back yard. I want to run them through with the rake handle.

I pull the rake again, uselessly. Stop to light another cigarette in the downpour, and devise the best plan of action.

There's a tight, hairpin turn on Forest Service Road 1706 coming out of the wilderness near Boulder Cave. We inch around it every three or four hunting seasons, whenever we decide - for a change of venue - to fill up with diesel or restock our water at Whistlin' Jacks in Cliffdell rather than the usual grocery at Eagle Rock five miles east. You can come out of the mountains either way.

The turn is tight and narrow. You come into it down a long slope, maybe a 35-percent grade on gravel and suddenly it's right in your face. If you don't know the area or you aren't familiar with this switchback on the map, you might just approach too fast and run your rig off into the forest, which banks there, and drops. If you slow appropriately, you'll turn the wheel as far to the left as your steering allows, and press through, certainly at no faster than five miles per hour, because the grade doesn't flow out or even up at all. You just keep going downhill, and pretty soon, you pop out on Old River Road on the south side of the Naches River from State Highway 410.

Meet another vehicle halfway into this turn and one of you is going to have to give way. Back up or pull over onto the brushy shoulder, which isn't much - maybe a couple of feet. I don't know how the hell logging trucks get around this corner; they must roar up and down through alternate routes.

When I was a boy, maybe twelve or thirteen years old, my father would take us - my older brother Byron and I - deer hunting up in the flowing hills of the eastern Cascade slopes around the Bumping River. I remember this curve well, and a day when rain fell as if it would never stop. The logging roads were awash with flowing water, some of it deep, channeling across the washboard surface creating by the heavy logging trucks, through deep muddy ruts, transporting soil and loose rocks. The cycle of water imposing its will on the planet - falling from the sky, moving earth, flowing and foaming, transforming the surface of earth - was clear in a way that no science textbook could make it, as my father drove our rig down out of the hills.

Byron, my father and I were nested in the cab of the truck, an old 1961 four-speed Dodge, wipers on and Dad gearing down into low gears. Dad had to reach out every twenty seconds to wipe condensation off the inside of the windows as the defroster labored against the wet. Rain was coming so hard and the road surface so unstable, he had left the security of the cab up top to lock in the hubs. But even with all four tires grabbing, inching our way down this road was slippery, and the rear of the truck, light from the empty bed, fishtailed more than once. Dad would utter *whoa* under his breath and steer into the slide, correcting, pumping the brakes. A few times, after moving across deep potholes or through long ruts, the drums and rotors of the brakes were saturated, and he got no response unless he said *shit* and pushed the brake pedal into the floorboard with zeal.

We'd determined that hunting that day would be an act of futility. All game would be hunkered down in deep thickets, or at the extreme bases of huge canyons, taking cover from the rain and wind. The few animals stupid enough to be out in these conditions would be, well, just that - *stupid*. And to eat the meat of any such animal would be risky. It was known that the *stupid* would roll right out of the meat onto the fork, off the fork into the mouth, and directly into the character and demeanor of the consumer. That dictum is as old as hunting itself.

Too, hunting in that kind of weather is simply miserable. No matter how tightly packaged a person is, water gets everywhere, down through the folds of raingear, seeking exposed openings and flowing onto skin. There is no protection for the back of the neck. And the sound of a hard rain in the forest makes detecting other sounds, such as those of approaching game, impossible. A waste of time.

So we opted instead to re-provision, and came down out of the hills about three o'clock in the afternoon, and rain and small sticks from the overstory around us slapped onto the windshield and hood of Dad's pickup. We couldn't see much, even though it was still light, and Dad had to crank the wheel hard when he first saw the truck at the left side of the road on the approach to the turn. Our truck fishtailed again and slid to a stop with the passenger-side front tire off the mud into bushes.

"Shit," Dad said for the tenth time since leaving camp.

"Shit," Byron agreed.

"Shit." Mine was tentative; we were allowed, somewhat, to cuss in hunting camp. Even so, in front of my father, cursing was still an unpredictable experiment at that age.

"What kind of fool'd leave his truck in the middle of the damned turn?" Dad asked, not intending Byron or I to answer but, rather, asking the question rhetorically.

The kind of fool who would do that rose from the opposite side of the stalled truck's hood, having heard the diesel signature of our engine, set both hands in the small of his own back and stretched. Reached up and adjusted his ball cap and turned his head just enough for Dad to see that he had long, stringy hair.

A man with long, stringy hair fool enough to stop his rig right at the business end of a tight turn: here was the kind of man my father normally would have very little to do with if he could help it.

The man stepped out from the side of his truck, around the front and we could see he was drenched from ball cap to boot, wearing overalls and a torn-up wool coat, and covered with mud. The pink of his bare, wet hands shown only in spots through the viscous brown of the muck. He came closer; it was clear he wanted to communicate with us, regardless of whether my father wanted anything to do with him.

Dad reached down and cranked the window handle a couple of times, clearing a slot in the glass about three inches high.

"Sorry," the man said. I noticed he was shivering and dark-skinned. "I got a flat," he explained. He must have sensed my father thought he was an idiot; maybe he wanted to appease Dad for any inconvenience he had caused.

"Could'na happened at a worse spot," Dad said, making no attempt to cover his irritation.

"Yes, sir," the man replied, an accent occurring to us. "I know."

"What happened?" Dad asked him from the comfort of the seat, but capitulating by cranking the window down another couple of inches.

As the long-haired fellow explained, I glanced over across the back seat through the gun rack and the rifles at his truck through the steamy back window. It was an old-model Ford, pretty beat up and the lightest limish color where rust hadn't overtaken the paint. The front end on the driver's side was high; he'd jacked it up preparing to remove the flat when we'd come along. It looked pretty precarious hanging there just before the road switched back, and it occurred to me that the shoulder would be soft. If the jack failed or slid, the pickup would probably roll onto the road below. My gaze swept back to the man and my father

64

talking, and in my peripheral vision saw movement in the cab. I looked back: a small face pressed up against the passenger-side glass. A girl, maybe three or four years old, watched us.

"There's a kid in there," I said to Byron. He looked back over his shoulder too, saw her, looked back at Dad and the man. Made no comment for a moment, then said to me, "Shouldn't be in the truck when it's jacked up like that."

"Nope," I agreed.

Dad was finally asking the man whether he needed help, the hunter's ethic overcoming his biases regarding men with long hair, men who might be Indians or Mexicans.

"No," the man replied. "Thanks," he said, adding that he just had to pull the wheel off and replace it with a spare.

"Good enough," Dad said, already starting to crank the window back up, reaching down with his other hand to engage reverse. The man stood there for a second looking at us, rain pouring on him, while Dad backed out. Then he stepped out of the way as Dad poked the accelerator and our rig lurched off of the brush and fully back onto the wet road. Dad pushed the gear shift over and into first, eased the clutch out and the gears grabbed. We pulled forward, surging at first then evening slowly into the turn. The man still stood in the road watching after us while we dropped around the hairpin. As we completed the turn and headed back exactly in the opposite direction from which we had just been traveling, Dad started to accelerate with care. We looked up now at the truck above us, maybe twenty feet higher than the level of the road here now, on three wheels and a steel jack, and we could see that the embankment was heavily eroded from the water, with clods of grass and open stones where dense cover once grew.

Thinking not much more about the man with long hair and his dilemma, we came out of the woods on Road 1706 shortly afterward. In total, it was maybe one mile between the intersection with Old River Road and the switchback turn where we'd left him staring after us in the rain. We had dropped five-hundred feet or so more in elevation; now we were at the floor of the valley carved out of the eastern Cascades by the Naches River. Here the mud road changed abruptly to asphalt, the boundary clear with a jolt through the shocks and a bounce on the Dodge's bench seat. Still the rain pummeled the road, and we could see it running hard in the ditches to either side, too urgent for plugged culverts wherever the flow was intended to run underground, so in low spots it spread out into our path. As we pulled fully onto Old River Road, we could see the Naches roaring eastward as if the river couldn't cover the twenty-five miles to Yakima fast enough. Manastash Ridge, to the northwest, was a green-black face looming in front of us but disappearing in ragged mist at a thousand feet. The mist looked threatening, as if falling to nine-hundred or eight-hundred feet - or even to the valley floor - was a foregone conclusion.

Crossing the Naches to Highway 410, all three of us looked warily through the slats of the bridge-rail at the turbulent water. Normally a clear rapids here, it had overcome its boulders and was now simply a black flow. Its dark surface bore limbs and leaves and whitecaps, and the liquid thing pulsed and frothed with outrage at its banks, that it still should be thus confined. Dad was happier than hell to be across the bridge, taking a right on the highway, reaching the speed limit as we passed the first welcome signs for Cliffdell on the right.

Cliffdell during hunting season normally was awash in hunter-orange, and the hunters wearing it. You normally could barely find a parking spot at Whistlin' Jack's, and had to queue up for the pumps if you wanted gasoline or diesel, a ritual with which all of us became familiar during the oil crisis a few years later. Today the town was all but deserted, the parking lots and lanes to the pump wide open, but an inch deep with rainwater in places. Dad pulled up to the diesel pump, shut down the motor and set the brake, and we hopped out of the warm cab into the deluge. It was gusty and cold; Byron and I both ran over to the eaves next to the entry and let Dad start to pump the fuel in on his own. We didn't last long in the rain and wind, the two of us, and before he had taken even a couple of gallons we cracked the door of the small grocery and restaurant, felt the inviting rush of warm, smoky air, and abandoned him entirely. The door shut behind us with a jangle from a bell tied to its knob, and the sound of the rain and river outside ceased.

"Hey boys," came a voice through gravel, a woman's, from behind the counter.

"Hello, ma'am," Byron replied, polite. "Dad's fillin' up," he said, offering explanation for our sudden presence, as if we were trespassers. "Out on the diesel pump."

"Nasty day for't," she said, clipping her words short, snuffing a spent cigarette in an ashtray next to the register. "Y'all huntin'?"

"Yeah," Byron said. "Well, not today, though," he amended. "Weather's not right."

"No it sure ain't," she agreed, looking out the window at Dad in the downpour replacing the diesel hose in its cradle. "No animals movin' in this," she said, gesturing out the window and upward, indicating for us the source of poor hunting weather. She lit another cigarette. Old, gray, ugly, she put me in mind of a sorceress. "Nobody right in t'head movin' in this," she said, wisdom from the exhaling mouth of an old soul, the proverb curling up from her lips and teeth and out of her nostrils with spent smoke.

Byron and I looked at each other. She was as weird as shit, we agreed, silently, with our eyes. She knew, of course, being wise, that we were latently mocking her with that communion of our eyes, but just then the door rustled and the bell jangled. Dad flung it wide open on its hinges and a gust of rain-spray and freezing air pushed in with him.

"Damn," he exclaimed, spitting the word out for emphasis as he stamped his boots on the wood floor and pulled his gloves off. "Colder'n crap out there."

"Yes, sir," she said from her witchy perch behind the counter, framed in candy bars and road maps, and the curling effluence of her Pall Malls. Dad, not the least spooked by her, walked over across the boards, digging at his hind end for his wallet, and laid a couple of notes on the counter. She made his change as he inquired about the restaurant.

"'Round the side," she said, poking her cigarette in a general direction. Behind her, through the steamy window, we could see that light was falling. "Burgers and fries," she incanted. "Beer, too," placing a hex on us.

By now it was about four o'clock, and out into the elements again went the three of us, 'round the side per her directions, to another door, and in. Dad ordered a round of burgers, fries and Cokes, and they came out steaming and greasy, cradled on wax paper in red plastic baskets. We knifed great gobs of ketchup out of a mulish bottle onto the potatoes, and forgot about rain and diesel and the flat-tired truck in the road with a tiny girl inside and a long-haired, dark man outside as the reservoir of our guts filled, mostly with tallow from the meat and oil from the fries.

We sucked the food down, barely stopping to breathe, rarely looking up, grunting at one another when we wanted more ketchup. Our dirty fingers had begun to run with french-fry oil and the juice of condiments when the cashier crone poked her gray head into the restaurant and hollered, although we were the only ones there, "Anyone headed back up 1706?"

My father stopped in mid-chew, a bolus of burger, pickle-relish and bread between his teeth, turned in his chair and answered with his mouth full: "Yeah, we're headed up that way."

67

"Fella out here could sure use yer help," she said, turning without another word back through the door.

Dad rose, motioning that we should follow. Byron looked at what remained of his late lunch, shrugged, belted down the rest of his Coke, and stood. The three of us left the restaurant, out into the cold again. Darkness had fallen, and the neon signs and lights of the store struggled to establish warmth in the valley, but were losing the battle. Into the grocery half of the structure, and there he was: the dark man from the hairpin turn. He stood at the center of the grocery, left hand in the pocket of his muddy overalls, shivering, right hand gulping hot coffee from a Styrofoam cup. On his face: a look of extreme concern, broaching restless panic.

He explained to my father that he had replaced the flat tire with the spare but that it, too, had been flat. Down the road he had come with the spare, propelling it before him like a boy rolling a hoop. For a mile he had pushed and steered and chased the tire, often retrieving it from the soaked woods when it veered off course. As light fell, concern for the tire had been replaced by concern for his daughter: too small for such an expedition, he had left her in the locked cab of the vehicle.

He'd reached Whistlin' Jack's just five minutes ago, had filled the spare with air from the pneumatic pump, but if anyone was going back up 1706, could he please have a ride.

Witch woman watched all this from her eyrie, smoking and shaking her head when he explained about the child. "This fella and his boys here are headed up that way," she disclosed. "They'll help ya," she said, looking at my father for confirmation of her oracle.

"Yes," Dad said, simply, shortly.

The man grinned through his discomfort and thanked my father a dozen times, saying *gracias* over and over again. Ah, then. Byron and I concluded, as my father had earlier, that he was Hispanic. How Dad in those moments must have wrestled with his conception of all Hispanics. In taking the uncomplicated step of providing much-needed transportation, Dad was about to perform an act of cross-cultural assistance.

The man hefted the filled tire into the bed of the Dodge and the four of us piled into the cab. We barely fit, Dad in the driver's seat, me next to him jammed between him and Byron, with the right cheek of my butt up into Byron's hip and my left shoulder set into my father's ribcage. The Mexican was at the passenger-side door, crammed into that space. Dad had to reach down between my knees to manipulate the gear shift.

Nevertheless, it was workable, and we got under way just as the rainstorm renewed itself and began to pump water onto us even harder than it had all day.

Again we performed the necessary ritual of wiping the inside of the window: with three of us it had been a fight. With four, it was ineffectual. And even when we got the window cleared, we could barely see fifteen feet in front of the truck through slashing rain. It was too much for the light of the headlamps, so we had to inch along between five and ten miles per hour on the highway, back across the fearful bridge onto Old River Road, and make a left on 1706 where water was now almost a foot deep at the intersection.

As 1706 began to rise, it seemed more and more like we were passing up the channel of a violent stream. Water rushed past us, and we could feel its push against the tires through the floorboards. I don't know how Dad was able to steer the old Dodge, but he somehow managed it.

Then the tailgate of the Ford was in front of us, inverted, with the bed and rear tires pointing up at the storm. Reflectors on its rear lights shown in Dad's headlamps.

"*Joder*!" the man cried. He fumbled with the latch, pushed open the passenger-side door, spilled out into the deluge. Byron followed, then me, before Dad had even set the hand brake. We ran around the front of the Dodge, stumbling and slipping in the current, and the Mexican completely lost his footing and fell on all fours in the muck. I followed suit, landing on my side in the water, and it was several inches deep here and flowing down the logging road.

Somehow Byron had been able to maintain his balance, and had rushed up to the cab, which was upside down in the muck. He couldn't see into the truck through the side window, so moved around to the front, in under the hood and engine. By this time, Dad was emerging from the cab of the Dodge, and the man and I were extricating ourselves from our fall, and he was crying and shouting with panic.

Byron told us later that the first thing he established was that the inverted cab of the Ford was filling with the dirty water, and that it was clear from the way water was foaming around the sides of the cab that if no action were taken, the road would be undermined here and a complete washout would result. Or the truck would simply settle into it, dropping the level of the cab further under the raging water. He could not see the little girl, though, and shouted at Dad for a light, then a giant sucking roar overcame the sound of angry water and part of the bank above failed and dropped yards and yards of mud and rock on the truck, and buried Byron up to his knees. The flow oozed in and covered most of the windshield, and my brother struggled to free himself, and Dad and I and the Mexican arrived with a flashlight just as he pulled himself free.

Dad knelt in the waters and pushed the beam of the light in across the driver's side window glass, and we could see her, curled up as in a womb, terrified, sitting on the cab's ceiling near the driver's-side rear window in a foot of water. And another gout of embankment gave way and pushed into the vehicle, moving it toward us, bed first; the inverted truck pivoted on the cab, pushing the Mexican over again into the mud.

Byron looked around for something to break the window. He could have used the flashlight, but apparently it didn't occur to him. Instead, he cocked back and drove his bare duke into the glass. It shattered with a comprehensive crack, lacerating the hand, but he didn't stop, grabbing the fangs of broken glass and flinging them away. Then he laid prone and propelled himself into the cab, reached for her as she struggled in panic like a drowning swimmer to flee him, misunderstanding rescue in her small mind. He snatched at her limbs, caught one, and dragged her back out of the cab.

She fell into the moving water, stood up, was knocked down again, and saw her father.

"Papa," barely aspirated in a little voice. And he scooped her up and cradled her and wept.

The bank above broke completely then, and by agency of a miracle we had just enough time to realize it, and all fled backward toward the Dodge, and the road failed, rolling the Ford down into the woods with the churning mass.

Byron received a letter from the Yakima County Sheriff thanking him for his bravery. "You have demonstrated all of the things that make us optimistic about the youth of today," it read in one of the more decorous sentences. Then, from the Washington state congressman of the district, a certificate with a curving banner on top in heavy, gothic script: *Award of Valor*. My mother framed and mounted in the hallway both of these articles of paper.

Every once in a while I wonder about the little girl. She would have been eight or nine years younger than me. We never learned her name. Maria. Juanita. Xaviera. Would she have grown up to be beautiful? I think so, perhaps crowned as the Ellensburg Rodeo Queen. Or maybe smart *and* pretty, a veterinarian or small-town lawyer. But once, years after the incident, at a Cle Elum honky-tonk called The Feed Bag, a waitress came up to our table to gather our drink order. I was overwhelmed with a surprising sense that I knew her, or that we had once been acquainted, or had shared common experience. It might have been her; embroidered over her left breast was the name Shayla. She brought our drinks then went on break. I left a larger tip than courtesy - or her service - would have called for, and thought I saw her smoking a cigarette outside as we left.

Shayla it is, then, albeit un-Hispanic. And she *was* beautiful. Exactly as I had so often speculated.

I finish with this memory in the same way I conclude a favorite book that I have re-read. Close the book carefully, admire the jacket held in my hands, feel its cool smoothness, my eyes wash across the title *Memory of Hard Rain*. I open it again to caress the leaves, the dry feel of good paper under my index finger, appreciate the type in which the memory is set. Remove the jacket for a moment to inspect the binding, the cover, cloth stretched across hardboard, the even cut of its pages. Replace the jacket and close the book again, turn it over, ponder the author's photograph: it's me, of course, but young, a boy, without dark circles under my eyes.

I place the memory delicately back on the bookshelf in a small, personal library, next to two sequels. One, the memory of Byron, not so lucky this time, succumbing to another appointment with water, drowning at age nineteen in Lackamas Lake drunk behind the wheel of his car, driven, flipped airborne to splash and settle in reeds and trout startled from wide-eyed sleep. Two, a memory of my father and mother, unable to cope with Byron's death, succumbing to another compelling water, the kind that comes in a pint bottle with proof on the label and a government tax sticker over the cap. These books I will take down on another blustery day, a day without leaf-raking.

For a day like today, they would be too much - overwhelming perhaps - to remember.

And rain and leaves fall and fall.

Blue Mountains Discourse

Richard and William got drunk together one autumn night and planned a hunting outing the next morning. They would take Agnes' automobile up into the Blues and come out with a bull elk strapped across the hood!

The next morning promised a perfect day of hunting conditions - cold, snow threatening - and they imagined rags of mist hanging down over the vague mountains to the west. Agnes filled thermoses of coffee, and Richard and William drank some off the top and poured in some whiskey for the road.

They ran the auto through the icy roads, crossing through Columbia County and then Prescott in Walla Walla County. Soon inebriated, they discovered that an auto became a much different animal than a horse. Twice they lost purchase on the slippery roads, sliding to a stop in a field first, then a light forest second, but arrived high in the Blues by nine-thirty in the morning - finished with the fortified coffee and ready to load bullets.

The pair hiked in to separate spots and Richard secreted himself in a blind overlooking a web of game trails above a canyon. It was an excellent, quiet spot to wait for elk to pass through.

Richard waited in the freezing morning for two and a half hours, then heard the first sounds of game moving in the thickets to his left. Cracks from snapping twigs on the forest floor and the breaking of small limbs across animal hides filled his mind with anticipation of a large bull and how fine it would ornament the hood of the auto on the trip home.

He raised his rifle, set it pointing in the general direction of the sound and bedded its butt in the crook of his shoulder. The sharp crack again sounded. Then out of the woods, at the focus of the sound, strode not a royal bull elk but a man. It was another hunter. A man whom he had never seen before - which meant an out-of-region fellow - smashing through the foliage as if he were walking to a Christmas party. The noisy ass was actually whistling to himself!

Here was an ignoramus, Richard thought, letting his grip on the rifle slacken. Even an idiot child with broccoli for brains knew that elk-hunting is a pursuit of stillness and silence. Even someone as slow-witted as William knew this! It was one of the great miracles of Richard's life that, given his impulsive nature, he could master chronic agitation for hours-long periods and sit without sound for a day of hunting. Yet there in front of him was a shit-brained, loud-mouthed corncob who had wandered into the area Richard had patiently cultivated all morning.

Just as Richard rose to quit the clearing, the man noticed him, waved, seemed to hail, and then further fractured the silence of the morning:

"Hello, fellow woodsman!" he called. Richard rolled his eyes at the fool's cheeriness and ignorance, and failed to reply in time to keep the man from turning in his course, and starting a climb up out of the ravine in Richard's direction.

"A fine morning," the man said as he crested the nearest rise and stood before Richard.

"Yes, t'was," Richard said.

"Sitting here long?" the man asked.

"Two and a half hours."

"Cold."

"Yes."

The man drew a flask from the folds of his hunting coat, from a pocket secreted deep inside his layers. "Have a spot?"

Richard accepted the proffered drink, mistaking it for apology, pulled hard on the flask, handed it back. He expected the man to bumble off, noisily, to intrude on some other hunter's surveillance, maybe William's. Instead the man sat down on the same fallen log where Richard had been waiting, took a belt from his own flask, began talking.

"Hunting is a great pastime," the man said.

"Yes, it is, when you can get it."

"I'll tell you a story about hunting, if you like."

Richard couldn't believe his ears. "I'd rather you just moved along."

"Come now," the intruder said. "I'm just trying to be neighborly - and you'll like the story." Here he paused, looked out across the ravine, and took another belt, offered the flask to Richard again. He sought no further concurrence, but simply commenced speaking.

"The animals of the forest, acting on behalf of their brother Elk, sought out Hunter for conversation," the man began, with a new voice, a sort-of singsong oratory that made Richard want to pull on the flask again. He did.

"Individually and alone, they each approached Hunter with a question about Hunter's annual trek for Elk," the man continued.

"First came Squirrel, scolding from a tree limb, then phasing into Hunter's language:

"'Hunter, on behalf of brother Elk, is it desire that brings you to seek him?'

"'Squirrel,' Hunter began, 'by way of illustration, let me answer you in a roundabout way. Let me share with you my thoughts on desire.'"

Richard pulled again on the flask, tipping it a little further back. He wondered whether this was going to take a long time, and the morning's feeling of drunkenness, catalyzed by two new snorts, began to return. The man continued his parable:

"'There's a continuous line,' and here Hunter stretched out his long arms, making squirrel jump from nerves, 'that terminates on one end with surrender and on the other with obsession.

"'Somewhere on that line - depending on circadian rhythm, phase of moon, a calliope of causes - one balances like a walker of tightropes in a high wind. The line is not a flat ribbon on a desert floor. It's a rugged stripe, with snarls that want to trip the walker up, so one risks falling into an abyss on either side. It's like a train track: I go to sleep between the rails so snakes won't get me in the dark. But sometimes there's a train, and I hear it coming just in time and scrunch down into the ties and cinders. It shrieks over me.

"'It seems as if it will never end, and then it does and there's a hoary rush of vacuum and starlight.'"

Richard sat listening, resigned to the intrusion, and pulled again. The interloper's voice droned onward:

"Hunter shifted his seat and initiated a new gesture, drawing his right hand in front of squirrel's face and holding the index finger and thumb a quarter-inch apart.

"'That line is the microscopic filament between need and desire,' Hunter explained. 'But it's a powerful distinction, and cruelly baffling. It's a fence that keeps one from thinking around corners.'

"It's clear squirrel doesn't completely understand, but images of pine nuts and the work of nibbling are in the back of its mind.

"'Desire is descriptive of the obsession of man with woman,' Hunter explained. 'With her eyes and their shades, with the shape of the back of her neck, with the rise of her breasts and their peaks. The secrets she keeps at the locus of her thighs. Her calves, lobes, ankles. When she wears a velvet dress, desire fires the imagination and evolves toward obsession.

"'Desire means the emphysemiac longs still for nicotine, the dipsomaniac for alcohol. It means one who uses narcotics in the dope dens, clear for so long and laboring under the illusion he is cured, cannot escape the seductive notion of opiating himself again.

"'Desire is at the root of the man who returns, again and again, to the tattoo artist, an addict to ink. First it's a small totem of military service on his forearm. Then he's covered like an autumn lawn under maples.

"'Desire is child's behavior still manifested in the grown. Give a boy a knife; he will discover that everything he encounters, up to and including his own flesh, needs cutting.

"'Desire is clean, cool, white sheets on a mattress.'

"'Then it's not desire that brings you to these woods,' Squirrel confirmed. 'It's not desire that drives your search for brother Elk?'

"'No, brother Squirrel.' Hunter answered. 'No. Not desire.'"

At this the man paused, as if he were finished with the story, and looked expectantly at his flask. Richard looked down at it, raised it to pull again, then handed it back to the man, who swallowed a draught. He handed it back to Richard and resumed, to Richard's astonishment.

"Next came Bear, lumbering up a game path, dropping scat every ten yards or so. His innards were acting up, and he was certain Hunter's motivation came from the need for food.

"'Hunter,' he asked in a low growl. 'Is it hunger that brings you here? Is it the search for food that brings you to hunt for brother Elk?'

"'Bear,' said Hunter, 'I'll show you something about food. It will help you understand more about me. I have never known hunger - can you imagine? I am witness to the symptoms of hunger only by way of walking past a local orphanage. Hunger is in the eyes, ears and throat of the children there, and their bellies are distended. Flies buzz around their mouths and deposit nits in the ducts of their rheumy vision.

"'Sometimes I feel guilty but I assuage my dread by eating another fistful of barbecued pork. Just look at my belly,' said Hunter, raising his shirts and coat, exposing ballast flowing down over a belt. 'Does this look like a man who understands the slightest thing about hunger?"

"Bear acknowledged that this man evidently did not hunt as a result of his hunger, and lumbered off."

The man eyed Richard, and Richard took another drink from the man's flask; he was, without question, drunk again. And he was decidedly tired of this fool's story, yet on this fool went:

"Fox, more intelligent than the rest, knew the root of Hunter's quest. It was to prove his manliness.

"'Hunter,' she said. 'You don't have to prove anything to anyone. We all know you are a man, and a fine one at that. Do you seek brother Elk to affirm your manliness?

"'Fox,' he answered, pointing, 'Manliness wells in me sufficient to break that mountain in half. I can lift a fully loaded rail car. I have enough manhood to reach out, grab the sun, and suck yellow juice from its hot face if I want.'"

"'Then it must be spiritual,' Fox said.

"'Do you mean spiritual as in God?' Hunter asked. "God? God? What is God? Are you asking me whether brother Elk is God? Or whether communing with nature is Goddish? Or is nature God? Is God in all of nature? Do you mean is the hunt part of my spirituality, like I'm supposed to pay homage to the animal whose life I take, and waste no part of him, and thank his spirit after I've shoved a projectile through him with a burst of gunpowder? Part of my own heritage, my tradition?

"'Is God the Jesus-God, the Buddha-God, the Allah-God? My ancestors? Maybe a lamp or a knob on a gate is God. Maybe our whole universe is a neuron firing between two synapses in the huge gray matter of God. Who can speak the name of God?'" - it began to occur to Richard, with the kind of clarity that only pre-blackout drunkenness may bring, that the man was rambling and possible insane and most surely blasphemous, yet the man went on, and Richard drained his flask and let it drop on the ground as the man began to babble - "'The Old Testament Jews wrote it Y-H-W-H, and spake it not. Nor, apparently, would they *vowel* it. So we might say brother Elk would, if he *were* to be God, be known simply and reverently as L-K, or W-P-T, as in *Wapiti*. Not voweled, and *never* spoken.'

"'Am I God? God, I hope...'"

"The hell..." Richard muttered and shot him in the chest. The report chucked loud in the clearing and echoed outside the immediate folds of the canyon and the man uttered the words... *solitude... I was going to... say... Hunter wanted... solitude* and slumped off the log backward onto his back with his legs sticking up in the air.

"You stupid, loud fucker," was Richard's brief eulogy, and he clung to a ridge of blankness.

He came to in the automobile's passenger seat. William drove through snowfall. Richard barely remembered a disturbing, unlit dream he may once have had.

The Kanasket Chicken Killings

There is no sound like poultry being dispatched. Many may be likened to it: a falling jet, the crashing of glass, glaciers calving, a child who shrilly encounters a snake. But a common chicken, in the throes of its own undoing, raises such a full cacophony no one in earshot can mistake it for anything else. Its deathsong is so separate and opposed to the daily undernote of gentle, rhythmic barnyard clucking. People in Kanasket know. *Grab the shotgun! Where's that coyote?*

And then there is the rising from warm quilts, pulling on the Levi's. Clattering out the side door off the kitchen, boots yet unlaced, to cross frozen earth to the chicken yard. The air is the temperature of raw metal. A sodium floodlight hums its cold energy out by Lake Walker Road, but it's dark here, next to the house. Henri DeLaats' breath billows in exhaled, burgeoning clouds - the flashlight beam, untrained until now, gives them columnar form.

Look! In the circle of light, a chaos of white feathers. Some of them still whirl in downy arcs above drag-marks in the bird-muck. The light migrates across a streak of blood in the long, distal shape of violence. There is a ruckus in the foliage that ebbs into the treeline. The sound moves onto the bluff above the house, receding, now sporadic, now ceasing. Something flees, cooling chicken corpse pinned between its teeth. *Vaarwel, my lovely leghorn.*

Henri steps into the coop to take inventory of the coyote's trespass. There is general unease, cluckings of discomfiture and reprimand. He counts them - now seven, one cock, four hens, two pullets. That's two hens lost in four nights, this the second violation of the coop. He imagines the coyote's jaws snapping around the hen's throat, licking its guts. Out there, beyond the light he shines back over his shoulder at the bluff. Henri's head wraps around an image: a strong mandible severs the bird's juicy viscera, sucking the contents of its reproductive tract. Albumen drips from the coyote's muzzle. The canine belies puzzlement when it encounters the shell of the incomplete egg. Henri, to validate his suspicion of the marauding pack, will check scat piles in the woods for bits of shell.

Indignant in the flashlight's beam, the surviving poultry levy an indictment with their pin eyes. Combs and wattles tremble in reproach. He should have built a better shelter for them.

77

But how could a coyote get in? The coop door swings out only after the latch is disengaged. There are no loose boards, no holes in the wire. Nowhere he can see where something has burrowed into the coop.

Nevertheless, Henri vows he will make reparations, make the coop a fortress, if he can find time. It's difficult, a mechanic by day at County Shops - the Cummins transmission expert - to find moments to tend the farm. But Henri's nearing retirement. It will be better then, he vows.

One hen is particularly disturbed, gesticulating with rapid back-and-forth head bobbings. The coyote must have come nearer to her than the other survivors. Perhaps she witnessed its grin and fine, long incisors. He makes a move to soothe her, reaches for her neck to pat feathers. She counters with spread wings, a carefully placed peck, drawing blood from the web between his forefinger and thumb.

"Shit," Henri whispers, then sucks the wound. "I'm sorry, baby." He turns to depart the coop, the cock eyeing the man in his periphery. It beats its wings once, to make clear the umbrage it has taken.

"Coyote again?" Andrea asks from a half sleep when Henri re-enters their bedroom.

"Didn't see it."

"We gotta fix it."

"I know." He squirms out of the Levi's, falls into bed, pulls the covers up. "We lost another hen."

But Andrea is already asleep again.

The sheets gather and wad around Henri's limbs, exhaustion and adrenaline waging minor conflict. The numerals on the clock are a glowing parade.

A farm at the foothills had been his and Andrea's idyll - and had, until a few nights ago, proved exactly in alignment with their happy expectations. Of course, they knew of the coyotes. In general, the Northwest was lousy with them, anywhere near the woods. Henri and Andrea listened, many evenings, to the baleful cries of the wild dogs, howls that raised gooseflesh and, admittedly, a sort of country-charming endearment. The pack, they had reasoned, must be interpreted as another set of neighbors. Like the occasional, more rare cougar or bear. Henri had believed that with the proper precautions taken, raising chickens at the forest's edge was a reasonable and desirable avocation. He never seriously considered the coyotes as hungry carnivores.

But tonight's incident gnaws at him as he churns. The coyote's trespass - he was *sure* it was coyotes - is a blemish he now fought to reconcile. What could he do differently? What new prudent measure must he enact? He could bolster the coop, adding lumber and wire. He could lay electric wire a few inches above the ground, surrounding the poultry. He could camp out at night, wait on surveillance for the beasts, with his rifle.

"Go to sleep," Andrea mumbles as he tosses.

The alarm invades the silence, brings Henri out of these concerns and into the full countenance of another: it is time to rise for work.

An hour later Henri is turning out of his gravel driveway, past the floodlamp, onto Lake Walker Road. His truck rumbles through mist that hugs the blacktop like a thick, used dishrag. The low-beams penetrate ten, maybe twelve, feet in front. The fog blanket is low. It will dissipate and rise as soon as the sun comes up.

He drives slow, glances up through the windshield to see stars and the waxing moon. He takes pride in the knowledge he possesses - that he has researched the almanac, as any good country man should - and knows the lunar cycle. That the moon, gibbous this morning, will be a crescent in a few days and new in a week. Coffee vapor from his travel mug, on the dash, rises to paste an ovum of condensation on the glass. He reaches for the defroster, hears the fan engage, senses the displacement of air in the cab and a frigid breeze against the bare patches of his face. A news report emerges from the radio speakers, but he isn't paying attention. Lake Walker Road winds here, changing elevation and arcing through hairpins at points - he needs to drive cautiously in this damned fog, with hands at ten and two on the wheel.

The gloom ahead births a shape, low-slung, coiling - Henri swerves and the shocks dip while the pickup's momentum carries it onto the soft shoulder and the passenger's side tires bite for purchase. The travel mug, stabilized vertically by its flat base, slides vigorously to the pocket formed by the windshield and dash. It explodes in ceramic shards there near the wing window. Coffee splatters the passenger side of the cab. The tires grab hold of the shoulder again. And Henri rights the vehicle, brakes to a stop.

What the hell was that? A bear? Henri fights for recognition, running a check on all the extant mammalian archetypes he knows. Bipedal - goes on two legs. Or did it flee on four, vanishing into the trees at roadside? Cloaked in fur - hirsute. Or was it bare-skinned, slipping behind blankets of groundcover beyond the periphery of the headlamps? Eyes that had reflected light - feline? Or were those absorbing eyes, sucking in light and observation? And teeth - he *saw* a flash of teeth, but can't, for everything that is in him, sift between these two options: were they sharp and long, or blunt, molarish? Henri sits cataloging the details of the surprise, steam from the broken mug and thrown coffee misting his interior. He gropes in the console for paper napkins left from a recent stop at Burger King - he routinely files them there for later use, instances such as this. His fingertips close around a tissue in the darkness. It occurs to him to switch on the dome.

Light overfills the cab. Henri releases his seat belt, scoots over to excise, carefully, the shards of the cup and wipe down the coffee. Goddamn - the carpet will be stained there. Coffee has splashed against the door, drips down the latch release and electric window-opener toggle. Fluid pools next to the floor mat. He wipes, first the dash, then the sidepanel top to bottom. Releases the napkin-wad to soak in the pool on the floor. He'll make a better go of it once he arrives at work. There are superabsorbent shop towels there, on rolls of ridiculous proportion.

But what *was* that? He decides it was a coyote, perhaps leaping for a brief second in his lights. It will have to serve as explanation for now, because it's time to be under way again - he'll be late to work if he doesn't shove off now. Especially since he'll have to wipe out the cab before he clocks in. A coyote is fine. Yes.

He engages the motor, drives a little faster than prudent through the fog. The smell of cooling coffee seeping into fabric permeates his pre-dawn.

All day, Henri is exhausted at work. Tiredness colonizes his limbs, and he views tasks through a film of half-sleep, a poor reproduction of sentience. No matter how much of the overtoned, ragged coffee he drinks from the shop's pot, it feels as if there are grains of sand behind his eyelids. Grease has worked its dirty way into the uncovered wound he received from the hen last night; it throbs. And as he fingers nuts and bolts, as he manipulates a camshaft through gaskets and heavy steel brackets slung from a grader's undercarriage, he seeks, but cannot find, a solution. Through his fatigue, Henri cannot even precisely define the problem.

Wait: A, there are chickens going missing. B, it is probably the work of coyotes. C, coyotes can be stopped. D, how? A plus B plus C equals D, a simple equation. He inadvertently fumbles a bolt, drops it into a greasepan, dips to retrieve it, smacks his head on the undercarriage. Stunned by the blow, he drops heavily to a sit next to the grader. He rubs his forehead where it met steel. Examines his fingers - no blood. Then he thinks, D, kill them, kill them all. He will wait tonight, in the barnyard, with an arsenal. Or a rifle at least. No matter how long it takes, how cold it gets, how close to his skin the fog creeps. Silently, unmoving, like a hunter, he will wait and exact vengeance. He will protect his flock.

Mind made up, for some reason the rest of his workday goes better. The threads of nuts engage the first time and spin easily. Parts go back together as if they have some urgent need to re-combine. The coffee - normally a distillation of acid that enflames the guts of workers there, or at least his - tastes better. Henri's shift ends, still in daylight, and he observes when he returns to the truck that he had, this morning, successfully dabbed the coffee from the interior. There will be no staining. This last discovery feels very much like a benediction on his decision. He believes the manner he has selected to deal with the coyotes is blessed, fair - it has the right backing. Henri grins: apparently he does his best thinking when his head is struck. Maybe if he had a mule around he'd be a genius. He fingers the knot on his pate - it, too, seems a material confirmation of his resolve. And this pleases him mightily over the next forty minutes as he winds through Maple Valley, Four Corners (careful to obey the speed limit - it's a ticket trap there), turns through Ravensdale, passes the Lake Retreat Baptist campground and the Bonneville substation, crosses the Green River and enters Kanasket.

Andrea is feeding the chickens when he pulls up. She meters palmsful of grain across the fowl-yard, seeds sifting from between her fingers. The chickens surround her like obstreperous planets, clucking satisfaction, bodies dipping like oil derricks as they poke their beaks into the feed. Henri steps down from the cab, laughing while he watches. How they can excise the grain from the mud and shit is beyond him - a marvel - but comical to observe.

"Hey, Babe," she says, turning toward him for an embrace and hello kiss. "How was your day?"

"Great," he says. "Well... not at first, I guess. I was tired as hell this morning. But I figured out what to do about the chickens."

"Yeah?"

"Yeah, and after that, the day seemed to just breeze by."

"So what are you going to do?"

"Kill me some coyotes, that's what."

"Oh, Henri, no..."

"Andrea, it's either our chickens or them damn dogs, and that's a no-brainer for me."

"But can't we just fix the coop, hang more wire and stuff?"

"With what?" Henri spreads his hands. "We don't have extra materials, I used 'em all up making the coop the way it is. And we ain't got a helluva lot leftover from my last check, and another week to go. What I do got is a rifle and shells, and the will to stay out and protect my goddamned birds."

As protests often do, Andrea's fades with the bare fact of economics. They are scraping it together, paycheck to paycheck. And Henri is trying to put every spare cent he can into retirement - working at County Shops is getting *old*, and so is Henri, before her eyes, so she can't blame him for that. Besides, the place at the foothills had been only half of their aspiration. The other half, the half yet to be, is a comfortable retirement for them both. Together, here, with chickens, and maybe a cow or two down the line. She had just the other day remarked how they had saved four bucks a week breakfasting on eggs laid by their own hens rather than store-bought. That's sixteen dollars a month to the fund, and no amount is too small.

"O.K., Honey," she says. The hens pause, sensing a shift in their fortune. The cock eyes his roost with magnanimity. Things are gonna change around here.

Henri rises after dozing on the unmade bed for a couple of hours. It's nine-thirty - time to get out there and mete out a little justice. His rendezvous with the chicken yard has been delayed past twilight by the notion he ought to husband some of his strength. He still has to work tomorrow, and he doesn't know how long he'll have to stay awake outside before one of the pack comes slinking in with the taste of chicken in mind.

Andrea has brewed a thermos of coffee, laid his rifle and a box of shells on the kitchen table. She offers to come sit with him, at least for a while.

"No, Honey, it's all right. You go to bed. I'll holler if I need help."

Henri has arranged a chair from the kitchen table at the corner of the pump house. Together with the house and the chicken coop, they form three points of a triangle, the driveway winding toward Lake Walker Road and the floodlamp to his back. He sits in a wool coat, John Deere ballcap and leather gloves, rifle across his lap, sipping the coffee. He cannot keep from checking his watch - it's almost as if the time, the hours remaining while he may still bag a predator and catch some sleep - is an obsession equal to apprehending the coyote itself.

Back over the house, the moon's wafer backlights high cirrus clouds - they seem almost as if they are resting upon the trees that crest the bluff: Henri is put in mind of a mint. He hears the chickens cluck softly from time to time, wonders whether they know of his sacrifice. Their sweet scratchings, the rufflings of feather, are soporific. Despite the cold, he is lulled by the warmth he imagines in their folds, under the tucked wings, in straw at the base of ovulating hens. He conjures a fact: a good hen can produce three-hundred eggs a year, he thinks, and catches himself nodding onto his chest. He straightens in the chair - it would do no good to drop the rifle in the dust, muzzle down, requiring another cleaning.

Henri dreams a coyote trots out of the woods, or is it prancing, perambulating on two legs? The beast seems anthropomorphic, a hominid. He sees that its rough coat of fur is mangy, that there are bare patches. But the canine turns in moonlight, drops to fours, and the coat is sleek and intact, healed. It revolves through full circles at the locus of the triangle, chases a tail that grows long then retracts between buttocks that shift between skin and coat. It stops spinning, faces him. The mouth opens and a child peers from within. The dogchild screams a challenge, piercing the night with a howl that rises in assault on the moon.

The cock is shrieking in the coop - Henri starts awake. His head snaps back, slaps into wood siding - the pumphouse. He staggers afoot, shoulders the rifle with the muzzle waving coopward, canters toward the sounds. Amid the rooster's urgent crowing, hens join in a terrified chorus. Weighted thumps emanate from the structure - bodies of poultry caroming off plywood. A yelp divides the night, high-pitched, a zealous cry of pain. That cock is not giving up so easy, Henri thinks. The old leghorn is gonna peck that son of a bitch's eyes out. Six pounds of beak-driving bantam up side the soft flesh of a coyote's head could, Henri supposes, bring the bigger animal down. He hopes, anyway.

There is silence in the wake of the coyote's yelp. It's long enough for Henri to wonder whether one of the combatants is dead or down. But a low, hellish growl evolves from a sort of dead space, the silence from nothing that emerges and grows to fill this corner of Henri's world. There is no other sound but the coyote's rolling throat. He imagines the rooster in paralysis, mesmerized by the insistent, overpowering glare of the dog. That coyote's hungry. And *this* time he wants the big boy.

The growl disturbs Henri outside the coop - he can scarcely imagine the rooster and hens not keeling over from terror. He wrestles with the notion of opening the coop door - what grim tableau will greet him? The irresolution vanishes as he hears a final, plaintive chirp from one of the birds, then flung dirt and chicken shit peppering the inner walls of the coop as the coyote pounces. He levels the rifle at the coop's door, reaches for the hasp.

Henri flings the door open ready to fire. The beast leaps straight at his throat. The rifle's report overfills Henri's property. Foreclaws slam into his lapels - Henri is knocked backward and down by the dog's momentum, ballcap flying, the beast's inertia carrying it through and over him with the rooster's neck fixed between its jaws. Henri twists in the frozen mud, fighting to gain his feet or knees or some position from which he can fire again. He sees the coyote chomp again on the cock for a better hold. This readjustment severs the neck - the cock's body falls away. The coyote sprints. It rounds the house so fast Henri is sure its forelegs never touch the ground.

He finds purchase just as the porch lamp comes on and Andrea is in the doorway.

"Henri, you O.K.?"

Henri ignores her inquiry, sprints around the house to discern a fleeing shape, he swears it is upright, disappearing into the trees. He shoulders the rifle, peers along the sight, thinks to fire a random round in the general direction. Maybe, with luck, the bullet will find its mark. But no, Andrea is at his side, slippers in the dewy weeds next to the house.

"Baby, what happened?"

"It's a coyote," he mumbles through confusion. "He killed the male." Henri slings the rifle across his shoulder, runs gloved fingers through his misshapen hair. Her hand is on his shoulder.

"Come inside, Henri," she says. "Let's go to bed."

Arm in arm on the way back to the front porch, they pause at the cock's head. Its upturned eye reflects stars, still shiny. Nerves in the body, three feet away, articulate their final neural messages. One leg moves forward, as if the headless cock wants to scratch earth one more time. Then it's still. Henri hefts the corpse into a trashcan.

He is freezing, even under the covers. Andrea undresses, wraps her warm body around his, eventually places him inside her. She loves sweetly, with tenderness and a soothing grace only thirty-three years of partnership can produce. He can fill her crags and wrinkles, those parts of her that used to be upright and soft. There are anomalies on that skin now, blemishes, moles, hair in odd places - age spots he'd see if he turned on the bedside lamp. But her succor is just as succulent as the first day she gifted him with it. And he, finally, is warm again.

But sleep evades him - the coffee, the cold, the excitement and fear, the lovemaking. While she offers a gentle, rhythmic snore, he stares at the still ceiling fan in weak light from the roadside floodlamp, diffused to the point of near occlusion by their bedroom curtains. The alarm clicks and beeps - it's time to rise for work again.

Henri lifts the phone, dials County Shops. Leaves a message on the tape machine he will not be coming in today. He feels, he whispers into the handset... not well.

In an alternative arrangement of circadian rhythms, busted up and interrupted by coopside nights and days spent in slumber, Henri watches the coop with an intensity so fervent, so severe, an observer would suspect blood must soon jet the from lachrymal sacs at the corners of his eyes. It is his third straight night.

He had waited there two nights after the cock was killed, seeing and hearing nothing but the wee-hours sounds of Kanasket autumn. On the third night he inadvertently fell asleep in front of the television news - Andrea had gone to bed, assuming he was awake and planning another night out. She went as far as preparing the coffee maker for him - spooning grounds into the filter, setting the timer, pouring in the requisite amount of water. At 9:30, the timer engaged the device's pump and heating coils, water dripped onto grounds. Fresh coffee filled the urn. But it went untended and unnoticed while Henri slumbered on the couch. After two hours, the machine's red indicator lamp went out and the coffee cooled. He slept the night through.

When he wakened with first light, he cursed himself, expecting the worst. And his fears were confirmed as soon as he stepped into the coop. Two were missing, a pullet and a hen. Their blood was everywhere, and the other hens simply refused to lay.

He had stayed out the next two nights, seeing nothing but the devolution of the lunar disc toward crescent, hearing nothing but the chatter of his own teeth. Counting hens. Four now.

Henri's life has been turned on end. But he has adapted remarkably, considering all of this. His new lifestyle - that of the graveyard shift, the night owl, the watchman - is reconcilable with a few half-truths left on the County Shop's answering machines, days of sleep, and a bald lie Andrea rendered in conversation with his supervisor over the phone. His boss had called to see whether Henri was all right, whether his whispered messages and ensuing absence should be interpreted as serious.

Now his gaze is boring new holes in the coop - they complement the wound ripped above the door by his rifle blast six nights ago. The moon is up in the west, migrating toward the horizon. It is a slim crescent, a single, long fang glowing in the exosphere. The leaves have started to turn in earnest this week - he hears them dropping from the stout, ancient maples that form the declination of treeline where the bluff begins to rise. The leaves drop noisily from high, snapping like dry paper against branches as they spin toward earth. The sounds are ubiquitous, urgent, creepy. It's difficult to distinguish them from the possibility of approaching mammals. Some slap so acutely on their whirling fall, he thinks the sounds must be deer or elk in the woods, cracking their antlers against trunks, snapping underhoof the superdry limbs and twigs thrown down in last spring's windstorms.

The falling of the leaves through clear, freezing space is hypnotic. Henri in his pumphouse chair, and his unblinking gaze, and the chicken coop are engaged in a gelid fusion. There is no other matter in the universe.

Some time passes. Henri's eyes waver and close, his chin sinks to his chest. His fingers relax, barely perceptibly, on the gunmetal and stock of the rifle. His breath comes even, exhalations of cloud that ascend toward Deneb, straight overhead.

All hell breaks loose in the coop.

There is no sound like poultry being dispatched. An airliner hurtles from the sky, panes explode in an outward rush of air and pressure and cavitation. An iceberg splashes into a cold, green sea. An asp imbeds its face in a small ankle - the concatenation of these sounds is full and replete in the denouement of Henri's remaining four hens. Henri is stunned awake as if an air horn has blown half his head away.

But this time he will wait. He raises the rifle, trains its business end on the coop's door. From the sounds it emits, the coop's interior must be volcanic, a slipping faultline. There are tremors from therein that must have risen from the core of the earth, cracking mantle and igneous strata all the way. The thuds of hens' bodies against the walls float across the triangle. Clucks and squeals and hisses - the birds sound more like a gigantic hog-slaughter in the midst of the coyote's onslaught.

And then there is a vast, wrecking stillness.

The door creaks open, hinges piercing the night, breaking through ice, chips and shards falling away down, back to the bowels of the earth, through the core of him. A snout appears, a hen dangling lifelessly there. The coyote levers open the door with its torso, emerges into the wane light cast from the road. Henri remains still, cursing the carnivorous fucker with black thoughts of hatred.

The animal comes fully into view - the coop door swings shut behind it. Henri takes aim from the chair. He exhales and increases the tension on his trigger finger. Through the sight, along the barrel, the chicken looks like a sack lunch grasped avariciously in the coyote's mandible. Henri's brain feeds impulses down a nerve highway to the muscles of his hand. The coyote rises. It takes on a new form. The form drops the hen from its teeth into waiting, pale hands with four fingers and an opposing thumb. A gout of flame jumps off the end of the gun. The recoil knocks Henri back into his chair. A report bounces up the bluff, echoes across the foothills.

A dead chicken and a dead boy - a young man - lay at Henri's feet. The boy is nude, technically, in that he wears no clothing. He's hairy though, unusually so, with a bright hole in his chest and a great cratered outblow that used to be his back, just under the right shoulderblade. Blood and feathers are matted around his mouth and filthy teeth. The boy's tongue pokes out, just slightly, beyond his dental bridge. It, too, is saturated with blood - whether the hen's or his own Henri cannot tell.

Andrea, wakened again by rifle shot and witnessing the last of this from the stoop, stands behind Henri with her hands to her lips. She is too terrified to scream.

Henri stands over the corpses. He has removed his John Deere cap and is massaging the side of his own head, where the hair has gone a very distinguished-looking gray at the temple. He is an amalgam of confusion. What he sees laid out for him on the semi-frozen earth in front of the coop simply cannot be. It is an impossibility. *Andrea, I swear to God it was a son of a bitching coyote.*

Changeling, shapeshifter: these are terms with which Henri is unacquainted. Yet they form a concretion in front of him now. There is nothing abstract or vague about the form lying still at his feet.

Andrea steps slowly backward, away from this phantasm. She will phone the sheriff. Everything will be all right.

Henri gapes nervously at his own hands, wondering whether he has done something wrong. And slowly, as the pool of blood widens, cooling, around the boy, Henri DeLaat suspects that yes, he has.

The Elk That Walked Through Camp

Grandpa and I returned early from an afternoon hunt. At seventy-four years old, with sixty elk seasons under his belt, he was tired. I was just frustrated and cold. All afternoon I'd hiked up and down ravines in knee-deep snow, pausing to sit on snow-covered stumps, snowflakes falling slowly, my enthusiasm falling more rapidly. There had been little sign of game: a few tracks here and there, hours-old turds heat-burrowed down into the drifts. Once I came across a fresher set of small tracks and spore, mud and sticks kicked up into the now-hard crust of ice, and drag marks from the hooves. The animal, most likely a mature cow, had been headed up further into the hills, counterintuitive given the weather forecast of more snowfall.

Now my mind was on building the evening's campfire. This was one of my camp responsibilities; in it, I took pride in the workmanship of my fires, in the even burning, in the colors of flame from various woods and pitch content. In the precise architecture, from foundation to apex, of the wood piled at the iris of a stone ring.

The campfire is the locus of the hunting camp. Around it meals are consumed; calories, lost in the day's exertions, are found again. Stories, true, not true, and between true and not true, are told. Cigars burn only here, only two weeks out of every year. We chew snuff and drink bourbon, tell jokes we'd never tell our wives or co-workers. Become re-accustomed to each other after fifty weeks. Sometimes we let something slip of our real natures, laughing quickly to cover the discomfort of disclosure and hurry on to the next joke. Around the fire, we are four court jesters.

The builder of the campfire has a serious obligation to facilitate all of this, then, and I was anxious to get started. We'd arrived back at camp a good hour before expected, and this presented me with the opportunity to build an unforgettable fire and say a prayer to the gods of good campfires on top of it. Grandpa had other ideas though.

The two other men in our hunting party, my uncle and step-dad, weren't expected for some time yet. The hunting party that had been camped across the road had filled their tags in the first two days of the season, and had hung two spike bulls from trees, loitering for a couple of days of drinking before pulling up and heading back home to Yakima. Grandpa knew that the lower legs, feet and hooves of the two dead elk would be laying over in their abandoned camp somewhere. He had devised a plan, and needed a partner to execute it.

"Let's go find the legs of those two elk over there and make tracks through camp," he said. He motioned to the other camp across the road. A grin spread across his old face. Born and raised in eastern Washington, a former Army soldier, then a carpenter for decades, he's prone to good humor. I was intrigued and - thinking back, privileged - to witness this streak of horseplay briefly played out in him.

We crossed the mud road, 1600 Road - which comprises the spine and ultimate homing beacon for all our elk-hunting operations - and set out to find, in the other camp, the legs of the unfortunate animals which, just about now, were probably being loaded into Yakima chest freezers in three-pound butcher-wrapped parcels. It took no time at all to locate the legs, piled neatly near the back of the site next to where the latrine pit had been filled.

"Here they are," I called. Grandpa ambled over and took hold of the foreleg I offered, gripping it like a ball-bat, inverting it to examine the hooves. We both exchanged forelegs for rear legs, examining them from severed shin to hoof. They felt like small logs, cold, with no give to them, having long since stiffened and frozen.

"These are perfect." He selected two and left the others piled again next to the latrine. We headed back to our camp, and he handed me one of the legs on the way. Both of us were starting to chuckle already, anticipating the success of our grand hoax, enjoying the presence of one another.

Entering our own camp again, we looked for places of undisturbed snow close to, but just off of, our habitual thoroughfares - the route to the pantry tent, our latrine, over to the woodpile, in a circle around the campfire's ring of stones. That way we could walk in the trampled areas and make the marks in the clean snow next to us.

The mechanics of the dirty deed were uncomplicated: Grandpa and I took turns planting the legs in the fresh snow at appropriate stride-length intervals, then pulled them out again, careful to leave convincing drag marks. This prevarication began at the road, wound up next to the tire marks out of camp we had left that morning, then passed the pantry and ran between the sleeping quarters and the fire pit. Here they crossed over one of our thoroughfares and recommenced next to the woodpile - we knocked a couple of pieces off the top of the pile for effect - and disappeared into the woods next to our latrine. Maybe twenty-five to thirty yards or so of bogus elk tracks in total.

We hid the legs behind the woodpile. Expecting my uncle and step-dad to return in about twenty minutes, we secreted ourselves fifty yards from camp in a natural blind. From there, we could survey the whole site, plus the road from where we anticipated their approach.

We didn't have to wait long before these two apes with rifles came up the road. They made so much noise we figured any elk in the surrounding thirty acres would bolt for high-country. They'd scrape the icy road with every step of their boots, and they were yacking away as if they feared speech would forever be stolen from them in a matter of moments.

"Cripes," Grandpa said, "listen to 'em." I already was starting to laugh in anticipation, hoping they'd find the tracks right away and we could watch their sorry asses run around camp pointing and gesturing. We started to watch them through binoculars so we could enjoy every minute of it, right down to their facial expressions.

My uncle hadn't taken five steps into camp when he drew up straight and grabbed hold of my step-dad's upper arm. He pointed at the ground with his free hand.

"Look at that," he said, and we could barely hear them from the distance. Snatches of exclamation came across to us though, things like: "...brass balls to walk through camp like that..." and "...shit, this is the bull I saw yesterday, I can tell from the hook in this hoof here, see..." All the while they gesticulated and looked around at the woods and up and down the road. They tracked the bull through camp, from the road to the latrine, taking their hats off and sitting down for a minute, shaking their heads in disbelief. Somebody should have hired them as big-game guides.

Grandpa and I were laughing our asses off, practically pissing our wool pants. We'd covered our mouths with our hands so hard we were mashing our lips into our teeth. Pressing those field glasses into our eye sockets so hard our eyeballs were touching the lenses.

"Look at those idiots," I said, now trying to figure out how far we could take this, while fighting back tears and wanting to take it much, much further. Our stomachs hurt from suffocating our laughter. Grandpa's eyes shone with fierce glee.

About ten minutes passed, and the two dupes calmed down a little. Grandpa and I decided to walk up and around a bluff, then come into camp as if we had approached on 1600 from the opposite direction they had returned. Without agreeing verbally, somehow we developed an unstated understanding that we'd not admit to our prank until we got as much mileage out of it as we could.

My step-dad heard us coming up the road. He rose as we entered camp.

"Come take a look at this." He steered us to the onset of the tracks. Pointing down, he said with all the conviction and faith of the Pope, "he came right through the damned camp." Here, his hand swept the length of the fake trail, and abandoned the motion pointing right at the latrine.

I think "Wow" was all I could manage. Grandpa came up with something more convincing: "You never know what a damned elk is gonna do. You can hunt them for fifty years, and I've seen all kinds of things, including this, but it's pretty rare…"

I got busy on the campfire, and Grandpa turned his energy to hanging up damp clothing inside the sleeping tent. We ate supper and gathered around the campfire. Every once in a while Grandpa and I would catch each other's gaze and fight laughter and confession.

My uncle and step-dad went on and on about the tracks, periodically rising to convince themselves again: Indeed, a bull elk had displayed the audacity to walk right through the very camp of four men who longed to shoot it, butcher it, and set it out on the kitchen table for the duration of the eleven-and-a-half months until next hunting season.

About nine o'clock everyone ran out of steam. We all went into the sleeping tent where the tent stove blazed at about 80 degrees. It was time to get ready for bed. I left the tent for a moment, gathered the two elk legs, and stuffed them - hooves up - in the semi-frozen muck of the latrine hole. This way the next user would open the lid - a normal toilet seat fastened to two four-foot 2x4s suspended between a pair of trees over a pit - and, if they happened to look before doing their business, discover our hoax.

I chose this method of admission without consulting Grandpa. It was a simple playing of the odds: when the two discovered what Grandpa and I had done, they'd likely kill us. I liked the odds much better if it was he and I against one of them with trousers on and one of them with trousers bunched around his ankles.

Ten minutes later my step-dad headed up to the latrine and bellowed into the deep, cold night his discovery. Grandpa and I went spastic with laughter, both nearly throwing up. Contrary to my fears, my step-dad and uncle were good sports, and promised only retribution.

Some day they will carry it out.

A Taste Like Fear

I sat back in a brushed felt chair in the Chocolate Room, gave an eager eye through rising cigar smoke to Dr. James Mullenix. We had just - the three of us - excised the tips from a trio of fine Hondurans, snifters at hand, in The Ruins' brown after-supper room. Scenes of foxhunts favored us from deep cherrywood frames. Over the hearth a fire cracked through kindling pitch and seared strong locustwood - its aroma worked its way into the room, merged with newer perfume from the cigars. It was, at that moment, altogether pleasant, the Doctor, the esteemed Randolph Harrison Chair in Applied Mathematics at the University of Washington, just returned from hunting escapades in East Africa. From the overstuffed chairs we implored him to share a post-repast adventure or two, Paul Oestinger, the zoologist-in-chief for the zoo project going in at Green Lake, and myself, an adventure columnist for the *Seattle Post*.

"You slick dogs," Dr. Mullenix said - he knew even dear friends must never fully relax themselves in the presence of the Fourth Estate or of fellow men of science.

I set my brandy down, held my hands up, splayed the fingers in innocent surprise - that he would abuse us so!

"My dear friend," I countered, "we are totally, completely satisfied with supper. And we are pleased to have your company again, after these long two months. All of us - to a man! - look forward to your presentation at the Traveler's Society, but please... please *do*... let us in on a small anecdote - not one for public consumption."

It was a bit of a speech, brought on by the brandy I fear. Mullenix recognized it as such. He had drawn on the Honduran throughout my oration, then blew forth a gust at its conclusion. In The Ruins' Chocolate Room, we mates had passed many such an evening, related hunting exploits too numerous to tally. He knew he had nothing to fear from us.

"Yes Doctor, *please*," Paul added. A simpler speech, and more effective by an order of magnitude than my less-than-persuasive bidding.

"I'm just bringing my notes together," Mullenix began. By this he meant the Traveler's Society talk, which was scheduled five nights hence. At the time, I supposed he dallied with this pre-explanation of his prepared remarks while, in reality, he sought a few moments to characterize the story he would relate. An instant or two to frame the arguments in his head, get straight in his mind - again and to the extent *possible* - what he had witnessed or, rather, *may* have witnessed. He also would have, in those moments of stalling, had to decide again how to deal

92

with the parts he had not himself seen, with his own Western eyes, but had been made clear to him or felt by him so deeply, so far down in the absolute cellar of his guts. Those things that had manifested themselves, whether corporeally or from something, somewhere, *other* than such.

"But I will tell you," he continued, "a strange story."

Oestinger and I exchanged grins - it was exactly as we had hoped. An anecdote for no one but us!

"Indeed," he said - and a shade fell across his eyes as if something had stolen his vision, and that rather than the deep brown painted walls and wainscoting and trim of the Chocolate Room, Mullenix was again on the Tanganyikan savanna with tall grass and acacia trees, baobabs, and in the company of his guide Mbele and a retinue of coal-black Maasai bearers - "Africa is a place of strange stories."

Mullenix had hunted God's beasts on all continents save Australia. Great striped bengals of Burma, slinking ocelots in Guyana, roan stags in the Schwartzwald. On the mantle of North America, he had subdued grizzly in the Selkirks, huge rams, elk, buffalo, cougar. And, of course, he had slain dozens of Africa's mammals - from the giant elephant to the lissome giraffe, the black rhinoceros, the majestic lion. He looked forward to, one day, loading his rifles and training them on beasts in Australia as well - that island continent of the freakish platypus, cassowary, kangaroo, dingo. He'd heard of fabulously succulent deer roaming Tasmania. And if not there, perhaps wild pigs on Sumatra - this was close enough, geographically speaking, to count as Australia.

Crows' feet creased the corners of Dr. Mullenix's eyes. I could almost imagine the perfect truncation of Kilimanjaro's cone, its flat peak reflected from his irises in the flicker of The Ruins' stone fireplace. I closed my own eyes for an instant and saw in his hands a huge rifle. I imagined without need to confirm with him it was a Model 90, Gibbs' Metford .570, capable of dropping any elephant or rhino with one shot - certainly the smaller lion and wildebeest and lesser antelopes. This - *this* - was the sort of story I thought we would hear.

He settled back in his chair with the cigar, raised an affirming gaze from its tip, tracing curls of smoke as they rose. Soon he was looking at the brown ceiling, still searching for a beginning point.

"Our party rose one day to the most splendid sort of morning - the sort I am coming to appreciate only Africa has to offer," he began. "We breakfasted on fried sweet potatoes, tender strips of waterfowl meat, which in some parts of the continent is called *biltongue*. Mbele, my guide, exhibited a certain enthusiasm that the day's hunt would well reward us, and he whistled and clicked as he saddled our horses. His gunbearers - six young men of the Maasai tribe, which he had assembled from the docks at Mombassa - fell in step as we left camp. Mbele kept always on my right. If we spotted game, he would require my rifle first from one of the bearers. It was a double-barreled .570, a beautiful weapon with a deep mahogany stock and a fulsome, substantial recoil. Only after he had delivered my rifle would he accept a second rifle from one of his fellow tribesmen. We hoped this second rifle was redundant - its purpose was to put down a charging animal if I were to be rendered, somehow, incapacitated.

"I have many early morning impressions from that horseback, Mbele the gun-bearer at my side. The Maasai retinue remained on the ground around us, trudging through the tall grass. There were the odors of moist earth and strange sweet pollens. The sun rose directly to the east from behind Kilimanjaro's broad, flat top. The morning was humid, with pockets of mist around baobabs and a high dew point. We spotted, over the course of the morning, a fleeing honey badger, a group of hyena and rock hyrax, several dik-dik.

"I rode quietly next to Mbele, turning a problem of calculus back and forth in my head. For the sake of a diversion - not that one was needed! - I triangulated our distance from Kilimanjaro's peak. Then I derived its height from the position of the sun above it, the time on my pocketwatch, and my knowledge of our current elevation. We were hunting savanna at six-thousand feet above sea level - the mountain rose another thirteen thousand feet, give or take a few hundred.

"One of our Maasai stopped suddenly and drew up to his full height. He peered over the high sawgrass, having a more intent look at an area that had, for some reason, interested him. Perhaps he had seen movement, perhaps not. I will tell you I have never seen an individual observe a patch of ground more fixedly than that warrior that morning. And he was a sight himself! Well formed, tall, with a fine carriage and the deepest ebony skin. He stood in a buckskin wrap, the hair on his head bunched tightly, absolutely still. His wide nostrils flared and I could hear the inrush as he tested the air for scents.

"Then he turned to Mbele and said one word: 'Simba.' He turned around to face the direction he had been reconnoitering and pointed. I lifted field glasses, let my eyes focus and resolve on the spot he indicated, and saw that his reckoning was dead on. A pride of lions loitered underneath a solitary baobab, three females awake and alert, one male in repose. Even from our distance, which I would judge to have been three-hundred, maybe three-hundred and fifty yards, I could see that the male was enormous.

"Mbele indicated we should ride around the plain a little and approach from the north. Another of the bearers offered up our rifles - my .570 first, a .500 Mbele would use second. He kicked his horse into a breezy canter, then a gallop. I followed. We sped to the north, eyeing the lions the entire time. They were watching us as well, evaluating our intent, I suppose, but as yet unalarmed.

"I can close my eyes and see in my mind this tableau at this very moment. Two lionesses are kneeling to the right of the tree. Their tails are twitching. The third lioness is to the left, standing. The male lies recumbent between the three, but he senses the beats of hooves, not so much the sound of them but their concussive footfalls through the earth he lies upon. His eyes open at the moment I am raising my rifle and he roars to his feet. He is stupendous, magnificent, regal - I place a bullet driven 2,300 feet per second by 750 grains of axite powder through his broad chest, into his heart. Still he has the strength to leap forward. Mbele, exactly in the role he is intended to perform, places a precautionary shot through the bridge of his face, shattering skullbone and facial architecture. The male falls immediately dead. Two of the she-lions bolt. But the third must have her revenge on us. I bring her down with two well-placed shots at the withers.

"It was some time before the retinue caught up with us, having stood back the several hundred yards while Mbele and I did the killing. Now they approached on a happy trot. They were eager to dress out the meat and ferry it, as well as the trophy heads and draping skins, back to our morning camp. It took three of the six to do this, nearly halving our presence that morning - which was fast becoming mid-day. Mbele and I paused for some bread and jerky with the remaining three bearers. We washed the luncheon down with our canteen. As the sun rose to its noon-time zenith overhead, we shared pleasant reminisces from the previous night's campfire.

"Mbele was re-telling the story from the night before, explaining what to me had manifested itself only as a sing-song exchange that had put me in mind of our own dear Presbyterian responsive readings. The tenseless kitchen Swahili of the interior is a language of fundamental instruments. Their voices were like the low notes of flutes that impressed me as *rising* - like sparks from the acacia-wood campfire. They had donned cloaks of barkcloth to ward of the night's chill.

"'My cousins,' Mbele explained, 'shared the story of the cloth of *Pembi Mirui*. It is the story of a tribesman who loved his wife so much he battled Pembi Mirui, a seven-headed serpent, to steal for her the gossamer cloth it hid in its belly. He succeeded in cleaving through the serpent's first six heads, but the seventh spat onto him a powerful poison. Only through the cleverness of a cat the tribesman had in his possession - a cat clever enough to bring along a serum! - was the serpent thwarted. Revitalized by the antidote, the tribesman cut off the final head, then slit open the snake's guts to retrieve the cloth. His wife is said to have received him with joy.'

"'I should hope so!' I said to Mbele, and we laughed together under a blazing Tanganyikan sun. The two of us, I believed, were becoming good friends.

"When we finished languishing at the feet of our horses, in the baobab's shade, we mounted again and set out for a ridge some two miles distant. We supposed, after some discussion, we might run across more lions, or some other worthy game. I had never taken, in Africa, a water buffalo, and mentioned this to Mbele. As we rode, he chattered about where we might detour to find a watering hole - this might be a good way to find some, he said.

"We entered a broad stretch of very high grass, moving slowly downhill toward a hollow. The grass grew up past the tops of our horses' heads. We followed the trail indicated by the wake of our bearers, who had spread out ahead of us. The horses tracked the divided stalks where the Maasai had walked through moments before, and in this way, we were certain to stay with them - there was no mistaking their routes.

"I was daydreaming yet again - whether it was of the pleasant night before or yet another algorithmic mind puzzle, I don't recall. Suddenly, we heard the tribesmen running back up the trails toward us. First we heard their shouts, then the sound of them sprinting through the grass. The three gun-bearers materialized through the foliage with eyes wide like specimens of mental infirmity. They spied us and halted abruptly, pausing, then dropping to their knees as if they were penitents.

"'What is happening?' Mbele demanded.

"The three of them looked only at Mbele - I tell you, they would not look at me or address me. '*Afriti*,' one said, and his cohorts shook their heads in terrified affirmation. '*Mkodi*,' the other two whispered. '*Ninakwenda*,' said the first man, and the others plainly agreed.

"'What are they saying?' I asked Mbele. But he silenced me with an upheld hand. He spoke to them in a long, low, calming language, but the first man vowed again, '*Ninakwenda.*' 'I am leaving,' Mbele told me it meant, after they left. They had encountered an evil ghost, a supernatural spirit, he said. Mbele's counsel had calmed them only a bit - he reminded the bearers, of course, of their retainer, of the vast difference in rupiahs to be earned gun-bearing versus working the docks. Nevertheless, they left, and there was no deterring them. I held my hand up in a vain attempt to persuade them to stop, to remain there with us. But they kept going, and soon Mbele and I, and the two horses under us, stood in a veil of hot, oppressive silence.

"We decided to press on, evil spirit or no, and witness for ourselves what had so frightened our men. As we proceeded downhill, the grass began to thin. Then we rounded a lone acacia tree where the tall grass tapered away and saw, fifty yards ahead at the center of a wide bowl, a watering hole. Mbele turned to me with a satisfaction that seemed to promise water buffalo this day even yet - though we would have had an excruciating time packing one back to camp without our bearers.

"The watering hole was empty at that moment, save a pair of egrets stepping among its gentle wavelets. As we drew closer I discerned a fish eagle standing at the edge too. And then a dark shape resolved itself on the near shore - it was difficult to make out exactly since the soil at the pond's edge was richly black as well. But there was a definite shape that emerged as we rode nearer.

"It was one of those moments where you start to imagine what an unresolved shape or thing might be. Then an idea, an archetype perhaps, suggests itself - just barely, as a whisper. And you say to yourself, 'No, that can't be it.' Yet the closer you come the more it seems to be exactly the thing you are refusing to acknowledge. It appears more and more to be the thing you wish to deny, until you are upon it and it is incontrovertibly the thing you do not want to believe, and you blink but it's still there. You close your eyes and utter a weak and tender, 'No,' the negation a refutal of it, a rejection, a parsing of that which is real and that which is created, unbidden, by the mind. You want this thing lying before you, at the muddy bank of a savanna waterhole, to be an illusion."

An attendant of The Ruins entered the Chocolate Room as Mullenix's voice had begun to rise. He glanced nervously at Oestinger and I, drew from his apron two fresh ashtrays to replace the soiled pair in which we had been dropping the ashes of our Hondurans. "Gentlemen," he said. "Please forgive my interruption. Will you have your brandies refreshed?"

All of us nodded eagerly, and I became self-aware of my racing heart, the tenseness with which I clenched my fists, my jaw. The Doctor's tale

97

had been engrossing up to the point just before the attendant's interruption - now what strange turn was it taking? Oestinger stared at the tip of his cigar. Mullenix closed his eyes and settled back into his chair. He had been on the edge of his seat, had, in fact, been gesturing somewhat wildly with the signals of a man who is flailing at myths.

"She was a sort of goddess," he continued, "although at first it seemed to me as if she was simply a mortal woman. She was clad in a loose antelope skin, a garment that had slid aside at the bosom to reveal one glorious breast and had gathered and bunched up at her hips. The shape of her was exquisite and perfect, but rudely exposed. Her deep nakedness drew our eyes in a violent magnetism, as she lay oddly contorted in the black mud. There were the tracks of herons around her. She seemed large from our mounts; when we dismounted moments later it would be clear to us she was well over seven feet tall.

"'My God,' I choked through the vise of my throat. Mbele, appearing stunned, averted his gaze, and whispered '*Mulungu*,' which also means 'deity.'

"The form at the feet of our horses, at the edge of the pool, partially buried in black sand and surrounded by the spoor of inquiring waders, had been radically traumatized. The broad nose of her once-elegant face had been smashed and gouged, the full lips bruised and bloodied at the downturned corners. Her neck had been deeply lacerated - not by an animal, of this we were sure. The cut was the work of a blade, so straight and fine. A man or men had done this, judging from the other manner in which she had been violated, below. I am sorry to speak of it, even now.

"For a very brief instant I harbored an illusion she might yet be living. But I soon abandoned this hope. Although no stench rose from her, and there was no external sign of putrefaction's onset, it was clear she had not been moved for some time. She had, for all purposes, *sunk* into the sand. I marveled that no marauding animals had visited upon her any act of depredation beyond that which she had clearly suffered in the incidence of her death.

"I wish I could convey the extent to which this disturbed us. Mbele, I saw after a while, was quietly weeping, and did not want to look at the body. I spent several minutes pondering a course of action, regaining my senses a bit, since they had received such a profound shock. Then I summoned from some unknown reservoir of will the courage to dismount. I thought, I suppose, that we might retrieve her from the mudbank. Mbele and I would pull her from the wet sand, take her back to camp.

We would send some of the remaining bearers for the authorities. It was impossible to imagine leaving her corpse here in the wild.

"Then I handed Mbele the .570 and dismounted. The horse was happy to be out from under me. I believe the animal must have sensed, through the saddle, my unease. With only the simple change in elevation from horseback to the ground, she seemed to grow - both physically, in dimensions that could be measured finitely, and in other ways - in her absolute *presence*. I looked upon her ruined face again. The mouth was slightly open with the pink pearly tongue visible. Her ebony hair clung close to her like a skullcap. The bare breast was a perfect coal globe, the nipple a dark button rising from a circle of sable velvet. My hands were drawn to touch the exposed skin of her and I felt, through primal soil beneath me, the rhythm of the earth's turning under my boots. I battled an unbidden, unwanted desire to look where her legs joined, to linger there between them with an un-doctorly gaze.

"Mbele stayed on his horse until he appreciated clearly that my intention was to touch her. Then he said, '*Hapana hapana!*' with some vigor as he dismounted, forgetting my Swahili was very limited. 'No, *jambo*! - she must not be touched by a white man. *Tafadali*! Please!'

"He moved closer to show why. My gun-bearer grasped her shoulder, pivoted with his body to lever against her, and thus she yielded from the mud bank - no rigor mortis of any sort had yet set in. Mbele lifted her shoulderblades. There, from her back, knobby roots of black wingforms emerged, and I could see now the feathers of wings partially buried there in the dark mud. My God! Imagine how this shook me, how it dumbfounded me to the core of myself! Here was a Negress seraphim so perfect, so obsidian, if she spread those wings a complete night would have fallen. She lay here, at the edge of a watering fountain. Where we had sought to slay a mortal, we had discovered a slain immortal!

"Mbele laid her gently back against the sand. He took a step away from her. He bent down to pull the antelope hide across her mons.

"'What shall we do, *jambo*?' I asked. "Shall we take her to camp and locate the authorities?"

"Mbele shook his head. 'She is *mzuri* - good, an angel.' He had a look on his face after he said this as if it was explanation enough, that with these words, I should understand. 'An angel, do you see?' He held out his hands, palms up, in a gesture of supplication. '*Malaika*.'

"'*Malaika*,' I repeated.

"'We will bury her there." He pointed back toward the single acacia at the boundary of the tall grass, from where we had emerged what

99

seemed like hours ago. I pointed out that we lacked spades, that we would have to go back to our camp to get them, then return here - in all, probably a hard ride of two hours would be required.

"'Should one of us stay here with her?' I asked. Mbele wouldn't answer aloud, just shook his head from side to side.

"So we left her there, rode - as I said - at least an hour back to camp, hard. Our Maasai bearers, both those who had left earlier in the day with the dead lions, as well as those who had fled us in the tall grass, were gone. The lion carcasses lay forsaken in the camp. After giving his fellow tribesmen a good round of cursing, Mbele and I rode out again.

"Sun was falling directly into the west - somewhere into Lake Natron, I suppose, some twelve miles distant. A purplish African twilight descended on us. Kilimanjaro, lit in pinks and fuchsias and mauves, appeared to leap at us from our backs. We retraced our route from the baobab tree where we'd captured the lions to the deep grass, and emerged, as we had earlier in the day, this time in the halflight.

"But the angel of Mulungu - this is how Mbele described her on the long return ride to camp - was gone. The edge of the pond was empty. We rode up on lathered horses to discover only the tracks of herons and other birds, small mammals, in the sand where she had been. There were no drag marks, no signs of movement of any kind, not even impressions where her partially sunken body had been. To read the sand was to reach this conclusion: she had never existed."

I sought to sip from my brandy again - forgetting it was empty - as the hairs on my neck stood. My arms broke out in gooseflesh, so unexpected was this turn in the Doctor's tale. I glanced over at Oestinger, who sat slumped in his chair eyeing his snifter. The ash on his Honduran had grown absurdly long.

Then The Ruins' attendant, looking sorry to have interrupted again, entered the Chocolate Room with new snifters all around. He bent to add two small logs to the fire. "Pardon me once more, gentlemen," he apologized. He bowed slightly, let loose the logs on the embers. A few sparks jumped at this, and he stepped away from the hearth.

"It's quite all right," Mullenix said, but it was if it had been spoken from the Dark Continent itself, from thousands of miles and many years distant. "I've finished."

The attendant made a small bow again and left them room.

The Doctor looked at Oestinger and me. He had finished his story and now sought an evaluation from us. There was a plea behind his gaze, and it was no longer the simple end of a story for him, the fundamental relating to us of something he had observed and encountered. His disclosure in that late hour, nested in the trappings of the Chocolate Room and the wealth and success for which it was metaphor, was far more fundamental. He sought not an approval for his story, or his ability as a storyteller. No, instead he sought validation of the rightness of the whole world. And, perhaps, for his own sanity.

Then he asked it, a question for which he must have known, even then, there was no sufficient answer: "My friends, what kind of place is this? In what place can one of God's own angelic beings be violated and murdered?" He raised his snifter and contemplated the brandy in its broad bottom. Then he sipped it, closed his eyes for the contact. He grimaced with the taste of those amber drops, the taste, for him, of fear.

I think of Mullenix today, fifty-seven years later, how the logician in him must have slowly lost concretion. How that taste of fear must have spread in his throat and esophagus, into his guts, so that it became an abstract hopeless whimpering humiliation. To have been so terrifyingly mystified as was evident in his begging glassy gaze, that moment when he finished his tale. I know these facts only: after some time at a state hospital - during which Tanganyika changed hands from the Germans to the British as spoils of the Great War - the Doctor returned to the East African countryside once more following a successful boar-hunt in Borneo. I received one correspondence from him - a waterstained envelope with a stamp bearing George V's portrait, a Dar es Salaam postmark. In it, he described a search for Mbele, but he was unable to locate his old *jambo*. He'd heard on the docks at Mombassa the gun-bearer had gone missing several seasons before, during the early months of the British occupation. In closing the note, he repeated his question, "What kind of place is this?" In the shaking scrawl of his penmanship I could comprehend his terror. I can suffer with him the same, whenever I re-read the letter.

I am ninety-six years old. I don't have any explanations for Mullenix's adventure - it has been a recurring question for me through the years. Occasionally I would experience more vivid recollections of Mullenix and his tale - at other times the bizarre story would seem unexplainable and unimportant.

I remember when Hemingway's "Green Hills of Africa" was published in 1935, or I would look at my favorite safari stories of Teddy Roosevelt, or Col. Patterson's "The Man-Eaters of Tsavo," or the excellent accounts of Gordon Cummings. It was at those times I would set aside the books after reading a chapter, sip a coffee or a brandy, light a cigar.

I would close my eyes and see only Mullenix and his black angel - wings unfurled for all time, Mulungu's handmaiden bringing the blessing of night to us all.

I hope Mullenix has found her. We can *all* only hope.

Fish Story

The day we heard Sixkiller's fish story, four of us had come in after skeet shooting, throwing clay pigeons at the autumn sky. The jumps of our shotguns had worn tender spots on our shoulders, as well as thirsty spots in our throats, and we sat at Cracker Heaven and passed recovery time. There was Money, Jimbo (his name is James; the last person, other than his mother, who called him that took a fist in the mouth), and Duff Benson, and me. We started watching a ball game after the shooting, refugees of the roar of powder and ejection of sulfurous shells. A guy could work up a thirst hefting a 12- or 10-gauge into position, taking its recoil.

Quincy has five avenues running north and south for a half a mile and five streets running east and west for an equivalent distance. That way, it's a perfect square and fits perfectly inside the surrounding geometry, which comprises platted farmland for coaxing alfalfa, sorghum and wheat from the Columbia Basin. Cracker Heaven lies on one of Quincy's intersections, its barkeep Dave Sixkiller, an Indian man who never drank booze himself. But we drank plenty to make up for him.

Cracker Heaven has all the normal one-story cowshit-town stuff in it - neon signs that spit and buzz as we walk in, a full-size cardboard cutout of one of the Miller babes whose breasts are too perfect to have any credibility whatsoever, a clock without an hour hand. There are mirrors and bottles behind the bar, and a guy can sit there on the tall stools and grow handsomer as midnight approaches. There's a condom machine in the men's room. I'm not sure what for; there are never, under any circumstances - at least that I ever encountered - women you would want to date who walk off Quincy's nothing's-happening streets through the door into Cracker Heaven.

Money, that day, was the first to strike.

"I remember hooking a steelhead down on'na Kelso that was longer'n a pool cue," he claimed.

Jimbo evaluated his beer glass; Duff and I looked Money over like the liar he is.

"Bullshit," Duff said.

"No bullshit, brother. He had scales the size a dimes. I fought him for fifteen minutes 'for he snapped the line."

"Yeah," I said. "I think you're confused, Money. I think it was a big smelt, down on the Kelso."

Money escalated the contest: "I think your mother's maybe a big smelt down on the Kelso."

"I think I *know'd* your mother," Jimbo said. Sixkiller raised an eyebrow over his tumbler-buffing.

"Anyway, that's nothing," I said. Then I fed them full of tripe about one time my grandfather and I were catfishing Silver Lake and these big, floppy bass started throwing themselves into his rowboat. "Just sacrificed themselves to the gods of catfishing, me and my grandpa."

"But you was catfishin," Duff said.

"Well, what do you want to eat, trashfish or a nice bass?" I said.

"How many?"

"Oh, I don't know, a dozen maybe."

It was a weak story, and its credibility with the three of them plus Sixkiller went early into the toilet. I couldn't make even the bartender suspend his disbelief for a few seconds.

"O.K., O.K.," I said. I drained my glass, grabbing at the pitcher. "You try." I motioned at Jimbo. He looked up at the tile ceiling, grabbed a few ideas, let them mix around in his fat head.

"My daddy killed a doe with a knife," he said. His lips turned up in a smile he could barely sustain.

"Oh come on," Duff said, spraying some beer through gaps in his teeth.

"Yeah, he did. He shot her, and she didn't fall over right away. But she didn't run either, so he worked 'is way across the ravine from where he fired, and when he got to her she musta panicked or somethin.' Anyway, she run right at 'im, damned near right over 'im if he hadn'ta ducked. Over him she goes, and he whips out his Bowie from his belt, reaches up as she jumps over him, slams it into her neck and down she goes bleedin'."

We marveled silently at this tale. Like a sap, Jimbo believed for a moment he had won us over. We were willing to let him suffer under this illusion long enough for him to order another pitcher, and for Sixkiller to draft it. We passed it around, all refreshed our glasses, and then there was silence as we studied the amber liquid with the sounds of Major League Baseball spilling from the ceiling-slung TV. A few minutes passed with none of us speaking. Then Duff adopted a pensive expression, as if he labored to find the right words. Finally he did and, as judge and jury, found Jimbo guilty.

"You know, Jimbo," he said. "You know, I known you a long time."

"Yeah, man, you lucky."

"Yes. Yes, I am. I known you a long time, but I never knew what a scum-bag liar you are."

The four of us fell into gut laughs, giggling like high-school boys. Sixkiller even cracked a smile.

"O.K., dickhead, let's hear your weak attempt," Jimbo said.

"Yeah, dickhead," Money and I chimed in. It was like a three-way game of Screw Your Buddy. We were as willing to turn on each other as take a leak. Conversely - and more importantly - the moment it mattered, we'd commit homicide for each other.

Duff then told, badly, a story about a royal bull walking right through hunting camp up near Bumping River, out past Naches on the way to Chinook Pass. How he and some buddies were up there one season and the bad boy wandered through in broad daylight. They supposedly just sat there and watched him walk through. No one had his rifle loaded in camp, and everyone froze in place, fearing movement toward a firearm would spook the elk, send it crashing into the pines.

"This was the biggest bull I ever seen," Duff said. "Never seen one as big since, and neither have any a you."

We howled at this sorry epic, all gestured a thumbs-down to him.

"No prize, Duffer," Jimbo said, then discovered he was out of smokes, and Cracker Heaven's machine had gone haywire. So Jimbo and I climbed down off our stools and made for the 7-Eleven across the intersection. Into the parking lot we strolled, mildly oiled, and negotiated the space between my scabbed-out hunting truck and Jimbo's Blazer. He'd left his window open, even though his shotgun hung there in the gun rack. He reached in, grabbed his wallet off the dashboard, and we were off across the street. Quincy people are unconcerned about the security of their wallets or firearms. We know better than to swipe stuff from each other.

When we returned, Duff and Money waved us over.

"C'mere." Duff beckoned with a flopping hand. "Sixkiller's got one."

"Got one what?" Jimbo asked.

Sixkiller had a fish story.

"This happened over at Trinidad Links," the barkeeper started. "You know, right on the river. It was maybe six years back, a couple years after they opened the course…"

Designers laid out the course so that most of it rode the eastern river bluffs soaring high over the water. But this topography surrendered nearer the waterline after a dogleg on the eleventh fairway, then ran parallel to the river for three more holes. The stretch culminated the fourteenth green, with the fifteenth tee box facing east, and uphill, a short par-three jump back onto the bluffs.

At 8 a.m. sharp, the course's greenskeeper carted around the back nine for inspections. These holes near the river were a consistent problem, with herons, other waterfowl, muskrats - and occasional fishermen - frequently engaged in trespass. He couldn't believe his eyes this morning, though. Before him, on the clipped hairs of the thirteenth green, enveloping the cup under the dominion of the flapping flag: elk tracks. Dozens of sets, like half a herd had come through during pre-dawn and executed a long-waited rut. Not only were the ungulate hoofmarks cut deep into the sandy soil, but the hooves had shorn away great gouges of grass, exposing the undergreen. Accurate putting would be impossible here without major repairs. The greenskeeper sighed, made an exploratory poke with one of his green spades. Nudged the torn surface with a cleated boot. Looked up, around, over to the west at the passing Columbia.

The tracks emanated from the river - there was no doubting it. He walked past a hoof-scarred sand trap to inspect the crest, the boundary of river sand and rough grass. Tracks and dropped scat dotted the banks and barrier grass, with the clear drag-marks of the herd's lift running up onto the fairway. The elk had emerged from the river all right, like mammals evolving from fish.

The greenskeeper executed calculations in his head. The math made him appreciate the source of his unease. The first tee-time this morning was 7:30, so the first group was an hour and a half to two hours off. He would have to bust his ass to repair the green. Repairs to the fairway and bunkers would have to wait - this was triage. Golfers could play their balls where they lied anywhere on the fairway, or move them to more favorable spots. He knew most of them did anyway, that winter rules ran from June 1 to May 31. But putting, that was altogether a different sort of prospect. No one would stand for playing out his short game on a torn-up green.

"Look," he said, back at the clubhouse, "we need to call the Game Department and get them out here to take care of these elk."

"Go ahead," the course manager said.

Sixkiller paused to light a cigarette.

The smoke curled around him, around his head, through his braids. It moved toward the ceiling, and I glanced at Duff and Money and Jimbo, whose gazes were fixed, intently, on the barkeeper. All we could hear was the air conditioning, and Sixkiller's intake on the smoke.

He took a few more drags, then continued...

Denny Willow saw the approach of a rain wall. It assembled itself like the weaving of a moist blanket over the rise off the river, dropping from low altocumulus onto round mounds of hills. Overhead, the sky still, light with cloud - almost white. And in the east, there were cloudbreaks of powder blue. The migrations of the breaks released, sporadically, the unmetered sweep of sun, so it painted with authority the hills on the river's west bank. They stood like masses of fool's gold under the gray of a front driven from the west, so that the hills seemed backlit from within by molten-gold fires. Their glow held out a false promise, a warmth that would never, on this day or in five months of subsequent days, materialize. The rain advancing above them was a foregone conclusion. Willow knew that inside of twenty minutes he and the boat would be soaked. And as the shower approached, he watched it move, a disturbance across slow, flat current, palpable and defined, until the first drops made small sweet circles in the river next to him. The circles multiplied. The sounds of their splashing became a steady white noise of tumult and rose up.

In no time, Willow was in the middle of a rainstorm on the Columbia River, and wrestled himself into Fish & Game-issued raingear. He glassed the waters to the west for swimming elk. Stackings of raindrops and wavecrests now occluded the eddies and whorls of familiar currents, those Willow knew like his own body, from his own history. Here, on the eastern bank forty yards off the golf course, the river ran shallow under him, maybe two fathoms. He waited, too soon rain- and wind-drenched, for the heads and racks of elk to crest water. He waited to turn them back. He would drift downriver a mile, then motor upcurrent again to his starting point, raining so hard now the propeller's wash was barely discernible. His fingers, first cold and then pruned and numb, grasped the wheel and throttles. He rose once to lift his binoculars again, misjudged the interplay of his body and balance within in the vessel, stumbled, carelessly slapped his bare hand against a gunwale. Pain jumped into the saturated digits like an egret's beak had closed on them.

So he resumed his seat behind the wheel, raised the lenses with the fingers that were still good, and clenched and re-clenched the traumatized hand to restore circulation and hope.

Willow had received this assignment with mixed feelings. Keeping elk out of a fancy new golf course was not exactly his idea of game management, and he believed that more pressing work elsewhere was left undone. Everyone had his idea how best to manage game herds, and the wanderings and intrusions of local groups of elk prompted no small amount of debate. No two persons agreed on solutions, no matter whether they both were hunters, biologists, public servants, interested citizens, or golf-course management. But something about the hoidy-toidiness of the course's manager, his raw umbrage that the wilds had descended on his fiefdom, rubbed Willow wrong.

On the other hand, Willow wanted to protect the intruders. He thought they must be attracted to the wide greens and open spaces set in the course, perhaps to the broad availability of delectable shrubbery there. He imagined the herd exhausting tasty sweetgrass and foliage on the west bank, spying eastward across the river the succulent strands of green, and making the swim. He knew this was absurd, but struggled with another explanation for the cross-water migrations. He'd seen the hoof-marks and sign - no question, elk had emerged from the water and tore hell out of the fairways and greens next to the river. That the groundskeeper had seemed to want the animals to suffer punitively, though, had bothered him. *How dare they stride across his turf? By what stretch of licentiousness had they gamboled across his fairways, lifting sand from the bunkers, slapping flags from their holes with an arc and thrust of antlers?* The man had exhibited a deep, concerned frown when Willow visited the clubhouse at the onset of his investigation, as if the world were deteriorating around him, and others didn't appreciate the seriousness of it all.

A reduction of all of this, in Willow's mind, sitting behind the vessel's wheel, taking rain into the bilgehollows of the boat below the draughtline: *The damned elk were here first.*

Nevertheless, his job was to deter them from the shore with volleys from flare guns, air horns and, finally, if necessary, rubber bullets. He was to patrol the one-mile stretch of riverbank, lying in wait from dawn until noon. Probably they wouldn't come. But to be seen in his black and white powerboat, from the golf-course clubhouse atop the bluff, would usher in the appearance of responsiveness. As a public servant, then, he felt as if his presence here, bred with his concern for the animals, would suffice. Elk or no elk.

The deluge subsided and he found himself on patrol through light showers again. The sky brightened above his position, and the cloudburst moved on to the east. He looked back to the hilltops on the west side of the river valley. They had lost their brilliance, returned to staid forms, giant dull hillocks of sage, scrub dirt and rock. The effervescing gold waned to the color of dried cornstalks, a uniform matte. As the brilliance of the hills muted, so too did the mottled splashing of rain, until it left, in its place, the sounds only of drifting. The slow caress of river water slapped against the hull when a swell lifted the keel out of the current. Willow stretched out his legs, hoisted the glasses again, let them fall and gazed across the water naked-eyed.

He first discerned the undulating humps of elk-forms across the water as a mnemonic: he had never seen Roosevelt elk swim a river, but recalled the graceful movement of other ungulates - gazelles, gemsbok, exotic deer - midway through scores of televised fordings on Wild Kingdom as a child, or the Discovery Channel as a grown-up. *Those are elk swimming toward me,* he thought.

Indeed, he counted five animals - the leader with a large rack floating over the water like the spires of a tallship. Trailing the old bull were four antlerless animals, cows or calves, it was impossible to tell yet across the distance. As they approached, the bull's neck swiveled in Willow's direction. The animal bugled with a great urgent cry - perhaps the old male was able to extrapolate their courses and saw that boat and beasts might intersect.

As Willow drifted toward them and they paddled closer to Willow, he was lost in their magnificence, in the wildness of them. Their bearing mesmerized him, their progress compelled him to sit and wait, and evasive action would have been impossible, had it ever come to mind. His fascination with them, extruding from the water only as heads, necks and rumps, was complete, unmitigated and perilous.

Then the elk were just off the starboard bow as the vessel drifted. The gunwale slid by. Willow saw exhaustion in the old bull's gaze. They were almost even with the stern now. Then the beast - just a foot away - lifted its forelegs free of water and dragged itself aboard. The stern dropped to the waterline, boat yawing out of level. The port bow lifted toward the cloud cover. Willow, still in the driver's seat, found himself face to face with the river's chop over his right shoulder, pressed to the starboard gunwale.

Willow shouted a curse. The boat corrected, then jittered under the elk's weight and struggle. By now, the cows too seemed intent on flinging themselves on board. Willow swore again as the stern - under the weight of the clambering beasts and the flailing of their heavy bodies - disappeared in froth. The elk let out bleats and bugles and wounded shrieks. They showed white crescents at the edges of their eyes, flopping around like musky, hairy sturgeons. Two more mounted the transom, and a deluge of riverwater overflowed the stern and rushed into the vessel. Willow heard the motor's hot manifolds pop with the contact, saw a gout of superheated steam erupt from somewhere down in the engine-case. The animals' odor, released from the envelope of water, was rich and wet. It combined with the hot smell of the engine, and oil and gasoline.

Then the bull rolled again, and the boat pitched, its counter-roll slamming the male and two of the cows back into the transom and port gunwale. The whole damned operation splintered and failed as if fashioned from balsa. The vessel's folding could have been no more rapid were it made of cigarette paper, stretched across spars of vellum.

The river swallowed Willow's shattered patrol boat. He had barely the presence of mind to disengage his boots from under the dashboard. Though drawn under momentarily by the vacuum of eroding displacement, he bobbed quickly to the surface in his flotation vest. Around him, the elk bellowed and squeaked, splashing with their sharp hooves. He treaded water at the center of them and knew, now, lucid with the stark shock of water, that he must escape their encirclement or drown.

Willow disengaged the preserver's clasps. He inhaled as deeply as ever before in his life, exhaled, and let himself sink. He propelled his body downward with hand-thrusts as well as he could manage, opened his eyes in the murk, and saw the nether forms of elk - bizarre half-animals - rise as if levitating, hover and move away. Their legs churned the water like fabulous beaters, ill-suited to propulsion but, nevertheless, tireless. They were as pistons underwater. From a blackish-green world he saw them go away from him, or he from them. He unlaced his boots and let them drift, and when he thought his lungs were sure to break open, reached upward and oared himself out of the gloom. His head broke the surface nose and mouth first. He sucked in and tasted rain-laced oxygen as he had never before tasted it, as an expensive gift, a capitulation and great reward of grace.

He turned, treading the river. He saw their bank-leaping egress at water's edge. They stared back at him as he drifted down-current.

Willow began, slowly, a stunned breaststroke to shore.

"The golf course people were outraged, and letting Fish & Game know it," Sixkiller said. "They'd take law into their own hands, by God. They said they planned to station volunteers on the banks with rifles, take some shots at them elk.

"Fish & Game made its position clear: 'I wouldn't if I was you,' warned the senior warden. 'You'll face some stiff penalties, maybe some time,' his junior added.

"The senior warden, while outlining the penalties for taking elk out of season, without licenses and tags, even on private property, was just as clear on another matter: 'We already lost one boat to this fiasco, and almost one of my best men,' he said. 'There will be no more government time or tax money wasted on this. I don't give a flip over whether you got green damage or not. You got insurance, I'm sure, and you'd best call in your chips on it.'

"'Fine, then,' snarled the course's owner, the pro-shop glittering around him. 'Don't know what we pay our taxes for anyway.' The greenskeeper all but dared the government men to do something about their plan, and when he shot - three weeks later - the bull and one of the calves, they did. Slapped him in cuffs and sent him to the Grant County judge. The judge fined him a few thousand bucks, which the course owner covered. Also got some community service, and banned, for good, from buying a hunting or fishing license in the state of Washington.

"Which was fine with him: he was a groundskeeper, not a hunter."

Sixkiller stopped, set down the glass he'd been polishing for twenty minutes. It sparkled on the counter. Duff and Jimbo and Money and I just looked at it, then at the barkeeper, then back at the glass again.

Last time I saw Dave Sixkiller was four or five months ago in a hospital up in Wenatchee. Money and I ran up there in my scabbed-out hunting truck to see how he was doing, which wasn't well. He'd had no response whatsoever to the chemo, except to lose all his hair. The poor bastard was bald and too tired to get out of bed, so Money and I pulled up a couple of chairs next to his bedside.

Sixkiller was intubated and hooked up to all kinds of medical monitors, intravenous drip bags, the whole works, laying there with a paperish robe on him. He looked like he was wrapped in a coffee filter. There wasn't much of him underneath compared to the version of Sixkiller we were accustomed to, before pancreatic cancer ate him in half.

He was happy to see us, though.

"Hey," he whispered. "Money and Zach." Saying our names produced joy on his face. He was alone then, not getting any visitors, no family, nothing.

"How you doing?" I asked. I felt stupid as soon as I said it. He was obviously doing like hell.

"Oh, you know." He lifted his hands in a gesture of surrender. "I'm toast."

"Yeah," I said. "I suppose so."

It was an honest moment.

"How do you like to pass your time?" I said.

"Tell me a fish story." Sixkiller closed his eyes for a moment, and I looked over and saw Money wiping at his. It was the first time I'd seen him cry since we were boys.

"OK, Dave," I said. "Yes."

The Valley of Mistakes

A volley of shots - small rifle fire - crackles in the folds and valleys of the Blue Mountain foothills. On one gold ridge straining up out of the Tucannon River valley, four boys lie prone, .22s and 30-30s blazing away at deer on the opposite ridge. The deer, four or five of them, writhe and fall. A couple of lucky ones break away from the group and sprint off, ignored by the boys. An adult with them, father of one of the boys, can't believe his eyes.

Another father, back at the cars on the road at the base of the ridge, hears the gunfire, eyes straining up the high ridge. Covering his eyes from the brilliant morning sky, he tries to discern what could possibly result in the insistent cacophony of pin against shell, pin against shell. It sounds like a phalanx of machine guns up there.

The father with the boys is holding his arms in the air, shouting, "Stop, stop!" And the space between reports grows and the last shot is fired.

"Wait!" he shouts. But two of the boys are already up, and down the hill, running for the opposite face, stumbling and slipping down, waving their rifles all over the place with the safeties off. The man and the other two boys take off after them, trailing them by thirty yards at first, but making up the gap by the time the group together reaches the runoff creek at the base of the ravine.

The father slips into the lead position, straining and sweating up the hill. The boys have set their rifles down near the stream, and run in his wake, one of them catching and passing him.

This boy, Mark, is 19 years old, a sophomore at Washington State University studying business administration. He has a proper hunting license, and is a graduate of the hunter's safety training course.

Mark and the father arrive at the deer a full fifty yards ahead of the other three boys, all sophomores at WSU, all properly tagged and trained. Harold, Ben and Greg - the on-scene father, George, is Greg's dad; the father at the cars, Don, is Ben's.

Mark and George, out of breath, discover a mule deer doe, and two of her fawns, all shot to hell and dead. The bodies are lying in the sun with blood flowing out of them onto the wild grass. One of the fawns has a foreleg twisted up in the air next to its ear, like it was growing toward the sky.

"Christ, they're mule deer," George gasps. He is carefully controlling his disgust with the boys and fighting the panic climbing out of his chest. "God damn it, fuckin' mule deer." He looks at the sky, puts both hands on top of his head, brings his elbows together and pulls his palms down his face, tracking sweat and sour fear.

Mark turns around and runs to the other boys, shouting, "They're mulees they're mulees," until he meets them. He's pissed and afraid and embarrassed and can't believe either that they shot a doe and two fawns. They looked so big from across the valley and they looked like white-tails too. "Christ, we're fucked," he says.

Harold, Ben and Greg, sucking wind, take a second to appreciate the weight of what he's saying: white-tailed spikes and bucks with multiple antlers are legal in this game management unit; they have just gunned down a mule deer doe and two mule deer fawns. Realization leads to disorientation, and they walk around for a bit and sit down and cuss and ask themselves and the wilderness *how*?

Still, there's a tangible problem right now in front of them, three illegally taken deer, and their awareness evolves on only two branches of action: confess to this abomination with local authorities and face the loss or abridgment of permanent hunting rights in the state of Washington, or get the hell out of the Tucannon River valley right now, get the hell out of Columbia County. Right now, get back to their books at WSU and keep shut the fuck up about it.

Three of them drag the corpses of the deer down the hillside. They're easy to manage, light, and track like loose bags of offal. The boys and George drop them in the creek just about the time Don arrives from the cars. They all turn him around for the road, stumbling over explanation all the way. Even among these close friends, the compass needle of blame is spinning for a magnetic source. No one believes he fired the first shot, nor recalls hearing the first shot, no one made the conscious determination they were looking across the bright valley at white-tail, not mule, deer.

In the cars, denial and unfocused casting of blame all the way back on Highway 12 through Jackson, Dodge and Pomeroy. Silence and shame for a while from Alpowa to Clarkston. A renewal of collective self-examination and confusion from Clarkston through Uniontown and Colton on 195.

Classes Monday morning.

On an autumn Saturday morning, Ben, Harold, Greg and Mark, juniors at Washington State University, and George, Greg's dad, pulled

114

over to the side of a country road that ran along the Tucannon River in northeast Columbia County, piled out, and loaded shells. They had passed on today's Cougar's game against Oregon State, Dad's Day, in exchange for a day of pheasant hunting.

A cool morning that promised to turn hot, the college boys and the adult enjoyed the clear smell of the air, admired the bright orange and yellow of turning leaves in willows, vine maples and oaks in copses down by the river. Wild grass at their feet was still coated with night frost, and their pantlegs sanded through the plants, boots crunched frozen ground.

For the boys, 20-year-olds, a year was a long time. Each had experienced an affirming sophomore year, and their junior year was beginning well. Each could point to a series of personal accomplishments and triumphs to balance, then quell, their confusion over last year's hunting debacle. Not one of them spoke of it, or referred obliquely to it by connection of events or train of sentiment. The clarity of the offense had faded, as it had for George, who had chalked it up as a zealous, but unfortunate, experience. All young people have them.

The party split up into a pair and a triad, one unit, the pair, to hunt ridges and ravines north of the river; the other to prospect for birds in the river valley itself. They parted at 8:15, George, Mark and Ben for the river, Harold and Greg for the hills.

The Tucannon River ran roughly straight from Marengo to the town of Tucannon for maybe eleven miles at this stretch. Further on, it would join the Snake River above Lyon's Ferry, but here, ranch-style farmhouses on large acreage lined its banks. Farmers would typically have a plot that ran one boundary four- to five-hundred yards of riverbank, two boundaries that ran perpendicular from the river across the flatland and county road, up into the opposite hills to the main ridge. The fourth boundary would be the top of the ridge, completing the parallelogram.

George had secured written permission to pheasant hunt with the boys on acreage owned by an old family friend. They had camped the night prior next to the friend's unoccupied farmhouse and driven out in George's van that morning.

At 10:30, George, Ben and Mark heard distinct shotgun blasts echoing down from the hills. An hour later, having flushed no birds themselves, they were ready to head back to the van. There they would meet up with Harold, Greg and, hopefully, the pheasants they had shot, and return to camp for lunch.

Harold and Greg were already at the van. But a third person was there with them, pointing up at the hills. As the three approached, it became clear that he was angry. He gestured up and down the hill, back at a house, pointing at a cable suspended 20 feet high across the road. The cable ran from under one of the eaves to a nearby pole, then hung from a series of poles from the house to the road, then on another line of poles to the top of the ridge. A television antenna.

Greg was arguing with the man, asserting his right to hunt on the land, promising written documentation as soon as George arrived. The man, a big sunburned farmer with a ball-cap on his head, was growing madder, describing the boundaries of his property, skeptical that a written permission note would be produced. He said that his television was broadcasting only static into his living room. Greg, or Harold, he insisted, had shot out his antenna, and he was calling the sheriff.

George and the other two boys walked up. The farmer turned to the arriving trio, and started in on an explanation. George stood listening, nodding his head every once in a while. He dug in his breast pocket for the letter of permission. The morning was getting on toward noon. It was getting hot, and he thought best that he and the boys just go, get the man's address and offer to compensate him for the cable, their fault or not, and get out.

The man became more perturbed by the minute, declining George's offered note. It didn't help that Harold or Greg would repeatedly interrupt the man.

"Excuse me," he said. "I'm talkin' here."

"Big fuckin' deal," Harold said, right into his face, and that did it.

"I'm goin' back to my house right now and calling the sheriff," the man blustered. He pulled out his wallet, fished in it for a slip of paper, and wrote down George's license plate number with a pen from his pocket. He turned and walked over to his driveway, and down the gravel path to his house.

The five stood at the van and watched him disappear in the house. Hoping for the best, George went over to the man's mailbox, wrote down his name and address, came back and said, "There's not much we can do here. Let's go."

The farmer never did actually call the sheriff - at least not that day. Unfortunately, as George and the boys drove out through town after pulling up camp, they decided to stop at a small roadside restaurant for a late lunch-early supper. And two booths over sat the same man with another farmer.

George decided to make one more run at the guy, to try to demonstrate contrition and offer to just pay for the cable. The farmer saw him materialize, got up, held his hands out in front of him, palms out, and interrupted George's pleas.

"No. No," was all he would say, no matter what George said. "No, no."

At home, in Vancouver, Washington, George comes home from work at the Sears Driving School and collects an envelope from his mailbox. Columbia County Courthouse, 341 East Main Street, Dayton WA 99328, he reads as the return address. Using his forefinger to pry the flap up, he tears open the envelope and pulls out a letter on Honorable Harlan Timlin's stationery. It requests his appearance in Dayton to show cause why he should not be charged with criminal trespass and malicious mischief in the Columbia County Courthouse at 1 p.m. on December 16, 1983. The bottom paragraph offers an option to contact the court with the names and addresses of the two youths alleged to have actually been involved with the destruction of property, specifically a television antenna cable, belonging to a Columbia County resident, on November 8, 1983.

He calls the boys at college, explains his dilemma, and they call the court.

On February 2, 1984, Mark sat in the witness chair at Columbia County Courthouse in Dayton, Washington, and gave testimony about what he heard and knew from the morning of last November 8.

There wasn't a jury or lawyers or anything, just the judge - HON. HARLAN TIMLIN, his nameplate read. He swore Mark in and asked him to state his full name for the court. Mark replied, "Mark Rader Milnor." With Mark's hand on the Holy Bible, the judge asked him whether he promised to tell the truth, and Mark said yes.

Over the course of his questions, Mark described the events as accurately as he could, and shared some of his perceptions with the judge and tried to throw in a few favorable comments about Harold's and Greg's characters.

The judge thanked Mark for his service to the court, then examined George and Ben. He put Harold and Greg in the witness box, and the

117

farmer, and established to his satisfaction that Harold and Greg had trespassed, that malicious intent was not present but that property damage had occurred. He fined them each $175, asking them to pay on the way out, and banged his gavel on his podium.

Greg had the money and paid. Harold was broke and asked for the option where he would make payments for four months and for the final payment, he would have to come back to Dayton and close out the fine in person. Judge Timlin agreed to this arrangement.

Three months later, Harold was ahead of his payments and able to make the final payment in person. He and Greg took off for Dayton on a spring morning, made the payment and, rounding a turn on the road back, encountered an oncoming vehicle illegally passing in their lane. Greg twisted the wheel to the right and rolled the car four times. It came to rest on its wheels, considerably reshaped, but its occupants intact.

Greg called Mark at his apartment while he was studying for a final exam. He asked Mark to come get him and Harold, so Ben and Mark climbed in Mark's car and headed down to Dayton.

By the time they got to the Dayton tavern where they had agreed on rendezvous, it was four in the afternoon, and Greg and Harold were dead drunk. All right from the car crash, but potted from bourbon. They loaded their sorry asses in the back seat of Mark's car and headed back for Pullman by way of Clarkston.

In Clarkston the quartet stopped to get something to eat, and Mark and Ben started drinking too, gin and tonics. Leaving town with a pretty good buzz, they stopped at a liquor store and bought a half-gallon of vodka and drove up to Pullman under the influence, passing the bottle across the seats.

Returning to Mark and Ben's apartment, the four of them finished off the vodka, mixing it with blue bubble-gum flavored Kool-Aid, Harold and Greg later puking blue chunks of Clarkston supper.

Drunk, Mark stepped off the back porch of the apartment with his shotgun and, just to hear the bang and feel the stock jump in his arms, discharged it into the air.

The recoil and echo blast back to me, unmitigated by time.

118

Always Sixty

Leo Bailey opens up on a strip of asphalt that's long and uncluttered. The forced march of his pickup's pistons through the floorboards, though, is overcome, then buried by two sounds: Charlie Rich on the cassette deck and the insistent ring of hammer on anvil he's heard between his ears for decades now. He keeps time to Charlie with the internal hammering - *and when we get behind closed doors* (clank) *then she lets her hair hang down* (clank) *and she makes me glad that I'm a man* (clank). Maple trees, pastureland and its cowherds, clouds threatening more downpour, all fall away outside the streaked windows.

Leo glances over at his new laborer from this nest of ringing, from his own communion with the road that comes translated through the steering column on the way to his first job of the day. Daniel, he said his name was. Having a rough go at it, as if there is someone, somewhere, who isn't. His last steady boss took to paper-clipping Twelve Step literature to Daniel's timecard. The pamphlets remained there, clipped, Daniel having not the brilliance, ambition or sobriety to remove them before punching the clock, so that after days and weeks of this, the tattered literature became a metaphor for his ability to remain employable. They'd let him, and his trembling morning motor skills, go.

Leo tried everything in his power not to regard the halfway house he routinely cruised for day laborers as a sort of human dog pound. Daniel had impressed him as someone who wanted to make his life better, just for that day. Whether sincerely or insincerely - Leo was no great judge of character. Leo's walk through the residents lined up and looking for a day's work concluded in front of Daniel, after he'd passed a dozen sets of hopeful eyes. Daniel seemed *clear* to Leo, and when he asked the man a question - whether he could help shoe horses - the resident answered promptly and lucidly. Through extraordinary effort, Daniel had controlled his trembling hand in the rough clasp of Leo's mauling paw.

"You'll be fine," Leo had judged, and Daniel showed stained teeth through a statewide grin.

Now Daniel is lost in the rhythms of the cassette deck and the sweep of windshield wipers, camouflaged there against the worn fabric of Leo's benchseat. Faded blue interior crossweave, Daniel in denim overalls, light blue sweatshirt, blue Mariners Safeway Giveaway Night ballcap, disappearing - wishing for a drink or at least a donut. The song fades and there's a moment of quiet.

"You ever shod horses before?" Leo asks.

119

"No."

"You been around horses much?"

"No, not too much."

Leo's quiet for a few more moments, then adds, "It's mostly a one-man job, shoeing."

Daniel wonders, then, why he is needed.

"I might want you to hold a horse steady, though," Leo says. It's fine with Daniel, who has never been within thirty yards of a horse except, maybe, a pony ride or two as a boy, and these memories are occluded and barely recalled. Considered as through a strata of dipsomaniac mist, he thinks he can recall what the hell a horse looks like, what - say - distinguishes it from a cow or a rooster.

The F150 now plies south through lowlands in a wringing-wet valley kept soaked by a stream with ill-defined banks. Anywhere within a hundred yards of the valley's center ground is prone to sopping disintegration. The legs of horses are swallowed to their fetlocks. Farrier work here is a muddy, filthy vocation, Leo thinks. He fumbles again with the blower lever, wanting to divert urgent air back at the windshield and thwart the spreading condensation.

Thankfully, this morning's client farms acreage just as the ground migrates in a slow rise to green foothills on the east. Most of her land is set above the valley floor that runs north and south - the rise like a shelf, with her barn, stables and horses higher and generally out of the spring muck. Of today's clients, this first will be the best - most of the others are in the valley or others hereabouts like it. It's 45 degrees outside, but the mountains behind the foothills are pushing a frigid wind around, bullying anything warm-blooded and stripping internal heat away from everything living. It will be a cold-ass morning, he thinks, with steam rising from the musky hair of the horses. While Daniel is still, Leo spends a moment pleased the first job won't likely be spent slopping through mud. The road veers east toward the foothills.

It has been eight months since he's trimmed and re-shod Brenda Schick's horses. A long time, unless she's using another farrier. Horse hooves grow a quarter inch a month, and he imagines her gelding Beau, a perfect roan half-Quarter, half-Arabian, will be suffering from splayfoot, cocked ankles, or some other manifestation of an uncharacteristic neglect. Brenda, a competition barrel-rider, is meticulous about her equine care. Leo, for a moment, is thinking along these lines before he remembers the appointment was set up by the Wilfords, who own the place one farm over from Brenda's. That's right - Brenda has been in Olympia for six months, living with her fading mother. The care she has ministered to her horses now is vectored elsewhere, and she has not yet faced the issue of a permanent living arrangement for her mom. The courage with which she rides around barrels has eluded Brenda Schick, and she must wait while it musters and neighbors caretake, less carefully, her animals. Leo doesn't know any details of this, except for gossip he's heard down at Kenny's, where he throws darts and takes his chances with a few pulltabs two nights a week and where - if he really thinks about it - he's seen Daniel in the shadowy corner, or rubbed past him on the way to the men's room. He just recalls, for today, finally, that Brenda is in Olympia, and she's a pleasant, single, attractive woman not quite young enough to be his daughter. And that she usually takes good care of her animals. It must be killing her to be away from them, Leo thinks. He slows the 4x4 rig and makes a right turn due south again into her gravel driveway. "Wake up," he tells Daniel. "We're here."

"Hummmh?" Daniel asks from midway through waking.

"We're at the job," Leo says. The truck lurches across the puddles in the drive, water-filled potholes that could be little harbingers of sinkholes, which could be prophesies of the whole sinking earth at the edge of this valley of saturation. For some reason, Leo is thinking whimsically as the Ford ploshes down the drive - the arrival and today's chores put him in mind of cowboy poets he's read, Badger Clark, and the resurgence of this melancholy artform at Elko. Leo likes to dabble in a little poetry now and then, mostly verse filled with anvils and tongs, blasting furnace heat from his forge, ghost riders in the sky that turn up to be all the great B-western actors like Hoot Gibson and Tom Mix. He'll let slip this fact - that he's a poet - from time to time at Kenny's. That he only aspires to be one makes no difference when his conversation is being consecrated, in the form of a flirty blessing, by a woman of, say, the age, shape and marital status of Brenda Schick.

Leo hears the rolling clank of metal implements shifting in the bed. The jostling has spilled some of his shoes out of their bins maybe. Or his nippers, cutters and hammers have come loose and are caroming about the lining. If a person were riding back there, they'd be sliced, hacked and lacerated by all the uncontrolled movement of sharp steel. Daniel is looking over his shoulder, over the seat back, through the twin rear windows of the truck's cab and the attendant canopy. But he can't see anything - the windows are too grimy and it's so gray outside anyway - it's all he can do to see out the front window. Besides, his vision isn't so good on sober mornings.

The driveway offers a choice to continue around in front of the house in a circle or to the right, southeast, upward, toward the barn. Upward is the route Leo chooses. The front tires depart gravel into muddy, sloped grass. The sudden climb is like a bear clawing out of its den in spring, and the whole truck seems to pause there on the flex of the rise, gather itself, then lift. With the resulting lurch, Daniel's head, which is barely on tight to begin with, bounces into the rear window from which he's still trying to survey for the source of those heavy metallic sounds.

"Ow," he says, without a hell of a lot of passion. He starts rubbing his forehead where the glass knocked the bill of his ballcap askew and fused, for a millisecond, with his pate.

"Careful, there," Leo says. "Watch that window." Which is exactly what Daniel has been doing, and he doesn't realize Leo is saying *Keep your head from plonking away at my rear window so you don't break it with your thick skull.*

"Yeah, I guess," is about all Daniel can manage, still massaging his forehead, adjusting and readjusting the hat. The truck continues around the east side of the barn, now the bear emerged from hibernation and looking for ripe berries to de-stem and suck juice from, gathering strength for a foray down to a stream where it can squish soft, floppy salmon in its paws. The truck is like that, *lumbering*. Leo brings it to a metered halt. He does a three point turn next to the barn where he can see Beau's stable, then the horse's brown head emerging, inquisitive. Finally he stops the rig with the hood pointed back the way he's come, *For a quick exit...* flashes through his mind.

He's disappointed when they dismount. The ground is soaked here too, and without Brenda's personal touch, the place has gone wild. Runlets of water have excised tracks in the soft ground, carrying off long-stemmed grass and wild weeds and leaving mud furrows. The whole place is a roiling, earthy moistness and Leo can see at a glance that the Wilfords have not concerned themselves with pasture- or manure management in Brenda's absence. Daniel is actually *tiptoeing* through the muck, for crying out loud.

The pair moves around to the back of the truck where Leo opens the canopy door and lets the tailgate drop. They look up to see that Beau and a couple of the other horses are fully out of their stalls into the stables where they can watch, with equine foreboding, the preparations. Leo points at tools and asks Daniel, "Why don't you get those out and ready, just pull them out."

"O.K.," Daniel says. He climbs up into the bed to start retrieving them. Leo departs for the barn to bring out the horses, Beau first. But Leo hasn't taken ten steps before he pulls up, reins in and stops. He realizes that two things are not right. First, Daniel has no idea whatsoever which of the hundred-odd tools Leo will need. Second, he hears the sound of heavy implements splashing into muck and then the muted clang of metal on metal tempered by mud. The idiot is throwing his tools from the bed out onto the bare ground. To Leo, it is suddenly as if Daniel were pitching naked infants off a railcar.

"Stop!" he shouts. He rounds the truck bed and sees Daniel frozen there with a handful of rasps in mid-pitch. They were next, and Leo looks down to see his twenty-five dollar driving hammer, his top-of-the-line hoof nippers at better than a hundred bucks, and his likewise-valued shoe pullers flung together with a metal salad of other implements and sopping barnyard filth. It's everything Leo can do to collect himself. It takes a supreme effort to keep from visiting demise on poor Daniel with the pointy end of the now-muddy clinch-cutter.

"Put. Those. Down."

There, Leo points, at the truck's bed. Daniel places the rasps slowly on the bed, crouched there as if he is abandoning his weapon to a sheriff's deputy and about to raise his hands in surrender. "I didn't mean to..." he starts, and Leo can see in his rheumy eyes that he is desperately ashamed and afraid. Leo knows, in this moment, that this fouled-up man Daniel has already written his name on Leo's heart. That Daniel would give anything to have done something right, intuitively, just once in his life. Because throwing expensive farrier gear in the mud sure isn't it. But throwing the gear in the mud was in perfect alignment with all of Daniel's lifelong actions and reactions and initiatives and undertakings. They have very simply, very clearly, all gone wrong, every one. Leo would have known this had he thought it through.

"Let me show you," Leo says, controlling his tone toward softness so that he sees Daniel immediately unwrap and relax. He reaches around the still-crouching man and retrieves a roll of polyethylene sheeting from behind a toolbox. He unfurls six feet of the clear visquene. "Here, I'll show you," Leo says. He indicates that Daniel should hop down from the truck. Leo lays the plastic sheeting out on the muck, anchors the four corners with three rasps and a sack of horseshoe nails. Then he retrieves each filthy tool, slowly cleans each with a rag. He nods that Daniel may do likewise, and thus gain repatriation, with another towel.

Leo and Daniel place the clean tools on the tailgate next to the vise, which is bolted to the gate's deck. Daniel asks why it's there. Leo explains that if there's any substantial shoe-shaping to be done, it comes in handy. "It's not heavy like the anvil, see?" Leo hefts the anvil in both hands but stops short of lunging at Daniel with the heavy object. He knows that Daniel will only drop it on their feet, smashing skin and bones all the way on the long fall. "So it has to be bolted there." Daniel spins the chuck and the long screw articulates, the vise's jaws growing wider. He may, at this moment, have an inkling as to the function of this tool. At least it seems so to Leo, who is pleased with the notion that Daniel may be *reached* in the intellectual sense of the word.

Soon the right tools - and only the right tools - are lying on the plastic. Leo is ready to bring out Beau. He asks Daniel whether he too is ready.

"Sure," Daniel says. Leo senses a lack of conviction. Daniel looks out across the farmyard, at the gentle slope from east to west, out from the trees here into the bare valley. Darker clouds are moving this way. He sees a rain wall falling from them like a discolored sheet, like the sheets he lays on at the halfway house. Sheets washed without bleach, although he doesn't know what bleach is.

Leo moves around the barn past Brenda's horse trailer to the rear door. He enters and takes a halter of yellow nylon rope from a multicolored array of halters hanging just inside. He goes into Beau's stall, calls Beau's name. The horse approaches. Leo observes that he suffers, as predicted, from mild splayfoot. The front of the hooves are turned out, the heels turned in as the horse walks closer. Leo comforts the gelding, encourages the big animal's approach. "Come on, Beau," he says, and clicks his tongue against the roof of his mouth. While he holds the halter out, Leo wonders whether he has any corrective shoes, which he may need to correct the splay. Beau shies slightly - the best way for Leo to describe it is that the gelding seems *skittery* - but finally accepts the halter on its neck. The rope falls across the animal's head, slides down its mane, rests there on the withers. "Good boy," Leo says, but the horse is still nervous. Leo leads him through the stall door, across the dry dirt floor of the barn. Beau's coat could use a good brushing. He vows there is no way he's going to let Mike Wilford pass him at Kenny's without remarking on this sorry-ass job of caretaking.

He walks backward leading the animal, sliding a little but then his boots finding purchase. By the tentativeness of Beau's gait he knows he will have to remove the front shoes and trim the outer half of each foot.

He might have to lower the heels on the rear hooves too, so the frog can carry more of Beau's twelve-hundred pounds - Leo thinks he perceives contracted heels there, on the rear legs. The gelding has been too long in the barn, with no moisture on its hooves. Odd, it seems, that outside it hasn't stopped raining for seven or eight weeks, but inside Beau's hooves desiccate into brittle shock. How close is the beautiful boy to split hooves, to coming up lame? Leo can't tell without a closer look, but he'll probably have to apply a dressing of oils and glycerins to the hooves, then return in a couple of days and check whether they have recovered some of the lost moisture.

Leo turns around, begins to walk forward at just the point where he and Beau round the barn's southeast corner and pass to the side of Brenda's trailer. For a fleeting half-second, Leo wonders that she'd left the trailer at this spot, on the slope next to the barn, wheels aligned with the flow of the hillside. Of course, Brenda would have had no way of knowing when she left to tend her mother how long she'd be absent. She would have guessed it would rain a lot. But she wouldn't have thought Wilford's husbandry of her property would be so pitiful. So it makes perfect sense that the trailer sits here, four tires and twin axles suspending thirty-five-hundred pounds, except for the part of the tongue that rests on a vertical slab of mortarbrick.

As the pair - man and horse - fully round the trailer, Leo seeks out Daniel, but doesn't see him. The back of the truck is empty, tools laid out as he left them on the visquene. The depressions in the plastic created by the weight of the tools is filling with rainwater, he sees, and then understands the mist has turned into a light shower. He had not noticed this before. He had been too focused on the severe state of Beau's feet. Now he hears the passenger side door of his truck close.

Daniel skirts the side of the vehicle, wiping a denim shirt-cuff across his lips, unaware that Leo has returned. He's looking mostly at the ground, evaluating each step for foundation but possessing failing faith in the ground itself. Each step is overly careful. So each step is careless at the same time. It is the gait of a man intimidated not only by walking in public, but when he is alone - or believes himself to be - as well. The gait of a man who is used to being struck.

Then, still looking down, Daniel undoubtedly sees Leo's boots. He stops short and almost slides into the weeds and mud.

"Uh... I didn't know you was back," Daniel says. His eyes travel up the length of Leo and rest for the briefest moment in Leo's own gaze, then dart immediately away, downcast again. But his eyes snap back when

Beau, over Leo's shoulder, resolves from a blur into stark focus in the cones of his vision. The look is one of confusion and desperate processing, as if Daniel must search frantically in his internal files for the meaning of this looming long-faced beast. He'd seen horses from a distance, of course, but its nearness pushed the air from his lungs, summoned a shaking from his guts. It was not as unnerving as his worst episode of DTs. But he considered, for a moment, whether the horse's presence was perhaps a living, breathing, animate bout in and of itself.

Leo spots Daniel's disquietude, misinterprets it as irresolution. "Don't worry, Dan, this is a damned fine horse," he says. "Come here and pat him, here." Leo gestures at Beau's muzzle, which assumes a longish, freakish, large countenance in Daniel's miserable interpretation. He exhales sharply and Leo is surprised, no *stunned*, to smell liquor. Where in God's name had he found some?

"You were drinking while I was getting the horse," Leo says.

The man Daniel doesn't deny or confirm it, just slouches miserably. Leo is looking at the button on the top of his ballcap.

"Where'd you get it?" Leo has the horse by the halter in his right hand, so he shifts the rope to his left hand as Daniel digs in the bib pocket of his overalls and surrenders a half-pint flask. Leo holds the silver receptacle next to his own temple, shakes it slightly, hears the sloshing of the last remaining ounce of spirits. "Was this full?"

"Not all the way," Daniel says, with a façade of cheer. As if the fact it had not been filled to the lip was a defense. Leo shakes his head, pockets the flask.

"This will *not* happen tomorrow," he says. Daniel is not sure whether this means he'll still be allowed to come with Leo but be permitted no liquor, or whether he will not be allowed to come at all. Rather than seek clarification, it seems safer to simply nod up and down, once. The less said about it the better, as far as he is concerned, and already time has passed and is passing, carrying him further from this most recent moment of failure, from the discovery of his fraudulence. Soon it will be simply another incident. It will lay atop a heap of incidents enveloped in his personal heritage. One built upon another, and eclipsed by the one that followed, so that all save the most recent are largely forgotten.

Still, the problem remains of Beau and his hooves and shoeing. Leo, having in his own mind clarified for Daniel the wages of sin, is ready to move on. He wants to believe that Daniel didn't get so far into the booze as to be rendered useless. He hands the rope halter to his partner, but

Daniel's arms dangle inertly, even though it's clear he appreciates Leo's intent.

"Look, Dan," Leo says. "I need you to steady the horse while I get ready."

Daniel summons all the courage he can find in a shallow well, accepts the assignment, feigns the enthusiasm of a new salesman. *I can do it*, an unsummoned, unwanted mantra, repeats itself between his ears as he takes the rope and nears the beast. It is so big and so close. Its head must be two feet long, and its eyes are like huge stones. He gasps when the eye he's watching rolls upward. Its white appears like a sliver of moon.

"You're O.K.," Leo says. He pulls a leather apron over his frame, dropping a fistful of shoe nails into the front pouch. He stoops to retrieve a hoof pick from the visquene placemat for the first, cursory cleaning.

But Daniel feels a hundred-thousand miles from O.K. In spite of the mantra, he believes he *cannot* do it. He holds the rope as far from his body as possible. His arm stretches to its maximum parallel to the valley floor downhill from the three of them - man, man and horse - a triad in still life that pauses, rests and awaits wild kinetics.

Beau, disturbed by a whiff of Daniel's brutalized confidence and expanding fear, grows restive. His gentle nickering, conferred on the familiar and authoritative Leo, is metastasizing into a fit of curt snorts. His shod, canted feet stamp and it's like a corrupt cycle - Daniel's unease feeds Beau's, Beau's feeds Daniel's - until the circle is so oppressive the drunk must return the reins to Leo. He just extends them in his hand and turns away. He waits for Leo to take them back.

Leo does. Without speaking a word of recrimination, Leo wraps the halter around his rough palms. But Daniel is convinced it's there, that he has irretrievably offended this day's benefactor. He watches as the experienced, sober man stows the hoof pick in the leather apron and stands tall under a cowboy hat. Leo is old, he thinks, but strong and broadshouldered. His chest, under the apron, is a stout unsunken plain. The flesh of Leo, where exposed, is toasted brown, robust, lined, where Daniel knows his own is pale and yellowed. Leo steps exactly where he means to, around the visquene leading the beast, clucking his tongue again at the animal. He looks around, determines to make fast Beau roped to a cleat on the front of the trailer. It's the only handy purchase within arm's reach.

Beau turns around so the halter is stretched to its fullest. His hindquarters face the trailer square on. Still unnerved from his ordeal with the unconfident man, he wants to follow Leo as the farrier returns to the plastic to get a pair of hoof nippers. Leo comes back with the trimming tool. Horse fastened there, he faces the gelding, eyes at the level of the animal's muzzle. He can feel the horse's exhalations on his neck, and it's pleasant.

Leo straddles Beau's left front leg. He reaches to gently tap the inside muscle of the upper leg, indicating *Lift*. "Good boy," he whispers as Beau complies. He slides the apron over to one side and rides the horse's leg, inverting the hoof and cupping it like treasure. Then he moves one hand to wield the hoof pick and starts making tender, exploratory strokes around the frog and bars.

Daniel watches this interaction from across an ocean of disappointment. He was not able to render even the simplest service. His misery is nearly total when this occurs to him: he could approach the horse now that it's tethered. He could try to soothe and calm it as Leo works. It seems logical. Where before there was near-total befuddlement, Daniel suddenly knows that this great work will redeem him.

Thus resolved, he takes a determined step toward Beau and Leo. This act sets in motion a chain. Beau, ears laid back on his sleek skull to begin with, jerks his muzzle up in alarm and stamps his left foot down between Leo's legs. Leo leaps backward out of the way; too many times he's been slow to react and had horses' hooves raise welts, carve lacerations, even - twice - break bones. As he slips away from the horse's front quarters, he slides down into the muck on his buttocks. The horse, to avoid trampling Leo and to move away from the threatening Daniel, backs clumsily away. Beau's rear legs, weakened by yet unconfirmed split hooves, stagger against the tongue of the trailer and find brief resistance there. But then his weight pushes the tongue off its mortarbrick support. Beau rears, neighing loudly. His cry is like a banshee's shriek. His rear hooves pedal for traction. But it's too late. The inertia of his own body carries his hindquarters into the front of the trailer. So slowly that Leo and Daniel both have time to comprehend what is happening and what is going to happen, the tongue raises and the trailer starts a roll downhill.

Strong and healthy, Beau may be a match for a horse trailer three times his weight. Weakened, enstalled for six months, footsore, knock-kneed, soaked with new alarm, the animal simply goes down to the ground like an anchor. But the trailer's weight, plus the sloppy ground and its irrefutable slope, may add up to disaster.

Leo scrambles to his feet, slips and falls again. "Dan!" he shouts, assembling himself once more. "For God's sake, Dan!" Daniel is standing there transfixed as if a giant bottle of cheap scotch has burst through the low clouds. He is as useless in this situation as the feather of a thrush.

Shocked, Leo watches the trailer carom down the slope, gaining speed. Beau's legs beat like helicopter rotors. Leo can see gouts of grass and mud flying into the air. The horse is screaming outrage that it should thus be dispatched. Leo without consciously doing so, but rather with a language from deep within himself - one he didn't know existed and won't remember when all of this is over - lifts a demand to God, or the gods. *Intervene*!

And so it happens that the trailer, through some force not understood, jumps across a pasture stone. The tire bounces there, and the anomaly transfers through the flexing axle and translates upward into the chassis. This sets up a bizarre sequence of harmonics that reorient the trailer and the horse it tows. Slowly, as slowly as can be imagined in the sheer velocity of this event, Leo watches the trailer turn and roll. It rolls so many times Leo has time to beg that Beau is not entangled in this crashing, disintegrating hurricane of aluminum and steel.

Leo sits in horseshit and mud. The whirling enormity comes to abrupt rest. Daniel sees this too. It is as still, suddenly, as a mesa. They are both convinced that Beau has been savaged, probably - no *surely* - killed.

When the horse moves, Leo is off like a missile down the hill. He arrives at Beau's side to discover the animal is whole, unhurt in any lasting sense, but choking from the twisting of the halter rope about its neck. Leo cuts the rope, as taut as steel rebar between Beau and the trailer cleat. The release of pressure invokes a hacking gout of phlegm and horse-snot ejected at Leo like birdshot. Beau leaps to his feat and canters away. He pauses at a distance that seems prudent, returns his roan gaze to the tableau of wreckage at the base of the hill. If the trailer had rolled another ten yards, it would have careened off a forty-foot precipice that, just there, rose nearly vertically off the valley floor.

It takes three hours to coax Beau back into the barn, into his stable stall. There, Leo fixes his hooves, re-shoes him in the stall, brushes his coat out. He notices little flesh nicks, abraded skin and a few shallow cuts, where before he'd marveled the gelding had totally escaped injury. He discovers Beau bleeding a small amount from the mouth. Newly concerned, he sees the animal had simply bit its tongue during the tumble.

All the time spent waiting for Beau to come in, he'll have to come back to shoe the lucky gelding's stablemates another day.

Daniel has been sitting in the cab of the truck this whole time.

Leo emerges from the barn. He stares at the quashed trailer fifty yards downhill. He inhales deeply, holds his breath then lets it out in a sigh that emanates from the core of him and disperses spent air for what seems like moments. When all the air is out of him, he looks upward and sees the clouds are thinning and a small blue hole has opened.

He almost forgets to breathe, then gasps his gratitude, for this day, for surviving close calls, for oxygen.

"I'm sorry," Daniel says in the cab sometime during the ride back to town. "I'm really sorry."

Leo feels every day of his sixty years, feels as if he always has been sixty and will always be sixty.

"It's all right, Dan," he says. Then he remembers Daniel's flask, retrieves it from his bib-pocket, spins the cap, hoists it. Sucks the last ounce of liquor - discovers, as he'd hoped, it's whiskey.

It burns down his esophagus and lights his guts. He opens the wing window, pushes the flask out and watches it bounce once in perfect syncopation with the familiar anvil-clank in his head. It disappears in the rear-view mirror.

"Everything is *all* right."

Bar Tag on Neil Young

We - Matt, Crank, Jeff and I - were sipping beers at the Five Point Café on Western, shuffling and dealing through a few hands of poker on a Thursday night. The cards were turning up fairly, with each of us winning hands and the pot distributing and redistributing itself with no major trend favoring any one of us. We tossed white, red or blue plastic chips onto beer-damp felt, their arcs through cigarette smoke concluding in melodic polystyrene clinks.

This was as routine for us as short sleep, our quartet gathering at the Five Point three or four nights a week to toss back beers and bitch about our go-nowhere jobs. We were regulars, there in the smoky tavern, halflight and neon mixing color and shade. Protest rock wafted from the Five Point's old jukebox, guitar and bass pumped through dusty tin. Stratified layers of still smoke, torn vinyl-covered chairs puking their stuffing, Jacqua's watery pitchers hoisted above her creamy, young figure, and droppers-in completed the inventory of the place. Unique among weeknights, Thursday traditionally was our weekly poker game. We'd all buy twenty bucks worth of chips, and usually close the place - one of us lucky with a fat wallet.

The lovely Jacqua came by to refresh our glasses, asked whether we'd order a couple more pitchers. It seemed reasonable - it was going to take a while to move the columns of chips each of us hoarded toward the lucky winner. I forgot my game face for a moment, Matt dealing me a third ace in a stud-hand that already comprised a pair of bullets and two jacks: a very winnable full-house. Janis Joplin belted from the jukebox. Matt saw my grin, folded. Crank and Jeff were intent on their cards, and Jacqua returned with sloshing pitchers. The bet came to me - I covered Matt's and raised him fifty cents.

"Bar Tag on Al Gore," Jeff said. We looked up from our hands, me from straight across from the door, toward where Jeff nodded. It was a close match: the vice president of the United States looked very much like the man who had entered the Five Point, pulling an overcoat from around himself and taking a station at the bar.

Bar Tag, a game we played to interest ourselves when the cards were slow, consisted of this: Match ordinary people with luminaries. Anyone comes in the bar looking remotely like somebody famous, you say "Bar Tag on So and So." You could win a beer that way, if your mates agreed it was a good resemblance. Over the months, we'd bar-tagged O.J. Simpson, Liberace, Meg Ryan, Jack Nicholson, Charles Manson, Tiny

Tim, Richard Nixon, Oprah, Fred MacMurray and Michael Jordan - those are the ones who come to mind right now anyway. There were probably dozens of others. Drunker as the evenings evolved, we'd Bar Tag everyone who came in, making spurious, silly matches - a robust woman as Boris Yeltsin, Muhammad Ali in the form of a rail-thin black guy who, nevertheless, possessed a boxer's face. It got so everybody looked like somebody else, until we were Bar-Tagging each other, Bar Tagging our own faces in the Five Point's nasty men's room mirror while we buttoned up.

"O.K., good tag," Crank said, breasting his cards lest one of us steal a peak. He raised his free hand, motioned to Jacqua. "I'll buy a beer for Jeff, here."

She gestured at the full pitchers on the table, but Crank insisted.

"No, a good beer, in a bottle, not this watery stuff." Jacqua grimaced at the truth, laughed, and moved off with her tray and terrific ass. "Much obliged," Jeff said, and lit a smoke. He exhaled into the center of the table, carcinogens whirling in cloud over the multicolored pot.

"Al Gore, that guy gonna be president in 2000?" I asked Jeff.

"Fuck no," Jeff said. "Not in this lifetime."

"It's 2001," Crank said.

"What's 2001?"

"When the dude's president. He gets elected in 2000, goes to the White House in 2001."

We eyeballed Crank as if he were a spaceman abandoned on earth by his mothership. "Thanks for clearing that up for us," I said. "Now, you staying or going?"

Crank scrutinized his hand, appeared to wrestle some huge problem of mathematics with limited capacity. He tossed his cards, face down, on the felt. "I fold," he said.

"Call," Matt said. "Your show."

"Full house, aces and jacks." I laid my hand in full view.

"Your pot," he said.

"Whatta you got?" Jeff asked.

"Forget it," Matt replied.

"C'mon, you're betting like a fucked-up stench - show us your tits."

But Matt had already buried his hand in the deck. "I don't remember," he claimed.

"Well then deal, bonehead."

We worked the pitchers pretty good, smoked about two dozen cigarettes, ordered more beer. The vice president left and no one was plugging the jukebox. Only our calls, bets, clinking chips and a TV over the bar on CNN at low volume broke the quiet. Folks came in and went out, none of them looking anything like anybody, yet. The winnings started to move toward Matt and, to my dismay, away from me. We were all starting to feel the effects of the beer, and I found myself making asinine mistakes and walled off from any good combinations or even single high cards. We mixed it up with hands of five-card stud and seven-card draw, five-card no-peak, Chicago and Follow the Queen. We violated our own no-wild-cards rule for a couple of hands to make things interesting. Jacqua came around to switch our butt-piled ashtrays for clean ones.

We started arguing whether the Mariners should trade Mike Cambray. He'd been throwing like a cross-eyed dog lately, his earned-run average climbing, batters walking or jacking his pitches into the stands, fans booing. Crank thought we should dump him for Pedro Ibañez of the Braves. "Naw," I vetoed, "not unless you need Ibañez for a card game." What about Tim Copes, right-fielder for the Diamondbacks? Everybody had his opinion, and we carried them, collectively, to the point of brinkmanship while Jacqua plied us with more watery beer and honey lips.

Then Crank opted for a set of five-card draw, dealing five cards to each of us while we threw in our nickel ante - a white chip each for the pot. My hand had three kings, minus the diamond, a five of clubs and a three of spades. Matt checked, I bet two blue chips - fifty cents - and Jeff folded straight away. Crank saw my fifty cents and raised me a red chip, a dime. So Matt had to throw in sixty cents to get new cards, and I had to toss a red chip into the pot to meet Crank's raise. I asked him for two more cards, exchanged my junk for two off the deck - nothing that would help transform my three kings into four.

And then Neil Young, the guitarist, walked through the Five Point Café's door.

"Uh," I stuttered, "Bar Tag on Neil Young."

Three heads swiveled toward the draft, Matt upsetting his mostly-empty beer glass on the table. We just sat and held our cards - except Jeff, who had folded - and stared. Damn, this boy looked exactly like Young, scarecrowy, lambchop sideburns, hair flowing kinda wiry-like but straight, if that makes sense, and cut straight off just above the shoulders. An unbuttoned flannel logger's shirt draped him, open, with a white T underneath. His Levi's were broken in real good, knees abraded almost to holes. A nice pair of mahogany cowboy boots with squared-off, rather than pointed, toes. Riding boots, I guess you call them.

"Holy rock and roll," Crank whispered. He turned back to me. "You win not only a bottled beer, you win an import."

Matt righted his glass. The man who looked remarkably like Neil Young took a few steps into the Five Point, stopped, and surveyed all of us. Our sorry little gambling table - our heads snapped back to our cards like the jaws of moletraps - Jacqua, the bar, a couple of other patrons. After a prudent second or two, Crank, Jeff and Matt peered around their shoulders at him again. I lifted my gaze from my hand. The visitor had a good, long look at the jukebox, resumed his walk, dropped a pair of quarters in. The first strains of a fast Steppenwolf number - I can't think of the name right now - followed him from the player to the bar. Crank, Matt and I all forgot our hands for a moment as he crossed the tavern, slipped up onto a barstool, caught Jacqua's attention. Of course Jacqua, all of twenty-two and working her cute behind through voc-tech, wouldn't have recognized a classic rocker like Neil Young if he, well, walked into her bar. Run the boys from Pearl Jam or Soundgarden or the Goo Goo Dolls through, she'd go monkey shit. But Neil Young - she'd just as likely recognize Bing Crosby or Harry Belefonte.

Still, she spent more time than we thought necessary getting his drink, long enough that we returned to our final bets on the hands we'd abandoned to goggle over his entry. I raised my bet another fifty cents, Crank called and Matt whizzled out, folding with all the courage of a bush-baby. Crank had two pair - fours and eights. I scraped the chips toward my dwindling columns after displaying my kings. Crank raised his hand for Jacqua, asked her to bring me a Heineken.

While we waited for Jacqua to return and Matt to deal, I stole another glance at the Neil Young look-alike. He sat at the bar, over Matt's left shoulder from me, studying some kind of mixed drink. It looked clear - maybe a gin and tonic or a vodka Collins. He stirred it slowly with a swizzle-stick, and the second tune he'd selected, *Desperado* by the Eagles, flowed out of the jukebox slow and sweet, like nectar. Jacqua appeared with my Heineken, and I had a long, cool belt straight from the bottle. Ice-cold and Dutch - now that was a fine beer. With no warning, the Bar Tag looked up over at us, directly at me, so that our eyes locked for an instant. I thought I saw him smile as he returned to his business.

I dealt the hand after Matt's, losing again, and Jacqua appeared to clear our now-empty pitchers and ask whether we wanted more. We said yes, then she added, "Fella at the bar wants to know if he can join your game."

"He gotta put up the full twenty," Matt said, "but sure."

"I don't think that'll be a problem," Jacqua said. She apparently had stolen a quick inspection of his wallet's interior as he fished out notes for his drink. She went back and collected him, taking his twenty and handing him a stack of chips. Leading him to our table, she pulled up another chair between Crank and Jeff, back straight between me and the Five Point's exit.

"Hey, how you doin'?" he said. His voice was unremarkable.

"Good," I said, for all of us. "Though the cards don't favor me tonight," I added, on behalf of myself.

"Thanks for dealin' me in," he said, to the group, really, although he looked at me as he said it. He appeared thin up close, but relaxed, out after no trouble. I couldn't tell the color of his eyes.

"Brian here thinks you look like Neil Young," Crank said, gesturing at me.

"Some people say that," he said. He started stacking his chips in columns that corresponded with their values. "Who's deal?" he asked.

"It's yours," Jeff said. "I dealt last."

He called five-card stud, won the first hand he dealt. Then he won the next, a large seven-card draw hand Crank dealt. The pot had grown large on that one, with so many cards. Over the next hour, it seemed the man who looked like Neil Young won every other hand, until Crank and Matt grew dangerously low on chips, Jeff not far behind. I'd gathered in a couple of the larger pots, however, and my stacks had actually grown, somehow, since he'd sat down with us. He had a fantastic poker face, betraying nothing, fingers splayed over the backs of his cards. I thought those of his right hand appeared callused, imagined them wringing sound from guitar strings as his other hand worked the frets.

After a while I began to imagine it really was Neil Young sitting across from me, right here at our humble Five Point Café poker table, downtown for a slow evening after a rigorous studio session or something. I wondered whether I should just outright ask him but, oddly, could not. If he *was* Neil Young, it would have been a horribly, cloying groupie-ish sort of question to ask. I'd have felt like a real asshole, for some reason. So instead I just sat across from him and played the cards that came my way. We were on our sixth or seventh pitcher between all of us - I think we were all at least partially drunk by then, although I could not speak for the Bar Tag's state of mind - when I received, as if

135

from lightning source, the most perfect idea: I wondered what Mr. Young's doppelgänger would do if I got up between hands, stumbled over to the jukebox, and plugged quarters for a CSNY number or two. If he was Neil Young, how could he just sit there and listen to *Carry On* or *Suite Judy Blue Eyes* or *Déjà Vu* without betraying his true identity, somehow? Surely he would inadvertently break into a bar of lyric, or articulate his fingers over phantom guitar strings. He'd tell us then, one way or the other. Because he looked so goddamned much like Neil Young I was expecting David Crosby, Stephen Stills and Graham Nash - or Bar Tags for them, at minimum - to step through the Five Point's door any second and pull up chairs.

I stumbled out of my seat, swerved around an amused Jacqua, and fell toward the jukebox. It loomed like a chrome calliope, old despite its blinking and flashing, but Wurlitzer classic. I had to close one eye to read the menu, scanned for anything by Crosby Stills Nash & Young - but there was nothing. My eyeballs rolled down the song titles again, top to bottom, top to bottom - everybody from the 60s and 70s but CSNY. How the hell could that be? And just as I was about to abandon this genius notion - that he would give up confession to the sound of familiar music - there, at second to the bottom in the fourth column of titles, I found a very reasonable alternative: *For What it's Worth* - the song that keeps repeating, "Stop, hey, what's that sound, everybody look what's goin' down..." by Buffalo Springfield, the real Neil Young's band before CSNY. Perfect!

I fumbled my quarters into the slot, nearly pressed the selection key, then thought, *Wait - I want to see his face. I want to observe when the first notes of the song come through the speakers.* If I selected *For What it's Worth* right off, he might recover his surprise by the time I returned across the room. So I picked a Jefferson Airplane number first, *Somebody to Love,* and then selected the Buffalo Springfield number, returning across the room as satisfied as a tomcat.

Jeff dealt as Grace Slick cranked through the song, and just as Jacqua materialized with a last-call pitcher and Neil's twin won the pot - taking Crank's and Matt's final chips - the opening guitar licks of my entrapment scheme curled profoundly from the juke's speakers.

He didn't bat an eyelash. Just stayed intent on the new cards Jeff had dealt, through the whole song, not a whisper, not a look up, no uttered lyric, nothing. Only the roll of tendered poker chips, our calls to hit, bet, raise, call and show interrupted Buffalo Springfield. He won the pot again as the tune finished in fading strains of outraged, lonely guitar, and the deal moved to him. He dealt three hands, mine, Jeff's, his, looked over the top of his new hand at me. And then, was there a *wink*? It happened so fast and was so minor I'm unsure whether it really occurred or an alcohol mist simply invented this confidence between us. I won that hand, cleaning Jeff out, but the victory was empty and joyless without a full confirmation of this stranger's potentially iconic identity. I placed my small winnings in front of me - there was barely enough, in total, to survive another hand. It was quarter-to-one in the morning. He and I remained in the game.

I called five-card draw, shuffled the deck. He anted. I gestured for him to cut the cards - he tapped the top card of the deck indicating his preference was no cut. I nodded, dealt ten cards, his first - alternating between the two of us. We inspected our hands - I couldn't believe it, I was staring at three aces, plus the king and queen of hearts.

"Your bet," I said.

He tossed three red chips onto his nickel ante. "Thirty cents to you," he said.

"I'll cover that and raise you twenty." I tossed my last blue chip and a white onto the pot. He scrutinized his cards for a few seconds, placed two red chips on top of my bet. "Pot's right," he said.

"How many you want?" I asked.

"Three."

I dealt him the top three cards off the remaining deck. He surrendered his three castaways, face down, retrieved the new cards, one at a time, from the felt before him. I buried his discards under the deck, watched his eyes for a surrender of clues.

"Dealer takes two," I said, dropping my two losers and dealing myself the top pair - trying to keep my eyes from growing plate-sized. A pair of kings! A full-house, aces high with kings. He was about to get his ass kicked!

He looked at my remaining pile of chips - two whites and two reds, thirty cents from the end of the game. He fished two reds and two whites from the jumble of chips before him.

"Thirty cents to stay," he said.

I tossed the last of my chips into the pot with confidence. "Call," I said, with maybe even a mote of uncharacteristic haughtiness.

Neil Young splayed all four jacks on the green felt, and a junk three of clubs. "Four Dead in O-hi-o," he said. "Whaddaya got?"

"Your pot," I said, stunned. "Four of a kind beats a full house any day of the week." Just for kicks, I showed my cards.

"Shit," Matt said, "you gotta *hate* that."

"You're a helluva card player, Mr. Looks Like Neil Young," Crank added.

"Thanks fellas." He just smiled, then added, "I enjoyed your company tonight."

Jacqua appeared again to tell us she was closing down. We were the last patrons, although we hadn't noticed when the few others left. We staggered out of our chairs, our guest following her back to the bar to cash his chips. He'd leave eighty bucks to the good, we'd leave twenty poorer each. Unless you counted the fifty cents, too, I'd burned playing the jukebox. Oh well, I thought, didn't much matter, and it was time to be getting home anyway, time to start that fifteen block walk up Queen Anne Hill.

The five of us exited the Five Point into a cold Seattle night, wind blowing up off Elliott Bay, the street empty. Except next to the curb - there idled a white Town Car, it seemed half the block long. Its driver door opened as we stepped fully onto the sidewalk, out from under the Five Point Café's canvas awning, a chauffeur unfolding grandly from the black interior of the limo. He opened the rear door, nodded at us, addressed the visitor.

"I trust you had a nice evening, Mr. Young."

"Yes, thank you."

He turned to us - four drunk ex-sorta-hippies, on in our years, pseudogamblers, each with his own private hard-on for Jacqua, job-bitching but good-salt types. Somehow he knew we all had about four hours to sleep. Four hours to rest and restore ourselves before getting up half blind with exhaustion, pouring bitter coffee in atop sour beer stomachs and driving off to work, each to his own small but proud role - Matt the electrician, Crank the lineman, Jeff the landscaper and me the bread- and baked-goods delivery man. He knew.

"Give you fellas a lift?" he asked.

A Known Turn in the Road

Exactly three years and twelve days after a rotten lodgepole pine, seventy feet tall but corrupt in its trunkwood, snapped and obliterated, in its fall to earth, the camp trailer of Ed Ferris' brother and nephew, killing them, Ed Ferris lost his way in the woods.

Mid-November, the second-to-last day of modern rifle elk season, and Ed had made a decision borne of frustration: to hunt elk at night, to poach. Three seasons of disappointment, of raw loss, of struggling failing faith. Add in ten days this season of unusually high temperature and clear Cascades sky despite radio reports of coming snowfall, no sign of elk at lower altitudes, not a single sighting and very little scat or other markings. In Ed's mind, these issues, independent at the outset, began to whirl and merge in his thoughts through the week. They drew to focus and culminated a belief that to bring home an elk this year - no matter the cost or risk - would fill this ache. Indeed, it would verify his deity still knew him, still held him in the palm of his hand.

Ed had spent three seasons hunting alone in the Nile game management unit, an imprudence he risked as he sought emendation for that hideous night. All week that season three years ago, the weather reports had warned of massive snowfall and potent winds. By midweek, the promise had failed to materialize. Turning in one night, Ed and the pair began to discern a change in the weather. Trees above them began to sway and whisper with the first gusts. Pine needles and dry sticks began, slowly at first, to rain into their campsite. The first dense clouds from the north, rushing from Manastash Ridge, suddenly eclipsed starlight.

Piling into the camp trailer after dousing their campfire, Willie, the thirteen-year-old boy, in camp for his second season, asked bold questions about the wind: "We'll be all right, right?"

'Sure," Ed had replied. "Of course," his brother added, as pine cones and larger sections of branch pelted the aluminum roof. They had played Canasta for an hour and a half, Ed and his brother drinking malt liquor, Willie drinking 7-Ups, by the light of a battery-rigged electric lamp.

Full, Ed stepped out of the trailer to urinate, grimaced as the cold wind raced around his member. He wondered about his warranty to Willie as the first snow began to laterally flow into camp. *Sure.* Prior to this dry week, October had been the wettest month on record for the eastern Cascades, and the wind was bearing down out of the west now, shouting above the canopy. The dining flies filled with air and rattled, and the end of a plastic bread bag flapped back and forth on the outside table. All around him in the woods he heard pops and cracks as limbs broke away, and in rhythm, the grinding of tree bark against tree bark as two trunks, somewhere in the dark, engaged in black friction.

As he buttoned up, the snow came fatter and harder, stinging his cheeks. An ember missed in the dousing of the campfire sparked, caught dry char, and blazed in a small nova. He had turned to retrace his steps, just beginning to believe there might be a reason for alarm, when a rogue current of the storm flicked down into camp as a finger of wind. An immense split and crack below the roar filled the woods around him. Then there was a large sound like his boot retreating from deep mud.

He turned toward the sound. Very slowly, from very high, a tree fell.

It smashed into the camp trailer directly over the dining table and sliced it perfectly in two. The halves jumped forward and aft away from the energy of impact, paneling and needles and Formica and aluminum struts and an eight of clubs and pitch flying around in a cloud that rose and settled. The light sputtered and was snuffed. There was the smell of propane all around him. He stood in the cold wind, bereft of sight in the blackness, and asked himself *What was that*, dully, from another set of rings around another planet. He understood, and did not hear himself moan lowly and say *No, no* repeatedly. And then a single sound - a limb slapping onto the steel hood of his Dodge Ramcharger - shocked him into movement.

Feeling his way, he stumbled over to the vehicle, felt the line of the left front quarter panel and traced his way up the hood to the windshield. He stepped around the mirror, found the door handle and yanked it open. Reached in, pulled on the headlights. They cast two beams just to the left of the bifurcated trailer, with enough sidelamp to reveal the disaster.

Under the trunk, threaded in branches and flotsam, both Willie and his brother were broken and dead. There was no doubt about it. Ed didn't even have to check their pulses. He returned to the Dodge, slipped in to the driver's seat, turned the ignition and snapped on a Citizen's Band radio, hailing for help.

He had waited ten and a half hours. The storm raged around him, dumping seventeen inches of snow on the campsite. He had shivered and wept, and ache welled in him whenever the thought came to him of his sister-in-law and her empty home west of the mountains in Chehalis. His headlights faded and the CB became inoperable as his battery gave out and dawn came. The winds died. Snow covered the abomination laid out in front of him. He had never in his life known a cold and a waiting so profound.

140

The sound of helicopter rotors roused him from a pre-hypothermic doze around 7:30, and suddenly the flashing lights of a chained-up Forest Service Explorer appeared in his rear-view mirror and behind that another rig with rotating lights. The next thing he knew he was in one of the rigs - he couldn't be sure which - spilling coffee from his shaking hands and getting the cup to his lips and it was hot, so hot. And the scalding had felt so good on his lips and tongue and inside his mouth as it burned and burned down his esophagus.

It burns even now, here, this week. Ed can recall across an abyss with bruising clarity his sister-in-law's stunned expression and collapse. The can clearly remembers the weeping at the funerals, cleaning gear out of his Ramcharger before taking it to the body shop to replace the hood. The inquiries by employees of the body shop as to the circumstances by which his hood had become dented. Returning to work. The cards of sympathy mocking, with each opening of each envelope, his own escape.

How shall it be explained, the incongruous fracture of reason that led Ed Ferris from the deaths of his brother and nephew to a determination to execute an act of poaching? For a man of Ed's character and deportment, it was an anachronism. Was it that resentment - against the tardiness of emergency response, against bad timing, against deities - had built so comprehensively a fence from his ethics that it couldn't be breached? Was it a misdirected salvo at equity - to take from the forest that had taken - no matter the cost? Or was it a pure anvil of frustration he must, compelled, beat upon? Whatever, for his own reasons, he chose to poach and in that choosing, chose to be iniquitous.

The initial step in that choice came at the end of the eleventh day of the hunt, when his plan had crystallized. After eating an early supper and checking his watch to verify the last moments of the legal hunting day had passed, he began to dress again for the wilderness. He went into his tent with a lantern and changed into fresh thermal underwear, two new T-shirts, put the used sweatshirt he had been wearing back on over these, and pulled a pair of utility overalls up across his waist and around his chest. Then he donned a wool hunter-orange jacket and left the tent, pausing to set the lantern on a chopping block at his exit, and button and tie the fly.

He walked over to the Ramcharger and retrieved his rifle and a hundred-watt headlamp that had been charging in the vehicle's cigarette lighter. He placed an orange cap with an embroidered deer's head over his hair. He pulled on a pair of gloves.

And at 6:15 p.m., walked out of camp into the evening.

He headed west, up 1600 Road toward the branch with 1608. As he walked away from camp and gained elevation, the temperature dropped quickly, but his pace kept him warm. Periodically, the trucks and trailers of hunters who had broken camp further in would approach, and he'd move off into the woods. When they passed, his eyesight would flare for a few moments. Then clarity would return, and he would pause and stare at the endless stars, at Orion, and smile in the absolute darkness.

At 7 o'clock, he came upon now-abandoned Lindsay Camp on his right, and the fork to 1608 Road on his left. He hiked up 1608 for five or six minutes and came to a gate where the Forest Service had closed the remaining two miles of that road, and its tributaries, to motorized traffic. Here he paused to enjoy a cigarette, drawing the smoke deep. The ember glowed like an alpine firefly, as a red-orange point of light that waxed with intake, then waned.

Ed finished the cigarette, accepting of the fact that he had just taken five minutes off the end of his life, twisted the burning cherry off the end and, still the ethicist, put the butt in his coat pocket. Past the gate, it was safe to click on the hand-held lamp periodically to get bearings and measure his progress up the road. He climbed with the road aggressively for five minutes, made a summit and as the road turned to the northwest and began to wind down into a valley, the forest opened up and the full panorama of the winter heavens emerged above him, unnerving in its expanse. Stars were layered upon layers and layers of stars. A meteor streaked across the sky every fifteen seconds or so. Far in the distance, to the south, he could see red lights on top of radio and microwave towers on Bethel Ridge.

He pressed further on into the valley, reaching its floor ten minutes later as the road turned back again to the west first, then further, due south. In years past, he had seen many elk down in this hole, and he knew its folds and ravines like the tips of each of his own fingers. Further on, he passed Roads 229 and 230 and reached the end of 1608 at 8:45 p.m. He figured he was at least two miles from any still-inhabited camp. A rifle shot would be ignored or dismissed as drunkenness in one of dozens of last-night parties.

Forest Service Road 1608 ended abruptly at the lip of a disturbing drop of hundreds of feet to Nile Creek. Ed stood at this abyss and shined his light into empty air. The light had no effect whatsoever on the void, except to cast sidelight onto the ground at his feet and up to the brink. He could hear the creek bubbling far below. He took a few cautionary steps backward to relieve, in his own nerves, the magnetic draw of the edge.

He smoked another cigarette, then shined his light into the nearby woods to find a stump to sit on for the night. He located a reasonable-looking one about ten yards from the road, sat down on it, and doused the light. Total silence fell about him. Not even the creek could be heard this far from the lip of the canyon.

Cold snaked through his limbs and into the core of his body. Within five minutes, he was freezing from head to toe. He started to shudder, then shiver without control. His vision readjusted, he began to discern, in starlight, objects around him, his own breath rising in front of him. He willed an elk out of the woods, knowing that at any sound he would turn toward its source, click on the light, transfix the elk, and take its life with one carefully placed shot.

Ed sat this way for several hours, hearing no sounds. During the second hour he believed he was as cold as an individual ever could possibly be. An hour later, he discovered that an individual could be much, much colder than he had thought an hour earlier. Still, he remained sitting and silent, determined not to make any sound that might betray his presence to passing game. Later, he mocked himself for how relatively warm he had been in the first hours. As the first stages of hypothermia and delirium set in, he cursed God for the cold.

The enormous snap of a stick washed in waves from somewhere into his auditory canals. He slowly moved his arms, as if he would shatter like an ice sculpture, toward the sound. He clicked on the light. A coyote turned to stare at the alien presence. It yipped and loped away.

It was at this moment that Ed had the first inklings of thought that if he were to stand and walk around a little, the metabolic activity that this generated would bring some relief from the cold. He rose and wandered, selecting another stump sometime later and, crestfallen, watched dawn break over a ridge he didn't recognize. The forest around him came to life, waking sounds from squirrels and birds.

Of course, with the morning, he was legal again, on the last day of the hunt. Internal to his thought, cynicism that he would take an elk on the last day of a heretofore-unsuccessful hunt warred with optimism that heat would return with the sun's rays. Resolved only to stick with it, he determined to hunt the rest of the day and make a decision, sometime over the course of the day, whether he'd remain out that night.

Needling at the back of his mind was the problem of location. He was unfamiliar with his exact position, although he assumed 1608 Road was somewhere to the east and that up over a steep ridge to the west was Flat Iron Lake and, higher, Clover Springs. During the course of the morning he heard distant rifle fire. He realized he was hungry and thirsty.

At high noon, Ed began to feel concerned. And strangely depressed. He found water in a small stream and drank deeply. As he walked eastward, up and down game trails, across fallen trunks, wading through marshy suck-holes and dividing thickets of vine maple, the first buds of panic emerged in him. They blossomed toward 3:30 as light and temperature again began to fall, and hunger rose and became excruciating, and his cigarettes ran out.

At 5:30, twenty-five minutes after the close of modern-rifle elk-hunting season in eastern Washington, Ed fired his rifle three times into the air as a distress signal. One shot for each syllable: *lost hunter*. He knew this was a universal S-O-S signal for hunters, but no-one had ever really explained to him what you wait for after firing the shots. Three shots in return? Then what?

Bitterly cold, he gathered sticks and dry forest duff, and started a small campfire. He fired three more shots, in rapid succession, at 7 o'clock. He spent the night huddled in the faint embrace of the fire's warmth and flicker, feeding it with larger wood until dawn. With the morning of the second day, he fired three more S-O-S shots, knowing that all remaining hunters in the area were - at that moment - rising to break camp and head back to Spokane or Seattle or Vancouver.

No response came, and he wasted his last shell in an attempt to kill a mountain hare and salve his raging hunger. The day passed again, and clouds came in from the northwest. A snowflake fell and then he couldn't believe his eyes as the clouds opened up and dumped snow as darkness surrounded him like a bleak, growing sarcoma. Then Ed sat on a log and cried, not for his loss, but for the loss of the season, and for his brother, and for Willie.

Ed Ferris lost track of time, of the meter of darkness and light. During one period of light, he cracked through ice at a stream's bank and bent to drink and saw on the water in his reflection a face that could have been another man's. This man had a full beard. But even beyond the facial hair, something was very different in the foundation of skin across skull, in the thrust of cheekbone, the shape of the eyes, their distance apart. Even so, his own familiar features were present as well.

He had long since abandoned his rifle and lamp, run out of fluid in his lighter, gained the upper hand on hunger. He wandered lost, and walked past trees and into ravines and up game trails that might have been familiar. It seemed to him as if he'd been in the circle of the woods for a while, or that he had dreamed of the rhythm of mountain seasons.

Some time after the light and darkness had cycled many times, Ed Ferris became aware that by simply looking at a tree he would know the number of growth rings in radius from the center of its trunk. Later, he began to imagine the distinction between random forest sounds and the hum of the thoughts of trees and plants and animals, even stones. Soon thereafter, he began to appreciate the sounds, and began to listen for history and instruction and music.

He found that he had been given all the names of the plants - the mountain currant, bearberry, myrtle boxwood. He understood the forbs of the understory, the arrowleaf balsamroot, cinquefoil, western yarrow, the vetch.

Placing his hand on a tree, its name would come to him: *I am Engelman Spruce.* Entering a stand of trees: *We are Western Larch.*

A lynx sat down next to him one afternoon and shared a poem, then a rumor of hard winter coming. Rain fell, and he would taste the heritage of each drop on the bitter buds of his tongue - stream to river, river to sea, sea to cloud, cloud to mountains. His news came on the wind: angels have been discerned on the wing in the form of ravens; the constellations have taken on new form and position. Glancing up that very night, he saw that, indeed, Orion had somewhat flattened, had raised his sword, was closer in pursuit of the Pleiades.

The beard grew longer and developed a personality of its own, performing oracle, and he named it *Schedar*, because it fell across his breast. He could separate its pointed end into two points and divine for water.

Elk and deer came to him now and communed with him in low, long language. In conversation with these ungulates, a brief greeting such as *How are you today, bearded one* would last for most of a morning. A fable of the forest, uttered from a royal bull's lips, would last many periods of darkness and light.

When the rut began, Ed and Schedar dwelt amongst the herd, and witnessed together the gatherings of cows, the violent competition of bulls. As the champions bugled and mounted the females, Ed and Schedar turned politely away and spoke pleasantries to one another, or engaged in protracted dialogue with spikes, yearlings too young and foolish to copulate.

One morning the chief bull of the herd, an old master with six branches on one side of his rack and seven on the other, gathered them together - sixty-eight animals in all plus Ed and Schedar - and announced, over the course of several days, a migration. The herd gathered itself and, in an orderly column, proceeded eastward for days and nights that merged in gray for Ed. After some time, the herd had traversed most of all the areas he was familiar with from his circular wanderings. He began to note here and there landmarks familiar to him from some remote past before the forest became his cosmos. He pointed them out to Schedar: a curiously formed boulder he was vaguely acquainted with, a Douglas fir he knew he had leaned against, an abandoned campsite. A known turn in a gravel road.

The herd walked in an autumn evening down the Nile Creek valley to the Naches River and waded down its middle to a bridge Ed knew.

"Do you know that bridge?" Schedar asked, sensing Ed's pause and wonder.

Yes.

Detecting light, Ed took Schedar out of the column of the herd and up the east bank of the Naches River, across the parking lot of a grocery and restaurant at the intersection of the access road to the mountains and a state highway. Schedar started and curled at the roaring pass of a tractor and trailer.

Ed arrived at the door to the restaurant, opened the door and felt a wash of heat. Stepping inside, he closed the door behind him and took measure of the interior. Six small tables, only one of them occupied by a pair of hunters - one with his back to Ed and the other across from the first, hidden from view. A waitress at the till to the left. Ed and Schedar turned to her to explain they were hungry but had no money. That they needed help.

Hello?

The waitress went about her business of wiping down the till. She took no notice of Ed and Schedar, even though she looked up and directly at them. Then she walked away through a doorway Ed assumed led to a kitchen.

Don't mind her.

Ed turned to the voice. A man was behind it, another hunter. He invited Ed to sit with him at a table, and got up once Ed was seated and disappeared into the kitchen. He returned with a bowl of soup and a hamburger on a platter, with a quarter slice of dill pickle, and set it down in front of Ed on the table.

I don't have any money.

Don't worry. The man smiled, and sat down as Ed dragged Schedar across the plate and pieces of the beard sought warmth between the bread, in the meat and condiments.

It was then that Ed became aware that the two other people in the restaurant, watching him, very much resembled his brother and Willie. Their faces could have been those of other men. They had full beards. But even beyond the facial hair, something was very different in the foundation of skin across skulls, in the thrust of cheekbones, the shapes of the eyes. Still, the familiar features of his brother and Willie were present as well, unbroken and whole.

Their reunion was pleasant and emotional, empty of the obvious questions normal folks would ask. They were like old, favorite clothing lost for a while, then found. They walked out of the restaurant arm in arm, the three of them.

Into the forest.

Perhaps as Ed Ferris and his brother and Willie stepped into the threshold of timber, he crossed a rubicon of heaven's gate. Perhaps not. Perhaps his traverse in that instant was only a weigh station along the way.

It is impossible to say.

Smoke Follows Beauty

Below an unblemished blue sky on a brilliant Cascades Sunday morning, the god Loo-Wit suffered a major seizure and the top eleven-hundred feet of Mount St. Helens' perfect cone slid toward Spirit Lake in a twelve-second seismic free-fall. Accompanied by a catholic roar, the mountain ejected one cubic mile of released ash, pumice and ten-thousand boulders heavenward. The mass ultimately reached altitudes where airliners cruise. It created its own infernal weather system, throwing lightning to the ground from a black, roiling cloud. Huge pyroclastic flows leapt down the volcano's flanks in an alpine tsunami, laying waste on their random routes, finally seeking lowlands and funneling through channels all the way to the Columbia River at Toutle and Kelso in a great, angry sweep. The compression blast of St. Helens' fury leveled twenty-four-thousand acres of old-growth forest. It buried or asphyxiated fifty-seven human beings, thousands of elk and deer, hundreds of thousands of other wildlife and, perhaps, a troupe of Sasquatch. It smothered Spirit Lake in a blanket of steam and gastric vapor, raising its shore two hundred feet. The cataclysm laid bare the rugged territory to the north and northeast of the mountain. It became like the face of the moon. Void. Silent.

Against this backdrop, the mystery of tension between man and woman and choice and consequence continued to unfold for Eric Ball. From sixty miles to the southwest, he watched from the roof of Engine House Pizza Company No. 1 on Oregon's Jantzen Beach with fellow employees of the restaurant. Barbie was among them, and only St. Helens's ash plume, which rose and rose, was capable of pulling his eyes, temporarily, away from her.

When scientists and diagnosticians began to warn people in surrounding communities that St. Helens was coming back to life after almost five quarters of a century, the perfect mountain became, overnight, a novelty. Those who lived in its shadow boasted to family and acquaintances across the country of a real live volcano, right in their own backyard. Geologists, appealing to the federal government and local officers of law enforcement, came up with the idea of establishing cautionary zones around the mountain as it fumed and spat, intermittently, ash and steam.

The Red Zone, as it was called, became their favorite trespass, their preferred boundary to cross as they crossed others, entering, they thought, young adulthood. Drinking, Eric and other friends would climb into Rusty's decrepit Vega and run up past Battleground out into Amboy and Chelatchie Prairie, the odor of mint strong as they crossed the brief flatland, and head up to Swift Reservoir. Wind blowing on them through open windows, they'd pass a bottle of vodka back and forth, pretend to like its sophisticated bite, and speed into their first months of driving privileges.

Pausing one night as they passed an intersection, they noted with delight the rural street sign: Rush Road. They got out and pulled the sign off with Rusty's tool kit: they liked music from a Canadian band called Rush, and, thinking themselves clever, they called their forays "Treks into the Rush Zone."

Spirit Lake was the High Adventure program headquarters of the Columbia Pacific Council of the Boy Scouts of America when Eric was involved, between ten and fifteen years old. The lake was, and is, nestled between Mount St. Helens and Windy Ridge in southwest Washington's Dark Divide, which separates the Cispus and Cowlitz watersheds. Its clear shores leapt up from disquieting depths onto steep, green slopes packed tight with cedar, hemlock, fir - ancient, old growth forests harboring secrets from the creation of North America.

In the waters of Spirit Lake Eric and the other boys swam and sailed, enjoyed spray from the powerboats that would ferry them from the docks at Harry Truman's lodge on the south side of the lake to the Boy Scout camp on the northeast shore. As campers, they'd spend the days enrolled in childhood seminars in pursuit of merit badges for Indian lore, hiking, first aid, astronomy and so forth. Or they would try for advanced awards - the Paul Bunyan Axman for felling a tree, or the Mile Swimmer badge.

A scout would work toward the Mile Swimmer for the entire week, swimming a quarter mile each day for the first two days, a half mile on the third day, three-quarters of a mile on the fourth, and the full mile on the fifth day. Spirit Lake was glacier-fed. Eric can to this day remember the full system shock of immersion, as well as the eerie fascination with the rumored depth of water below his body. He can recall the mechanical movement of his numb limbs as he swam, following a rowboat over the regimen of those five days, in the high summer of 1975.

They would, Eric and his patrol, go with a counselor out on the lake in a longboat at night and gasp at stars. Unrefracted by atmosphere, in competition with no other sources of light, they were like an inverted bowl of diamonds. The scouts would reach up for them and delight in their mythology, wonder about their systems.

The night Eric earned the Mile Swimmer award, the scout troops gathered together for a campwide fire at a tiered arena that featured half-hewn logs as benches. They would start the final fire of the week by stacking tinder inside a fabulous pyramid comprising lengths of split logs, then firing a flaming arrow into the mass from fifty yards away. The flames would leap instantly into the summer night, ravenous and throwing sparks, the lusty sound of pitch popping across the lake.

Camp leaders, as on other nights, would lead the assembled boys in traditional campfire choruses, give awards for patrols that had distinguished themselves, and periodically settle into the ritual of fire-staring. Wholesome, All-American fun.

This night, the final night, though, was a special night for the counselors. It was traditional that on the eve of the return of the boys to their suburban homes in Portland or Longview or Vancouver or Oregon City for the counselors to provide them with the gift of an unforgettable story. One they would, and must, carry with them wherever they went, for as long as they lived.

As the fire's light grew low, the lead counselor stepped into the dancing half-light of the circle. He assumed a serious air. He stuffed his hands in his pockets and began to tell the story of the naming of Ape Canyon, an abyss merely five miles south of the lake.

"Back when our grandfathers were boys like you," he said, "the shores of Spirit Lake and its surroundings were different. Indians in this area named Spirit Lake because of strange things they had seen that might have been visions but seemed too real and could not be explained away as normal. Strange animals in the water, odd mists hovering in old places, mists with shapes and stories in them. Strange tribes of hairy giants, who moved off and disappeared quickly whenever they were seen."

He removed his hands from his pockets and began to gesture.

"In those days, white men, miners, came to Spirit Lake from Kelso to search for gold. They made a camp just south of here. So successful was their search that they built a rough cabin there. In 1924, four of them moved in to work their claim, thinking nothing of the large footprints they would find from time to time in creekbeds.

150

"One day, one of them - a man named Fred Buck - was prospecting a ways from camp and had a strange sense he was being watched. Turning slowly to look" - and here the counselor turned dramatically to face a new section of the assembled boys - "he saw in the trees a creature that seemed like a man, only about eight feet tall, and covered with thick brown hair.

"Fred Buck fired a shot with his rifle over the head of the creature, and it fled into the woods. Returning to the cabin, he tried to convince his fellow miners of his strange encounter. But they thought he was drunk, and ignored him.

"A few days later, one of the other miners saw a similar creature and, terrified, shot the monster three times. It toppled over the edge of a cliff into a canyon five miles from this place, and the miner ran back to camp to tell his story. He convinced his partners to accompany him to the spot and see the dead creature. But they searched all day at the bottom of the canyon without finding the body, and the remaining two who had not seen the creature still didn't believe.

"That night the miners were awakened by thuds and violent banging and scratching on the walls and roof of the cabin. It went on for five hours. Not one of them was brave enough to open the door and look outside to see what was causing the noise. The next morning, after the terrifying sounds had stopped for a couple of hours, they ventured out to find dozens of massive boulders lying all around the cabin. The walls and roof were chipped where the boulders had hit, and there were enormous claw marks around the door and in several places on the walls. Huge footprints, twice the size of a grown man's, surrounded the cabin in the dust.

"The miners packed up that morning and fled back to Kelso. They enlisted a posse of men to return to the camp and search for the creatures. When they returned, they found the door thrown off its hinges and the inside completed torn apart."

He paused to let the enormity of this sink in. Every scout's eyes were fully wide, unblinking.

"No sign was ever found of the creatures. The camp was abandoned. But from time to time hikers and hunters report a sighting of the hairy creatures - now called Bigfoot or by their Indian name, Sasquatch - or a terrifying howling late at night is reported by campers, throughout the years since, and even *recently*.

"The ravine the creature is said to have fallen into is now called Ape Canyon. It remains there today, one of many great mysteries of Spirit Lake." He concluded with this inescapable fact.

Dismissed, the boys filed back to their cabins along dark trails with flashlights. They glanced sidelong at the impenetrable forest to their right and left, outside the circle of light to the front of them and to the back.

In the summer of 1978, Rusty and Eric, best friends, were fifteen and counselors in training at Spirit Lake. They'd met in the same home room in seventh grade, and had become inseparable over the course of the next two years. They had alternated as patrol leader and assistant patrol leader of the fabulous Cobras, unsurpassed in lashing, woods lore, calling forth fire without matches, winners of top honors of red, white and blue ribbons for their patrol flag at district camporees.

They had looked eagerly forward to the opportunity of spending three weeks as counselors at the lake, to fraternize with the more mature boys, to view themselves as leaders - lieutenants, if not generals yet.

Their barracks was a two-story lodge on the shore of the lake. Cots and lockers filled the upper level. A boathouse that led out to the main receiving dock for the camp made up the lower level. They'd spend preparatory days cleaning the camp, then relaxing in quarters while an eight-track tape of Cat Scratch Fever - the possession of one of the older, full-fledged counselors - cycled over and over.

Three-quarters of a mile from the Boy Scout camp, to the west, the Girl Scouts of America had established its own camp, and for counselors, one of the highlights of the two weeks was a Friday-night mixer. The Boy Scout staff would embark in a longboat and cross the inlet that separated the two camps over the deep waters, and begin to sing *There Ain't No Flies On Us* as they approached the girls' dock.

The adult counselors had set up a dance with Kool-Aid and snacks. And knowing themselves to be goofy and awkward, the scouts stood around a lot - boys on one side of the lodge, girls on the other - until a few of the more confident began to mix, drawing the rest in. Rusty and Eric were introduced to their counterparts: two counselors-in-training, like them, Paige and Sharon.

Paige and Sharon were exact opposites. Where Paige was short and athletic, Sharon was taller and pudgy. Paige had a short, cute bob of raven hair; Sharon had long, strawberry blond tangles. Paige, Eric and

Rusty noticed, had breasts. Sharon, they assumed, also had them, but it wasn't quite the same. Paige was a gregarious talker with a figure like a gymnast; Sharon, silent and introspective, shaped like a big bag of flour. Paige: *fox*; Sharon: *dog*, was their assessment. A walk through the sea of their burgeoning characters - both Rusty's and Eric's - wouldn't have gotten your ankles wet.

They were cabin-mates though, so Paige insisted that Sharon be included in all aspects of all their conversations, which got easier as they became accustomed to one another over the course of the evening.

"I think she likes me," Rusty said, as Eric and he returned, in the dark, in the boat that night.

"Who likes you?" Eric asked, addressing his best friend with foreign scorn for the first time in their friendship. An unfamiliar, unbidden horn rose through Eric's scalp.

"Paige. That's who." As if Eric was an ignoramus for failing to detect this obvious thing.

"That's funny," Eric said. "I was about to tell you the same thing."

"That's bullshit, man."

"You're bullshit, man."

Strange, alien silence - a gulf between them.

The following Friday night they again mustered for the mixer with the Girl Scout counselors. All week as Eric went about the serious business of counseling, Paige was a sweet beacon in the back of his teen-aged mind. He thought constantly of her giggle, her eyes, the freckles on her tiny nose. Her shape. Rusty and Eric had spoken to each other the next morning as if their odd verbal duel the night prior had never taken place. They had continued to speak and engage for the ensuing six days. The relentless task of whipping campers into shape, guiding them to young manhood, had pushed them momentarily beyond smaller concerns, beyond jealousy.

The boys docked and clambered out of the boat. Rusty and Eric pushed to be the first ones onto the shore. They both sought her out, but it was clear from the start she was paying more attention to Eric. She put her hands on his arms and twirled her hair when she'd talk to him. They danced, and she bestowed upon him a most heavenly kernel of information - she was sixteen, a year older than he. Eric felt giddy.

Rusty was relegated to a time-passing role with Sharon, which is not to say that all four of them did not interact that evening. They did, and shared jokes, laughs - Rusty even danced with Paige, and Eric with Sharon, to a fast song. But the last song of the night, a slow rock ballad, belonged to Paige and Eric. No one else was there, and Eric put his arms all the way around her and felt the small of her back. He ground his thigh into hers, just a little, and pulled the soft mounds of her breasts into his middle, and breathed her in.

It was during that confusing dance that Paige softly whispered the invitation of invitations: *Come over to our cabin tonight.*

How? Eric whispered back, barely, skin tingling.

The trail, from the west end of your camp. Pushing, pulling, sighing. *It hooks up to us. Our cabin is the first on the right.*

She pulled her lips away from his ear, pulled her head away, grinned, looking straight in his eyes. Eric Ball felt very much unlike a Boy Scout.

"Don't forget Rusty," she smiled. "For Sharon."

The song ended. Their limbs disengaged. Hot clothing grasped Eric's skin, bonded in place with cool perspiration. And his head rushed and rushed.

"Come on Rusty, don't be a dick."

Later that night. Rusty had been sore all evening, Eric could tell. Even at fifteen, though, he was too much of a pre-gentleman to betray his jealousy in front of the girls. Even so, back at camp, he was being obstinate. Eric knew that Paige would be disappointed with him if he didn't arrive with Rusty in tow. He also knew that there was no way he was going to undertake the expedition three quarters of a mile to the Girl Scout camp in the dark, by himself, only five miles from Ape Canyon, drawing closer to the myth of Bigfoot with every step.

"You're the dick," Rusty said.

"Look," Eric tried, "I don't want to hike up there by myself, and it'll be cool."

Instantly Rusty discerned the actual motive behind Eric's insistence. His bruised ego properly mitigated, he began to let slip small signs that he might be willing. He started out by enumerating reasons why they shouldn't go, demanding logic from Eric's responses.

"If we get busted, we'll get in huge trouble - probably get booted."

"If we get caught, we'll just say we were out memorizing constellations - we'll take a star chart with us."

"We gotta get up early tomorrow."

"It don't make no difference. Tomorrow's an easy day. All we gotta do is work camp clean-up."

Rusty's objections faded into strategic discussion regarding how the pair might possibly carry out the plan and return in time for reveille. Finally he capitulated: "O.K., Eric, let's go," He added, through a forced grin, "You're still a dick."

They grabbed the star charts they would use the following week to counsel Tenderfoots who opted to seek the astronomy merit badge and rolled them up in a tube. They grabbed their jackets and a flashlight each. The pair left their quarters at about 9:30.

Camp was quiet, and the woods were an absolute void outside the light of their flashlights. Circles of light bobbed up and down and back and forth on the trail as they hiked out of the area, uphill through the ancient forest.

Cresting the hill about ten minutes later, they paused in the trail and agreed, just for a moment, to switch off the lights. Darkness and silence were so comprehensive that disorientation attacked within five seconds. Quickly, before Eric fell over or panicked, his fingers fumbled for the switch on his light, and clicked it back on.

"Chicken shit?" Rusty whispered.

"Shit chicken." Eric stared ahead at the trail. He half expecting a battalion of Sasquatch to jump out of the woods, pursue, catch them, and feast on their flesh. Or the ghost of Fred Buck, any second, washing over them in a vapor. Making them go mad.

Under way again, the boys and their modern torches pioneered the trail through deep black. And at exactly the moment when Eric first thought *It must be up here soon*, the beams of their lights played out into emptiness, and they entered a clearing of cabins and heard a whisper, Paige's voice: *Over here.* Their lights swept in unison to the door of the first cabin on the right, spotlighting Paige's fine form in the frame.

"In here," she said. Eric and Rusty very quickly complied, in out of the chill. Their boots clomped on the wood floor, resonating with too large a sound for their comfort, and that of the girls. "Shhhhh!"

"Sorry," Eric whispered, and sat on a cot, Paige's. Rusty looked around, saw Sharon sitting shyly on the single remaining cot in the cabin and, resigned, sat down next to her. Paige walked over to a dresser and lit a candle on its top. The flame sputtered then grew steady. Rusty and

Eric switched off their lights again, and stowed them in their jackets. They set the star charts down on the cots. The candle cast a minute glow, and flickered from moment to moment. Were their shadows, or were they, quivering?

The four of them talked for a while, Paige dominating most of the conversation - she was from Camas, a town on the Columbia River famous for its paper mill and resulting stench, a characteristic Eric didn't choose to point out at that moment. She had a driver's license... She this, she that. Eric was eating it up, a court servant sucking on a queen's toes, a little sycophant. Rusty was bored out of his mind, sitting next to the nearly invisible Sharon, who once in a while would pipe up with a statement that, even as it rolled of her tongue, all four of them knew was eminently and instantly forgettable.

Sensing this, Rusty suddenly remembered the story of the naming of Ape Canyon. Retrieving his flashlight, he held it under his chin and switched it on, pointed upward. Light rushing from it inverted his face's normal topography of shadow. He looked diabolical, speaking to the other three from a black and white horror cinema. Somewhere in the middle of the story, Paige reached over and grasped Eric's hand, lacing her soft fingers with his, sharing tensile heat. Eric thought he could feel her pulse, slow at first, then quickening.

Rusty concluded the myth, and they lapsed into silence. As Rusty and Sharon looked around at the four corners of the cabin for further inspiration, Paige leaned over and uttered in Eric's ear, barely intelligibly, so lightly he wasn't sure whether she actually aspirated syllables or sent a message by coy telepathy, *Ask me to go for a walk.*

Turning to her, Eric followed her instructions, precisely: "Come take a walk with me," he whispered.

They rose, grabbed their jackets.

"Back in a sec," Paige assured Sharon, and Eric caught Rusty's glare of betrayal, shrugged his shoulders barely: *Well, what else am I supposed to do?* Paige and Eric departed the room, out through the door and into the darkness again before he clicked on the flashlight.

They walked back up the trail for a minute, his hand in hers. Nervous, led, needles of uncertainty poked into his chest from deep within his back. He felt as if any moment he'd have to jump out of his skin. In the cool air, searching for words, knowing that whatever he said would be inadequate, he selected a safe, reliable question: "So... what did you think of Rusty's story?"

She stopped, turned to him. Looked up at him, full, in his face.

"Is that why you asked me for a walk?" Gently chiding. "To ask about Rusty's story?"

"Not... really," Eric stammered.

"Turn off the light." It was an urgent, authoritative command, sighed through smiling lips under amused eyes. Brown eyes, even in the half-light.

In darkness, her mouth found Eric's and parted, a warm wet circle. Pressing with her lips, then her chest, then her full body, they clung, waters of Spirit Lake washing over them, transformed from ice to warm shower. The penetration of her tongue and its urgent movement in him drew his tongue, hesitant at first, into her. They moved in this way for a moment, sharing and enjoying moisture. In his mind, there was blankness except for some vague sense of enigma, barely aware of a growing hardness between his legs. And her scent, *Oh*. Inexperienced, Eric's teeth clicked lightly against hers and she giggled quietly. She pulled away. She held his hands in front of them, then released them and reached forward, upward, and held the sides of his face. She said *Eric* and it was a melody. She kissed him again, lightly, darting her tongue across his upper lip and barely inside again, teasing, then retreated.

"Let's go back," she said.

"Let me have one more." The words felt thick on his swelling tongue. She did.

Rusty and Eric were, of course, busted the next day. An idiot, Eric couldn't help crowing to a couple of full counselors who he had mistaken as confidants. His foolish disclosure, breast-beating, spread amongst the staff - not about Paige and the kissing of course - but, rather, simply the act of going AWOL from camp and ingressing the Girl Scout camp at night, was enough to bring a stern lecture about character and the Boy Scout promise and pledge and oath from the camp director. Sanctions, in addition to the sermon, came in the form of prohibition from the final mixer and in kitchen patrol - KP - for Rusty and Eric's final week.

Which is not to say that the punishment was insignificant: KP for about a hundred pre-teen chimpanzees in Boy Scout suits is no damned picnic. Which is also not to say that, leaving Spirit Lake after three weeks, Eric did not feel it had all been worth it. He regretted, though, the unbelievable error of failing to get Paige's phone number, or even her last name.

And as summer faded to fall, and Rusty and Eric entered high school, the scent of her and the taste of her mouth, the push of her sweet tongue, Spirit Lake around them, under them, over them, rose periodically at odd moments, unbidden. Football season started, and their interests in all things Boy Scoutish waned, traded without a mote of consideration or backward glance for girls and cars and cigarettes, and parties where they experimented with alcohol. Still, thinking of her, his young chest felt an ache of loss. Magic, but loss.

On March 20th, 1980, the Juan de Fuca Plate slipped gently, insistently under the hot, liquid folds of the North American Plate. Perhaps no further, no more incrementally, than the width of a single strand of baby squirrel's down. But this penetration proved enough, and geologists recorded an unusual number of spasms from St. Helens's core. From deep in the earth's mantel, something pressed upward and outward, rising, trembling in its ascent.

Earthquakes surged in waves of construct-altering harmonics, outward from the mountain, slowed then damped by evolved forms of the ancient crust. All over Washington and Oregon, needles shuddered in seismic labs. They tattooed the disturbances on the paper skin of rotating drums in glass cases.

During ensuing days, the frequency and magnitude of the quakes doubled, then trebled. Interest kindled from the area's, then the nation's, then international volcanologists. The United States Geological Survey began issuing cautionary news releases, holding periodic press conferences at headquarters in Vancouver. The Forest Service, landlords of St. Helens and all its environs, mobilized to sanction roads to the area. The rangers evicted tourists and non-essential personnel - lookie-loos - in favor of access for scientists, technicians and, occasionally, pool reporters.

Soon the flanks of St. Helens were probed and monitored. Sophisticated gizmos recorded every quiver, every emission, the composition of groundwater feeding into nearby watersheds. Laser surveying equipment recorded the constant expansion of a new, massive tumor near the summit. As earth pumped its essence up from the red source of friction miles below, quakes continued to proliferate in rolling, urgent foreplay.

St. Helens belched a small, disappointing eruption on March 27th, and the news wires went wild. Associated Press rushed a twelve-paragraph story, paraded as news but editorially, a finger-wagging at government officials for their unnecessary closure of the area. UPI's coverage was straight, quoting geologists who warned that although this eruption appeared minor, it didn't necessarily mean the conclusion of seismic activity. News helicopters from Portland buzzed the summit as a cloud of steam and ash spread upward and eastward, sowing minute particles of silica throughout eastern Washington, flummoxing automobiles and cleaning systems. *The Columbian* and *The Oregonian* both sported front-page headlines.

Average citizens were underwhelmed. Gossip quickly turned to other matters of springtime. But the Rush Zone remained. The squadron of diagnosticians on the mountain did not depart.

Eric spent the spring dividing his time between high school and a mediocre social life, playing rock and roll, and decked out in a white shirt, red suspenders and black slacks as a busboy for a pizza joint on Jantzen Beach. He and Rusty were still tight, and Eric had long months previously reconciled the empty loss of all the potential Paige had represented. Believing they had made a profound discovery, Eric and Rusty, as well as other friends, had begun to experiment more frequently with marijuana and alcohol. They chased away, temporally, all things unresolved. *Made you look forward, yeah.*

From midway through Eric's junior year in high school until their class graduated seventeen months later, he performed as frontman for an outfit called High Seas. They'd play private parties, a few school dances and hoped they could hold it together long enough to play Portland clubs when they turned twenty-one.

A long-haired kid named Larry played lead guitar. A kid named Ron played drums, and Rusty plodded through bass guitar parts as Eric sang and shouted, trying to catch the eyes of girls. Conscious of ungainliness, gangly, he'd try to strut like Mick Jagger, the cock of the walk, and end up looking like an epileptic chicken. Still, Eric could sing, and they could play. Girls liked to hang out with them between sets, bring them beers, and flirt. Share their dope with the band.

Every gig they ever had began with *Stranglehold*, a roaring number that started out with tasty guitar licks and burned onward for seven minutes - long for a party tune. Their sets variously included *Rock and Roll*, a Led Zeppelin cover; *Feel Like Makin' Love* by Bad Company; Lynyrd Skynyrd's *You Got That Right* and *Freebird*; *Light Up*, an obscure, bouncing Styx song; three or four numbers by ZZ Top, a dozen other covers. They'd always end with Pat Travers' *Boom Boom, Out Go the Lights*, a crowd favorite with lots of participation by those gathered around.

To practice, they'd jam in Larry's garage, rigging together crapped-out amps and soldering pickups for Larry's and Rusty's guitars. They experimenting a little with pure ad-lib sessions, mostly just strumming over-amplified blues chords or throwing plastic cups and wadded-up newspaper at Ron when he'd try a drum solo, acting like he was Keith Moon but falling far short. They'd smoke cigarettes and a little pot, drink a few beers, and collapse back in bean-bag chairs listening to Pink Floyd on a popping turntable, zoning out. Stare without much initiative, in blacklight, at posters of Jimi Hendrix and Jimmy Page and that sweet grandmother who's raising her middle finger defiantly.

On April 10th, High Seas had a gig at the house of some out-of-town parents of this kid named Corny. Arriving about 6 p.m., they set up, tuned up and tested their amps and speakers. Classmates and strangers from other high schools, as well as some older kids who might have been college students or already in the workforce, started showing up about seven, and Corny tapped the keg.

About 7:30 Larry and Rusty strapped on their guitars. Ron plopped down behind the drum kit and took a few exploratory whacks on the toms and cymbals. After a second or two, Larry pulled his strings in rhythm, the first grinding notes of the intro to *Stranglehold*, holding that meter for several bars, then grabbed his whammy bar with his right hand, pulled the neck of his guitar upward, shut his eyes tight and grimaced while his left fingers wrought pure iron from above the frets. Ron and Rusty hit dead on as the song kicked in. Eric snatched the microphone from the stand and snarled the opening lyric. The audience whooped. Guys started playing air guitar, and Eric surveyed through a beer buzz for the good-looking girls. When he found them, he sang with his mouth and eyes and body.

Seven minutes later, High Seas launched into *Finding My Way*, a Rush cover, played six or seven other cuts, and took a break. Sweating, Eric sat down on a speaker and lit a cigarette. Larry sauntered over and gave him a high-five. The quartet had been on the mark, completely in step, had the illusion through alcohol that they had a tight outfit executing their songs with surgical precision. A pretty girl from Eric's high school, a sophomore, came over with a cup of beer, inviting him outside to enjoy the cool air. She introduced herself as Kelly.

"I know your name," Eric said, which was bullshit. "I been watching you for weeks." Not precisely true either. But she was tall, with brown eyes, and what was true was that he had noticed her in the hallways. Eric forgot what she was talking about the second words came out of her mouth. He got to the end of his drink, tipped the plastic cup up and sensed, through a storm front of blossoming alcoholism, grit in his mouth.

Lowering the glass and pointing its orifice at the porchlight, he noted grains of sand tumbling and turning in the fluid dynamics of the remaining ounce of beer. It reminded him of parties down at Frenchman's Bar on the Columbia, when sand got everywhere - in your beer, in your shoes, in your car, in your pants. Eric looked up at Kelly. She was staring around her at strange precipitation, smiling oddly, her shape rotating.

Someone who had been listening to KGON-FM during the set-break ran out of the house and yelled *St. Helens blew!* Eric and Kelly recognized the sandfall as volcanic ash, and they giggled as their hair turned gray, and covered their beers with their hands.

This bizarre development lent an aura of risk and delight and celebration to the night, and High Seas blazed through three more sets. Who knows how, or what led to it, but Kelly and Eric ended up in the back seat of his car, making out with heavy, sour breath and his hands on her breasts, up under her tight shirt, hot. He attempted a foray into her pants, but she rebuffed that expedition: "I'm a Catholic," she kept saying. "I'm a Catholic."

Oh.

Barbara Jeppers pulled into the lot at Engine House Pizza Company No. 1 in a brown Toyota Celica. Eighteen years old, she was an order taker and cashier at the gaudy pizza joint, layered in a white blouse, black skirt, nylons and white tennis shoes. She had completed the thirty-minute drive from Hillsboro just in time to clock in.

Walking through the back door, twisting brown hair with blond highlights into a knot and inserting a comb, she pulled her timecard from a metal rack, popped it into the clock, replaced it. Down the short foyer, in the walk-in refrigerator, Eric was mixing pizza sauce in five-gallon buckets.

He looked up: "Hi Barbie." He smiled, winked.

"Hey Eric." She was friendly, interested. "What's up?"

"It's my birthday."

"Na na na na na nah na na Today is yer birthday," she invoked John, Paul, George and Ringo, pantomiming a guitar player, bobbing her head, brown eyes flashing from below an attractive line of mascara. The lids had a trace of blue.

"Thanks." Eric rose from the red slop in the bucket. "Nice place to spend it, huh?"

"Could be worse," she flirted, turned and headed for the front counter.

For five hours, Barbie took orders and rang up checks. Eric bused tables, wiping them down with a wet white rag, running the sweeper back and forth across the carpet, stooping to pick up sausage balls and rogue disks of pepperoni, globs of hardened cheese, crust. Cleaning up kids' spills. Dusting the antique fire engine that dominated the decor at the center of the eatery.

At closing, eleven o'clock, one of Eric's tasks was to clear the beer lines in the bar's taps. This resulted in the discharge of quarts of unmetered beer, and Eric drained these into plastic containers that used to house bell peppers, grated cheese, mushrooms, myriad salad bar items, dressing, croutons. Four of them, Barbie, Eric, Scott and Vicki, sat in the parking lot after closing, after management had gone home, and drank from the containers, a couple of quarts each, and listened to Santana and Steely Dan on the tape deck.

Vicki offered the option of driving to her house, also in Hillsboro, since her parents were gone. She didn't want to be discovered drinking here in the parking lot. All were in favor; of course, by the time they drove the distance to Hillsboro in Barbie's cramped Celica, westward from Portland into the hills, the quarts were finished and all everyone could think of was going to the bathroom.

After relief, the quartet spent some time doing nothing, looking at Vicki's albums and posters, and Barbie remembered it was Eric's birthday. The real birthday song was slurred, and Vicki and Scott were starting a pairing-off ritual with tickles and feigned modesty. They disappeared from the room for a while, then Vicki came back with flushed cheeks, bent and whispered in Barbie's ear. She disappeared through the door again.

Barbie looked at Eric, who was kind of wrapped up in a song, reached out and shook his knee, raised her eyebrows, smiled and said, "Let's get out of here."

Eric's mind filled up with possibilities. She led him by the hand as they walked back down the driveway to her car. They drove around for a while, way past midnight, and ended up back in the Engine House parking lot next to his car.

"It's my birthday," he reminded her, pleading.

"Not any more," she looked at her watch. "Not technically."

"Still, you could give me a birthday kiss."

"Yes, I could."

She leaned forward across the gearshift, caressed his right cheek with her left hand, and he moved toward her. Their lips met, and her tongue raced across his, retreated and moved across his cheek to the vicinity of his left ear. The odor of the restaurant had moved into his hair, his scalp, as it had under her fingernails, which now gripped his shoulder.

The two engaged in this for a while, and he wanted to progress further, feel her up. She was attracted but even through the alcohol she had confidence and a basic knowledge of herself. She knew what she wanted, and it wasn't a roll in her Celica with a drunk busboy a year younger than she. Even if he was a lead singer.

"No," she whispered. She grasped his roving hands with gentle firmness. He looked up. "No. I'm sorry," she said, smiling. "Not here." It was 3 a.m., three hours after the technical conclusion of Eric's birthday.

Then they were out of the Celica, leaning on his Buick. She tried to explain, over his aimless objections, that she *was* attracted. But she wanted something as important as being with someone to be meaningful, and she wasn't sure if that's what she wanted from Eric that night, right then.

Eric was having none of it, coming down from the beer and tired. "Fine," he said. He asked her for one more kiss, which she bestowed. Her eyes tried to tell him *It's O.K., maybe another night.*

"I'll see you around," he said. He turned for his car, fumbling in his pocket for keys.

His cold casualness offended her. As if she'd be *around.* She struck him on the side of his arm, and was immediately sorry. Eric jumped behind the wheel, potted. He started the car and laid rubber halfway out of the lot.

St. Helens completely exploded, and the news blared through the tinny speakers of a transistor radio Eric had set up on top of the dishwasher. He ran around the restaurant telling everyone, and someone came up with the brilliant idea to climb up the ladder to the roof and watch the eruption.

Half the staff at Engine House Pizza Company No. 1 filed down the foyer to a small storage room. The manager climbed up the ladder and flipped the latch on the roof access hatch. Then he threw it open and disappeared up into the light.

Barbie and Eric had been friendly since his birthday. She and her skirt preceded him up the ladder, she perhaps unaware, perhaps not, that his upward gaze took in every square inch of her nyloned calves, thighs marked by the boundary of hosiery, the skin of her bare upper thighs, the round tight cheeks of her bottom. Brief eclipses of her black underwear, occluding as she climbed.

In a testosterone-provoked prevarication of teenaged anomie, Eric had boasted to the other members of High Seas of his birthday night with her. He had reminded her it was his birthday. She had said she'd gotten a present for him. He had said *Where is it*, and she said *Right here, all you have to do is unwrap it.* And she meant her, her clothes. High Seas were suitably impressed, believing his boorish shit.

Eric emerged onto the roof of the restaurant behind her, joined others looking off to the northeast as the top eleven-hundred feet of the mountain blew and blew.

Eric Ball, his wife and two children take a day trip to Mount St. Helens National Volcanic Monument in 1994, drive off Interstate 5 at Castle Rock and wind up past Silver Lake, pause for an hour at the visitors' center there, then press on up Highway 504, tracking the north fork of the Toutle River.

They pause at the Coldwater Ridge Visitors' Center, then proceed on towards the Johnson Ridge Observatory, finally to Harry's Ridge. There, a different Spirit Lake opens up before Eric like the sea of another planet. Its shoreline two-hundred feet higher, its alien shape clogged with perhaps a hundred-thousand logs that migrate on the water with the winds, the lake lies at the foot of St. Helens. Eric thinks that from here, the mountain resembles a huge granite armchair, says so to his family.

But he's years and years away, even as he speaks. Sounds, images, odors of his own personal heritage: in training for the Mile Swimmer; Rusty's facilitation of his encounter with Paige through the telling of Ape

Canyon's naming; Kelly drinking sandy beer; Barbie ascending. Eric descending.

A camp song rises out of the cliffs in front of him, over the barrier railing and he sees a young boy, a child, at the fork in a trail. *Stop him stop him* he silently cries. But little Eric chooses the wrong path, runs down it and disappears. And a report fills the firmament over the woods and he's falling, falling into an abyss. But he gets up and lumbers away.

Confused, he shakes his head, snatches of clarity fleeting and wound about and through the retardation of emotion, integrity, accountability, the magic and toll of alcohol and substance abuse.

"You O.K. honey?" his wife asks.

"Yeah," he says, explaining his disorientation away, to those he loves, as shock at the great gap between what he remembers of this region and its topography, and what's laid out, right here, right now, in front of him. Still hiding, perplexed, disordered, unable to fully appreciate his late bloom, his progress.

Still with open cuts that nearly heal, then crack open and bleed, at such moments as these.

Eric Ball herds his family back into the car and they drive home, three hours. He's unusually talkative, covering an unrequited wish for alternate history, to trade the rock and roll singer for the Boy Scout, having re-bound his own eight-foot-tall hairy mythology deep, deep within. Telling himself over and over, maybe naively, it's not too late.

Hunt At the End of the World

On opening day, I sit overlooking a tangle of timber and logged slopes, at a clearing's edge. Dawn is breaking, sunrise evolving bands of orange and pink, the pink flying from light and overcome by gold, then gray, as overcast settles the east.

Intermittent corn snow begins to fall, although it is clear directly overhead. I can still make out some fading stars. Snow pellets skip off my coat and trousers, mingling at my boots with bark sloughed from the pine stump of my chair. The bark appears cut with a jigsaw. Ambitious enough, one might collect all the pieces of pine bark in these woods and derive a glorious picture.

I listen for sounds of movement. I'll have to wait a good while, silently, before any elk will approach this place. Hiking down, my boots on the crust of yesterday's snow sounded like bursting glass. Elk are not interested in big noise, and flee from it.

As light mounts, the gibbous moon, still bright in the darker unclouded west, is ready to set into the hills of Clover Springs. Camp robbers, hopeful for a tossed peanut or breadcrust, circle and land nearby. They move off when it's clear I have nothing.

Sun breaks through the clouds for a moment and finds me through interstices in the woods. I see sunlight through needles, bending around and through the melt of nightfrost. Light fractures into prismatic colors - sapphires, rubies, tourmalines hang from branches. I know these jewels are transitory.

I hear a raven's reedy honk and its wings beating air. Looking up, I spot the jet-black bird. It ceases moving its wings and glides. The wingtips curl up as it soars an arc, looking down for movement.

It is a morning, here, in these woods, like ten million and one-hundred million before.

I lift binoculars to the moon. Craters and seas leap forward in the lenses. The clarity is stark and solitary. I note the Tycho impact crater topped by Oceanus Procellarum and Mare Imbrium, south to north. The declination lies on a line through Mares Fecunditatis, Tranquillitatis, Crisium and Serenitatus, in the eastern hemisphere. My arms tremble from cold. The moon trembles in my grasp.

My focus strains and an anomaly flares on the silver surface a couple of degrees north of Tycho. A red dot appears, like a gunshot. I take the glasses down, look at my rifle - *has it fired?*

The raven, or another, flies between the moon and I, then swoops up the canyon. I hoist the field glasses again, find focus. The wound is larger.

It spreads, a plasma circle, overcoming Tycho and washing the southern reach of the Procellarum Sea. I am oblivious to anything else. An elk herd could sneak up and exact proactive revenge with its antlers.

Twelve minutes into this the moon is fully red.

And it cracks latitudinally and explodes in scarlet. I hear gunshots, near and far, from across canyons and ridges all through hunting grounds: other hunters are witness. Vehicles honk on the logging roads as lunar detritus fades in carmine streaks. The front of a pressure wave moves at terrible speed toward me, toward all of us.

I feel an alluring tingle in my hands and behind my eyes, in my mouth at the roots of my teeth. It calls my name, tells me the world is changing forever.

The wave enters the atmosphere, quickening, sucking cloud into the vacuum behind it. It strikes the ridge of Clover Springs and throws high trees and stones. I hear its rush as it buffets the cliffs of Glass Creek, one ridge over, where I once saw a gray wolf ford the stream.

In my peripheral vision ravens unite in a troop, take flight.

They circle, waiting for the wave.

It flies through us, our viscera, our bones, our hearts, and rushes on.

Expecting obliteration, I'm stunned to find myself - and the woods around me - whole and unperturbed. The wave has moved on, leaving only silence in its wake.

Mists gather at the bases of trees and in low, ancient spots. I hear rustling under blowdowns and roots. I see the bones of elk and deer and other woodland creatures rise up and unify. Ligaments, flesh and hide grow on them. They ascend on a breeze.

The first things to go are my hands. The bones of my wrists separate from the socket of my forearms. The hands with which I caressed my wife and children fall at my feet. The rifle clatters.

The ravens fly by. The whirlwind of their passage blows out my teeth. They tinkle like little bells, bouncing off the rifle barrel at my feet. My tongue moves, finds only pulpy maws, and falls out onto my lap.

All is strangely as it should be. Nothing about this is frightening. I understand this disintegration involves the loss of senses. The last thing I smell is cold air. The last things I hear are wings.

My legs fall off.

My arms drop from their shoulders. My torso slips from the stump in a slap of wool-wrapped flesh. My head separates and rolls downhill, the clearcut spinning past, then comes to rest.

I feel the optic nerves behind my eyes unbind. Muscles relax and separate. Lachrymal sacs feed final tears.

My left eye pops out, rolling in frost. It rests staring at sky. The right eye detaches a moment later, landing light as a feather on moss, pupil pointed west. I can see two separate images at once, and it's exhilarating.

A female elk wanders into my left eye's vision. She spies my eye as a morsel, nudges it with her snout, consumes it. The fluid inside bursts between her teeth. Half my vision goes black. Now I am one eye, staring west at blue sky and green mountains.

An eagle snatches me, and I am carried up. From here, the world, purified by lunar pulse, is so beautiful.

Embers Rising

The cat circled our camp for a couple of hours. It stayed just beyond the circle of firelight. We could hear it growling every few minutes. Blown-down sticks, barkless and bleached gray in daylight but indiscernible now, cracked under its paws.

"Did you hear that?" my Uncle Owen asked. He glanced over my shoulder at the woods.

"What?"

Owen held his forefinger up to his lips to shush me. He gazed with intensity into the dark. Firelight reflected in his pupils. He had the look of a man who listens for something, anything, and hopes he will not hear it again.

"That growling noise," he whispered, finally. "Like a cat."

"I didn't hear anything."

But now I listened too, hearing at first only the crackle of split logs in flames. Then pitch popped. Sparks ascended like hornets into the tree limbs overhead, then went out. I smelled the fire's smoke. As I strained to listen, an airplane droned high above us. Its engines made a deep hum on approach. Their pitch changed as the craft moved overhead, then to the west, and trailed off.

Then I heard the cat as well: a low, searching moan, glottal and thick.

The cold air - maybe twenty, twenty-five - dropped several degrees when I heard that animal. I glanced backward, knowing there would be nothing to see but still trying to penetrate the blackness. My scalp tingled under my hunting cap.

"Shine a light out there," I said.

My uncle looked at me as if I were an idiot.

"Not without a gun nearby," he said. Our rifles lay on the front seat of the pickup. We had left them there, with the doors locked, for hunting the next morning.

The throaty whine came again from the treeline. We could have risen and walked over to the cab, retrieved one of the rifles. But it was several yards away, outside the ring of reassuring light. We could have climbed into the canopy right then, waited until dawn. But that would have been several hours off - ten or more. So we simply sat, and waited, feeding the fire whenever it burned low. Believing in light. Hoping the cat would move on.

We guessed a mountain lion, a cougar, made the noises. We had both heard that if you run across a cougar in the woods, you should hop on top of something big, make yourself tall, and holler at it. None of this lore helped at that moment, though, with the cat circling us.

Smoke stung my eyes as I bent to put the tips of two thick branches in the fire. I had in my head this picture of cavemen fending off the razor jaws of saber-toothed cats. One torch for my uncle, one for me. We'd defend our camp with fire, if we had to.

I asked Owen whether it could be a lynx or bobcat. He shook his head. "Those sounds ain't made by little animals," he said. "Them're some big-ass feet, with claws at the end of 'em."

Snapping limbs. The heat of flames. Low, long guttural sounds from a hidden throat. The faint outlines of branches at the edge of firelight. A black, occulted sky pieced from fragments in the interstices of pine and hemlock limbs moving slowly in slight breeze. The exploding of small pockets of pitch. Woodsmoke. Embers rising. All of these things I remember.

The fire burned low, the wood running out. We could have stepped beyond the light to gather more, but that wasn't going to happen. Not even if the growls and footfalls stopped.

"We're gonna have to decide where to sleep," Owen said.

The tent was out of the question. There was no way we were going to bed with only canvas between the cat and us.

"It's gotta be in the canopy." I pointed at the pickup. It would be tight, but both of us would fit. I pulled my sleeping bag out of the tent and unrolled it on the pickup's bed. Then Owen got his.

In our bags we lay on bare metal, surrounded by metal - a sarcophagus of ice. Our breath made clouds. They would condense on the windows and freeze in a thin layer by dawn. With stocking caps on we watched the ceiling, wan firelight leeching in through the windows, bags up around our ears. Sometimes an ember flared in the firepit, and the canopy's ceiling glowed orange. Owen's breathing grew deep and regular, and I realized that what I had hoped would happen - that I would fall asleep before him - had not.

For a while I lay trembling. I imagined the cat moving closer to camp as the fire burnt itself out. I thought I heard it prowling through gaps where the canopy's bond with the pickup's bed panels had rattled loose. I wondered whether it might turn the handles on the door - it seemed unlikely, but the canopy could not be locked from inside. I thought I'd never get to sleep.

I woke some time later.

Dim, rectangular fields of light marked the canopy windows. The night must have cleared. I pushed the little illuminating pin on my wristwatch: almost a quarter of three. This meant more than an hour before we'd rise to prepare for the day's hunt. I had to urinate. I dozed a while, discomfort gnawing my guts.

Then I heard it. Filtered through steel came that growl once more, close and insistent.

This is what I heard: the cougar calling me. Telling me to rise up and look out. It beckoned, commanded, pled at once. It compelled me to do its bidding. I couldn't resist. Something cracked sharply - a talon clacking on the side of the pickup? Loathing and strange fascination soaked me. I waited, holding my breath, not wanting to make the faintest sound.

Indeed, a faint skein of ice crystals coated the inside of the windows. When I looked, a man stood there next to the canopy. Or something with mannish shape. It went on twos. For the briefest moment its eyes glowed like embers. Then they grew black and bottomless, their blackness unlike the night around them, for chaos dwelt at their core. Its lips peeled back across sharp teeth and offered a growl - that growl we had heard hours ago outside the false security of firelight - and it peered into me from a face pallid as the moon. It peered into me and knew all my secrets. I will never tell anyone the things that mannish shape knew about me.

I fell away from the window. Owen shifted under me and cursed from inside his bag. His name came out of me like a groan and a shriek mixed. "Owen!" I shouted.

The form receded, moving away without footsteps. It didn't behave like anything normal. It didn't walk. It... glided. And then was gone.

We looked for prints around the canopy and firepit the next morning. There weren't any. Aside from impressions from my uncle's boots and mine, the ground was void of them. Neither were there any prints in the surrounding woods. Owen and I rounded camp in ever-widening circles under flannel cloud-deck threatening snow. He wanted so badly to show me what fresh cougar tracks look like. He maintained, and does to this day, that it was a mountain lion prowling around us that night. But we found only the cloven-hoofed impressions of elk and deer.

We searched for an hour. A clean, silver-smelling snow began. If we missed tracks, they were covered fairly quickly. Soon a couple of inches coated everything except the still-warm firepit. Wisps of steam rose from its mound of ash then dissipated.

We boiled some coffee and ate pastry rolls. Then we left camp to hunt.

Something for Nothing, But Only Once

What is that, a *face?* It jumps off the end of a burnt log, a long femur of jackpine sent halfway down the mountainside in a Cascades windstorm years before now. It looks like the unfinished cartoon mug of one of my son's Pokémons, a gob of carbon chub, charred knots for facial topography. You see weird things in the woods. This one has been rendered weird by the elemental force of fire. The same force that boils deep below us on this mantle, the very same force that has pushed the mountains up around me, once carved into the end of this fractured trunk this countenance.

It was a creative fire.

I think the best way to get into this is to describe the sort of day it was. If all the things that were normal about it are considered then perhaps, too, this will resolve itself.

I have hunted elk and deer in the Nile game management unit for more than thirty years. I know every fold of every canyon, each rock face, the tumble of the creek beds: Nile north fork, Nile south fork, Orr, Dry, Glass, Rattlesnake. They all flow into the Little Naches, which flows at the base of the Manastash Ridge to the north. I appreciate how the wind can change silence into the sound of a rushing train. I have seen the sun rise in the east, pause, and sink again. The moon has presented itself to me in wide daylight, and exploded in carmine streaks. I've held my ear against the bark of a western hemlock for seven days and heard the faint meter of the earth's turning - it's like a seashell lifted from sand. The forest here is magic.

I have hunted these woods in raging windstorms, huge Cascades blowouts in which I could hear the forest floor around me being pelted by flying sticks and larger limbs. Tree trunks would engage in urgent friction above me, and I'd conceal myself at the base of one, clutching my Remington .300, praying for the integrity of that particular tree's trunk. Other times snow would fall, dry corn snow first as the system would move up-valley, then fat, wet flakes that would saturate everything. Hunting in snow is quieter. The sticks don't break under your boots. Still yet, other hunts would be like high summer, and I would want to shed my orange coat and cap - run nude in the wilderness, in the native heat.

To be sure - I've shot a lot of game in these mountains over the years. There was the big daddy bull in 1977, which came crashing over a ridge in front of me, presented himself chest on, and froze. That animal was a perfect five-point - the graceful tines sweeping back over his withers. I brought him down with one shot to the brisket. There was a spike yearling, an inexperienced youth curious and compelled to a roadside rendezvous with our parked pickup truck. We emerged from the woods sticky and out of breath, dropped him aft of the bed. That was in 1986. The next year - I remember because it was on the same logging road, 1607, near the haystack rock - a mountain lion menaced me one afternoon. I got up in the back of that truck's bed and *shrieked*, which is what you're supposed to do if you encounter a cougar in the forest. It snarled from the side of the road, eyes aflame with gold, and turned tail. I could have shot it, I suppose. I think, though, that would have amounted to an unforgivable trespass.

So the morning I observe the face in the end of a charred log is like any number of these previous mornings. I am hunting over between Roads 1605 and 227. I'd hiked up a bluff on an infrequently used logging trail that branched from a switchback on 1605 and ultimately connects with Clover Springs at 6,350 feet. I'd parked my truck there at the tight curve, where the valley drops away a thousand feet and runs out to the Feeding Station. The dawn hike had been a moderate climb, good for a morning like this one - overcast with a cold rain or, perhaps a wet snow, threatening. It is probably just above freezing, and I am nicely nested in a wool parka, two or three levels of shirts, thermal underwear, jeans and boots. My gloves hold the .300 out in front of me in a ready position. I trudge up the trail attempting lightfootedness in my boots, blowing gouts of steam each time I exhale. The forest is quiet, as it typically is at sunrise.

I enter a meadow from the south and choose a stump that rises from yellow grass against a tree trunk at the perimeter. It will be an appropriate place to rest and watch the field for a while. It is a grassy, open space surrounded mostly by cedar trees, notable because the red giants aren't that plentiful in this part of the Cascades. I pause to refresh my chewing tobacco. I sit here for a few moments recording the waking sounds of the forest - the small pips of squirrels, the calls of mountain thrushes. I hear the flap of a raven's wings before I can see it, wending above the trees on a foothills air current. The sun breaks through a thin spot in the clouds, washes everything in pinkish light for less than a minute, then disappears again like an unfulfilled promise. In these ways, the morning is like every other.

One of the curious traits of waiting while elk hunting is that no matter where you loiter, there appears to be a slightly better place downwind or across a ravine, or at the top of the next ridge. There are no elk *here*, the reasoning goes, at this moment. So maybe they're over *there*. This sort of thinking is, of course, circular. Elk are not public creatures and eschew discovery. They will flee, rapidly, at the slightest incidence of detection. An elk can discern a hunter from two ridges away, spook in this discovery, and be a mile away through thick forests in less than five minutes. All the hunter hears is the fading crash of hooves, breaking limbs, the clatter of antlers against treetrunks.

Nevertheless, even after more than thirty seasons and moderate success in the field, I am always tempted by this notion: that I will cross this field, right here, or climb that ridge, right there, and just as I crest the rise, a royal bull will be waiting for me. His muzzle will snort steam, the antlers rising in great horned symmetry. Their tines will splay perfectly, the main branch running parallel to his back, the last set clear back to his rump. I count them in my fantasy: one, two, three, four, five, *six... seven*. He will trumpet beautifully, wave his rack around in the air, and wait for me to drill him with a .300 Remington Ultra Magnum bullet driven 3,300 feet per second by 180 grains of exploding gunpowder. It will hit him at 2,145 foot-pounds - he will go over with one shot, a trophy animal. I will have steaks and jerky for months, and a fine rack to mount.

There it is, I think. Sitting at the edge of the cedar-ringed meadow on a near-freezing morning, I see a blind at the other end of the field. It is formed by the root ball of another tree that must have gone over in a storm. There, in the tangle of roots, is a sort of shelf that could be used as a seat. From the new location, I would be able to survey the field that opens before me now, plus the woods to the north, which are moderately packed with hemlocks and Douglas fir, ground cover, a network of game trails. The attraction, though, is that I know there is a small creek at the base of the draw over there. It may be a place for elk to wander through after drinking.

Resolved, I hoist my rifle and circuit the meadow, clinging close to the concealing overstory of the cedars. It takes ten minutes by the route, stealing ten or eleven quiet steps, pausing then to listen. I'm alone, of course, the mode of all elk hunting. I start to shiver, the cold having crept in and taken possession of my body while I sat. Only with the rise in metabolic activity brought on by walking is the cold properly distributed. Thus it seems to grow for a while after rising, after the first steps. But it diminishes quickly as well. This is not a truly cold morning; sometimes, we hunt in temperatures closer to ten or fifteen degrees.

I arrive and climb into the root ball; the seat is like a boatswain's chair. True, once I'm settled, I am afforded a much more comprehensive view of the meadow and the woods around me. It is a better place to wait, and surely, now, my cross-field migration will be rewarded with the appearance of game animals. *Big* game animals.

I wait in the root ball for an hour, until I have to urinate. Then I wait another fifteen minutes, before I choose to climb down and take care of my bodily function. The noise I make dismounting the roots sounds like an automobile crash, and any animals in the area will have heard it and fled. There goes an hour and a quarter. Then I climb back into the root ball and wait another half an hour, and no game shows itself. I hear, from time to time, sounds from the forest that I know could presage the showing of brown hide, musky odor - the footfall of elk. But they remain hidden, if they are even there at all. The sounds - little snappings of twigs and clatterings against bark - could have been produced by smaller deer.

I lean back against a soiled root pillow raised like arthritic fingers against the gray sky. And catch my first glimpse of the log, its carbon end, the nose, mouth, eyes. I'm staring at it suddenly, amused with the way the features emerge. It's like imagining shapes in the clouds, bas relief in the bark of a pine tree, whispers in human language there, surely, in the song of baying coyotes. They're all there. A rock face becomes the wizened expression of Old Man Mountain. The shape and arrangement of deer prints in snow is an algorithm. Somewhere a set of them holds the secrets to the universe, or tells a story so dramatic or tragic it could tug at the heart of a despot. Water flows around boulders in the shape of a forest nymph's hair.

The log is twenty feet long and lays alone at the edge of the field. Its bark skin has long fallen away, aided by termites. The long, naked wood is bleached gray, like part of the giant skeleton of these hills exposed. I trace its length to the larger end, which lies away from me. There I can see the fractured stump from which it tumbled. It was not cut by loggers in the fashion of many of the downed trees in these parts. This tree must have taken on a disease, been weakened in the heartwood. The sap had ceased to enervate, sucking life from the topmost branches first. Needles near the crown turned from deep green to yellow to red, and dropped in a final shedding. The tree became a snag, magnetic, hungry for lightning to strike. Is that how it happened?

I close my eyes and see it fall. The trunkwood, corrupt now, ceding strength to exterior elements. There is a single omnipresent *pop* that fills the meadow - the trunk shudders and the few remaining needles separate.

Then a series of cracks and groanings in the wood. The tree falls from a very great height, keens over like a failing mast, pulverizes earth as it smashes to the floor. The whole meadow resonates with its glorious, final thump.

Seasons and seasons have passed since that day. The gray log is pitted with charcoal - the tracings of the controlled burns that are a process step in the logging of these hills. The lumbermen cut the large trees down, then limb them and burn stacks of slag for days. They squirt a commercial version of napalm into the piles, so the green branches and needles will burn in spite of their wetness. This is a fundamental of timber management - leave the land clean for more growth. Although it's a long cycle, it works, or so they say.

Sometimes the napalm fires roar out of control, leap a fireline and burn some unintended acreage. That may have happened here, too. There's no way of knowing for sure. The broken end of the log, the end facing me, is scorched deeply in the area where the fantastic has emerged. It is a black creosote face.

I'm staring at it, daring it to speak.

There are no elk in this area. The elk are over at Glass Creek.

I remember - the deep canyon of Glass Creek is two ridges over. Road 227 connects two branches of 1605 upwards of where I parked this morning. Then there's an unnumbered spur off of 227. It parallels for roughly a mile one of the deepest canyons in the management unit, in some places a sheer two-thousand foot drop that terminates in scree, aspen, vine maple, and the rushing creek. One year, I remember now, I sat under a tree near the lip of the canyon and watched, through high-powered field glasses, a wolf ford the stream. I tell people that and they say it must have been a coyote. It was not. The animal was too large for a coyote, and silverish-gray.

Glass Creek is one of the main migration routes from the Bumping Lake area, high country where the entire herd summers. They winter at the feeding station, move up to high country during the spring rut, and move back in through this area in autumn. They spread out - it's as likely to discover a sub-herd here, or anywhere within twenty miles of here - but today, I am suddenly convinced, there are animals over at Glass Creek.

There are no elk in this area. The elk are over at Glass Creek.

I look at the end of the log again. Those burnt lips were *moving*, the charred eyelids *fluttered*.

The charcoal nose blasted a gout of dried, burnt sap.

I just saw it.

Despite my warm clothing, the hair on my neck is standing, and I'm fiercely cold. Suddenly I'm put in mind of psychedelic flashbacks - *Oh, that's what this is!* - and what a *fine* place to experience one. I remember the high-school health class propaganda warning us about this, how the illegal drugs never went away, never departed your system. They stayed there - especially the LSD - like little cellular demons, part of your corrupted fabric, waiting for a moment when you were alone or in need of high performance, say, in a job interview or driving down a crowded street. They would just take over. The health texts called this a *bad trip*.

I recalled once I thought I was having one while watching an episode of Quincy. He was doing an autopsy for a crime victim who turned out to have what would have been some variety of inoperable cancer. And watching, I was convinced suddenly that I *too* had The Big C, that it was inside me, malignant and metastasizing. At the core of me were rotten, vile cells growing radically out of control, and further, that the core blackness of me was justice for my experimenting. The walls and ceiling seemed to waver and I had gone to lie down, sweating fear.

But there's nothing about the log that suggests fear this morning, neither are there any other of the sensual disturbances - auras and light-bendings and the odor or timbre of certain colors, drippings of the fabric of reality, which are the classic hallucinatory hallmarks. It's just that the goddamned face in the log was speaking to me. I saw it!

There are no elk in this area. The elk are over at Glass Creek.

I've walked this land many times before; I mentally stumble on the notion that there may be a hidden meaning here. On the other hand, *no*, it just means what it says. And so I reach this conclusion: I should go over to Glass Creek and check it out.

It's a half-hour hike out, and a gentle drizzle has started. It beads up on my wool coat and gloves, fogs the optics of my rifle. I'll have to wipe them down before aiming, so I pause to administer a dry cloth to the lenses. I reach my pickup, load in, close the door. It echoes in the cab as if I were outside. I do a three-point turn, slowly reversing on the narrow gravel road.

Fifteen minutes later I am in the turnaround that terminates the spur off 227. The canyon of Glass Creek is arrayed before me, an enormous trench carved into the mountains. I remember the wolf, try to recall the route I took to the overlook where I saw him. I can't, so I step randomly into the woods to the west of the turnaround. The drizzle has taken a turn for the colder; a weak frozen rain is falling now from deep, rolling clouds. Their grayness envelops me, surrounds me like a shroud. I see the tattered rags of low fog clouds pushing themselves up the canyon. They'll be here soon, and visibility will be neatly halved, then quartered. Ultimately, at cloud's center, I may be able to see as little as twenty yards ahead of me. Dampness will creep in and inhabit me, cold to the marrow, waiting, wishing for elk.

I am barely fifty paces down a game trail from my truck. Suddenly, the foliage, which is an ivy-like salal that rises into thick, neck-high shrubs, shakes and rattles to my left. I've spooked a large animal, and instead of fleeing, it counter-intuitively approaches, bursts forth from the foliage shaking and burning to be slain. It's a beautiful bull, four feet high at the shoulder, three tines on the left antler, four on the right. It stands long enough for me to count the points, to observe it had lost one of the left tines in a rutting fight, long enough for me to raise my .300. He is twenty yards away, nine-hundred pounds in a tawny overcoat, buff rump, deep brown shag head, bright black eyes. He's so close I don't really have to sight down the scope. In lifting the rifle, I snap open the safety. I pull the trigger and the shell explodes in the magazine, producing an instant tinnitus that will fade in my right ear.

The bull staggers backward, snorting steam from its wide nostrils. He shrieks outrage, to be ravaged thus, stamps the needle floor of the game trail. He gathers to flee, and I discharge the spent shell, engage another, shoot again. He is thrown backward again, then recovers and stands, trembling. I can see the hole I have opened up in his chest. He sprays red mist from the nostrils, shakes his head to clear internal passages, perhaps to negate what he knows is coming. The muscles under his skin bunch and ripple like migrating cords. He expectorates blood in a blast, brilliant on the trail, and vital fluid oozes from the wound. The bull turns slightly, and I can see blood jetting from the first entry hole now as well, up on his neck. He folds at the front knees, kneeling as if I am a deity. *Give me more life*, he prays in low, long, desperate language. Then his hind quarters sink as he tucks his rear legs in under himself. The gorgeous bull rests there, lifeblood flowing free, gasping air through moist holes and tortured pipes.

His head tips sideways until the rack snarls in low-hanging branches. The bull's eyes grow dim as I approach. I've chambered a third shell in case he kicks out in pre-death panic. But it's superfluous - he's dead now. I know because his death rattle overfills the woods, echoes off the opposite walls of Glass Creek canyon.

Gutting the elk is easy, plunging my knife into the soft underbelly, carving hide away in a Y-shape. Hauling the carcass from the woods

179

forty yards from my pickup is the easiest extraction I have ever experienced, although the freezing rain has transformed again, now falling snow.   I pull him from the woods counterclockwise after quartering him with a bone saw, make five trips - right hind-quarters, left hind-quarters, left front-quarters, right front-quarters, head.   I am saturated in his blood and guts and melted pink snow and my own pouring sweat, and the smell of his musky interior is in the hair of my beard and head, on my skin, under my fingernails.

After the fifth trip, I return to the scene of the shooting to retrieve my saw, knife, ropes. I gather these butcher's tools in a knapsack that soon leaks blood of its own, scan around once more for any items I may have forgotten.   The trail is a half-frozen puddle of pink water-ice - precipitation mixed and stirred with the core of him. I leave the gut bag, the stomach, urinary tract and anus, his penis laying in the mud.

I know, as I hike out slick in the bull's fluids, that it's a one time deal. Something for nothing. You *can* get away with it once in a while. I know if I return to the clearing next season, all I'll encounter is a half-rotten log - like a hundred-thousand other half-rotten logs that dot these hillsides and mountain meadows.   There will be no magic there, no illusion, no repeat performance. Another year's worth of sinking into the meadow floor, the old bleached bone. A silent face, no face at all.

Or perhaps it won't even be there.

About the Author

Born in June 1963 near Seattle, Brian Ronald Ames was reading the newspaper by the time he was five years old. In elementary school Brian, 12 years old, submitted his first story - how Coyote and Fox, in fits of mutual foolishness, created the comets. "Coyote and Fox" was made into a "film-strip," a projected medium. Brian joined Boy Scouts, started spy clubs, built forts, and went hunting with his grandfather for the first time.

In 1976 Brian's parents divorced. But he gained two stepparents a year later. Today he is blessed with two families. One of them came with two more sisters - Kris and Kate - to join his natural sister, Michele. Brian rode his first horses and briefly had his own mount, Molly, a half-Arabian, half-Quarter horse.

At Vancouver's Hudson's Bay High School, Brian discovered cars, girls, cigarettes. They were impossible distractions, but he got A's in English. Mt. St. Helens blew its lid in Vancouver's backyard, and in 1981, he left for college. At Washington State, he enrolled as a music major, then changed to political science. But for electives, he took reative writing courses under Dr. Alex Kuo, and discovered a passion for poetry and yarn-spinning. For two years, he co-edited *Wind Row*, the university's award-winning literary magazine. Finding love over manuscripts and proof galleys, he wed his co-editor, Natalie Hanford, in 1984.

Both graduated in 1985, leaving Pullman to begin careers in the Seattle area. Ames contributed poetry to *Wind Row* until it folded in 1989. He wrote during this period also for The Boeing Company. His daughter, Rebecca, was born in 1986. Douglas, his son, was born in 1989. The family moved to Huntsville, Alabama, for two years in 1990, then returned to the Seattle area. There were several starts and stops on stories, novels, poems. None of it was working out.

In 1998, Alex Kuo read with Sherman Alexie in Seattle. Kuo invited Ames for supper afterward, inquiring pointedly about writing. "Are you writing? No?" The following day Ames received an e-mail from Kuo: "Try to find time to write. It's important that we continue."

Ever Kuo's student, Ames has since written over a hundred short stories and essays, three unpublished children's books, and an unpublished novel. His work has appeared in print and on the net, most notably in *Glimmer Train Stories*, *The Massachusetts Review*, *South Dakota Review*, and the Pocol Press anthology "Unusual Circumstances: Short Fiction from Around the Globe." His day job still is at Boeing.

About the Illustrator

Todd Mueller was born and raised in Denver, Colorado. He resides there today with his wife and three children. He has an associate degree in commercial art, and started as an illustrator for KMGH-TV in Denver at the age of 20.

Mr. Mueller has been an illustrator, graphic designer, and art director in the Denver market for 17 years. He has won various awards in the TV and cable industry for his design and animations.

More of Todd's work can be seen at his online portfolio at: http://homepage.mac.com/toddmueller.

www.ingramcontent.com/pod-product-compliance
Lightning Source LLC
Chambersburg PA
CBHW070027260626
47159CB00005B/1973